LEGALLY HOT

**Anthologies from
St. Martin's Paperbacks**

THE BODYGUARD
CHERRY ADAIR
GENA SHOWALTER
LORIE O'CLARE

MEN OF DANGER
LORA LEIGH
RED GARNIER
ALEXIS GRANT
LORIE O'CLARE

RESCUE ME
CHERRY ADAIR
LORA LEIGH
CINDY GERARD

LEGALLY HOT

**LORA
LEIGH**

**CHEYENNE
McCRAY**

**RED
GARNIER**

St. Martin's Paperbacks

This is a work of fiction. All of the characters, organizations, and events portrayed in this novel are either products of the author's imagination or are used fictitiously.

LEGALLY HOT

"Sheila's Passion" copyright © 2012 by Lora Leigh.
"Deadly Dance" copyright © 2012 by Cheyenne McCray.
"Caught" copyright © 2012 by Red Garnier.

For information address St. Martin's Press, 175 Fifth Avenue, New York, NY 10010.

ISBN: 978-0-312-38913-0

Printed in the United States of America

St. Martin's Paperbacks edition / January 2012

St. Martin's Paperbacks are published by St. Martin's Press, 175 Fifth Avenue, New York, NY 10010.

10 9 8 7 6 5 4 3 2 1

CONTENTS

SHEILA'S PASSION

LORA LEIGH

PROLOGUE

Vengeance.

It had been so long coming.

So many years waiting, searching.

Hating.

Ah God, the hatred.

It was like a wound festering deep within the soul, growing more tender by the year, refusing to release the acrid bitterness that filled it.

And it all centered on one man. On a monster who had destroyed countless friends and family. Who had, with a single, thoughtless decision, caused centuries of traditions to be wiped out. Destroyed as though they had never been.

And there had been no price extracted for the betrayal.

There had been no punishment, no atonement; there hadn't been so much as an "I'm sorry" or a sprig of flowers on the gravesites of those who had died because of the choices he had made.

And many had died.

A son had begun the slaughter as his father, the one so many followed, stood by, helpless, his loyalty centered on the daughter he had adored.

The daughter's life had meant more to that father than the traditions that had sustained a people for so long. That daughter had held his loyalty, his entire focus, rather than the people who trusted him with their lives.

There was a reason why marriages were arranged within their world. A reason why children were fostered out to other families throughout the years. There was a reason why fathers were often separated from their daughters and sons from their mothers.

To maintain the sanctity of tradition. To ensure that family love and loyalty never came ahead of the decisions which may not be in the child's best interests.

Giovanni Fredrico had broken the trust of his people in his attempts to save the daughter he had so cherished. The child conceived with the woman he had wed after the death of his first wife—Giovanni had broken tradition and married for love. In doing so he had begun the destruction of all that had been given into his safekeeping.

Had the families known it was a love match rather than a marriage of tradition, as they and her family had sworn, it would have been dissolved with her death. She would have been killed by order of the other families immediately.

Watching Giovanni now—Gio the Giant, they had always called him—regret welled, but it hadn't paid Gio to teach his son that it was love that mattered rather than tradition. Gio, with his ready smile, his pocket of candies and coins, and his genuine love for children. He had been as treasured as any favored uncle by those who knew him. Those who lived beneath his rule gave him more loyalty than to their fathers, mothers, or kings.

And there were many who knew him, many who depended on him.

No child went hungry as long as Gio ruled the families.

No child was abused as long as Gio's punishment awaited the abuser. But in the end he had destroyed them.

The world had changed since that fateful summer when Gio had betrayed them, though. Since the day Gio had followed his heart rather than the tradition of the families, and taught his son that the heart mattered more than the unwritten laws.

The sanctity of family was no longer adhered to as it had once been. The innocence of a child mattered to no one. Abuse was rearing its ugly head, hunger was striking families who once knew prosperity, and crime was becoming an act of greed rather than a business.

Because of Gio the Giant and the son who had followed his dreams rather than destiny.

Gio had betrayed the families, the children, the wives, the fathers and brothers, sisters and mothers who had trusted in him, who had relied upon him. He had betrayed them all for the love of the child who had meant more to him and to his son than the responsibilities he had accepted when he had taken the reins of the Fredrico family and their vast holdings.

But even with all his faults, the blame did not lie with Gio alone. He had only severed the final link in a chain that had been thoughtlessly weakened by another.

The blame did not even lie with the fragile, delicate child he had betrayed them all for. The one who had suffered with her blood and with her shame as she was so carelessly used against her father, who loved her more than he loved the people.

No, the blame lay with the son.

It was the son who had set this nightmare in motion.

It was the son, Beauregard Fredrico, named for the childhood friend Gio had so missed after his death and the brother of the woman he had given his heart to.

The friend who had betrayed *his* own family as well.

Had Gio cursed his son?

Perhaps he had, for Beauregard Fredrico had followed the example of his father and his father's friend when he had turned his back on the people who had already begun to depend upon him. He had betrayed all their honor and walked away from Italy as though the land and its people had not been burned into his soul.

Eight years.

This search had gone on for eight long, horrendous years, and finally, the end was near.

Here, in this little town called Simsburg, Texas, the prey that had eluded fate for so long had finally been located.

The selection had been narrowed to four men.

There was no doubt, it had to be one of them.

Only these four, who were a part of Gio and Serita Fredrico's lives now, had no past to call their own.

They had not existed before that fateful summer eight years ago. Before that summer when Beauregard Fredrico had supposedly died.

Just as his sister, Serita, and his father as well, were reported to have been killed by the remaining members of the families who eventually turned on them.

Four men.

Hardened, cold-eyed, so unlike the man Beauregard

had been the last time he had been seen. Weak, uncertain of himself, angry with the world. That had been Beau as a young man.

It was not the mature male he had become.

He would be a challenge to identify and kill now, but vengeance was demanded.

So many generations of families had been destroyed because of his selfishness. So many lives lost and destroyed because of his traitorous actions.

So many lives had been wasted because of his choices.

Entire families had been lost.

And now, it was time to destroy Beauregard. No matter the new name he had taken, the man he had become, or the reasons for which he had made his choices. No matter the arguments those left behind had made for his life. None of it mattered any longer.

It was time to satisfy vengeance.

And vengeance demanded blood.

But blood demanded proof.

And there was only one way to prove Fredrico blood.

By threatening the one thing they held dearest.

The only true weakness a Fredrico was ever known to have.

The women they loved.

Beauregard, unlike Gio, had not fulfilled his responsibilities first, though. Nor had he kept the woman he had loved as a mistress. No, Beau had left Italy. He had betrayed them all, and destroyed not just his own family, but those who followed the Fredrico family as well. And he had to pay.

ONE

Sheila was stretched on a rack of such torturous pleasure she was certain she couldn't survive it. There was no way she would come out on the other end intact.

She always thought that at some point during the hours she spent in Nick Casey's bed, however, that something other than her orgasm would be found.

Each time, she swore she wouldn't allow herself to be seduced, and each time he touched her, each time that sensual dominance swirled in his dark chocolate eyes, she found herself seduced. Seduced. Ready. Willing. He mesmerized her with his kiss and made her more than willing to beg for more. To plead.

Breathless. Devoured. Fucked until she was screaming mindlessly in a pleasure so intense she was certain she would die from it. That was how she felt. And the pleasure became the center of her universe.

"Oh God, Casey." She arched to him, her tone so rough and hoarse she didn't recognize it as her own.

But oh God, his touch was so good. Everything he did to her, every kiss, every stroke, every caress was ecstasy.

Sheila spread her thighs wider, her heels digging into the mattress as she lifted for him, feeling his tongue sink into the tender flesh between the folds of her pussy.

Broad, strong hands gripped her hips, holding her in place as he licked at the sensitive flesh, then pushed inside the saturated entrance with a slow, destructive thrust.

A long, low cry tore from her lips. Casey tasted her, his tongue moving inside her, possessing and enjoying her with exquisite pleasure. Rapture suffused her senses, washing over her and racing across her nerve endings with a wave of electric intensity.

There was nothing quite like Casey's touch or the addictive sensations that tore through her.

His hard, calloused hands roved over her body and stroked every response she would have kept hidden. Awakening nerve endings and hungers better off ignored. From the depths of a sensuality she hadn't known she possessed, he revealed desires she hadn't known existed inside her.

He had only to make her think he was going to touch her and her clit swelled. Her breasts became swollen, her nipples tight and hard. The very thought of the pleasure to come had her ready to explode.

His tongue slid from her pussy, flickering over the entrance, licking gently and driving her crazy with its fiery touch. Inner muscles clenched as she fought to get closer while her clit ached in a desperate need to come.

He was wicked with his touch. Diabolical.

Teasing, deliberately seductive, the tip of his tongue

eased up the narrow slit as his thick, heavy lashes lifted to stare back at her.

Deliberately, with teasing, provocative licks, suckling kisses, and flickering strokes of his tongue, he began to make her insane with the lust beginning to pound through her. Heat flushed, sweat dampening her flesh and making her whole body slick.

She couldn't help but stare back at him, locked by the dark arousal in his eyes, suspended within the swirling, nearing ecstasy he was creating.

It was exquisite.

It was so incredibly ecstatic she could barely breathe.

Fingers of powerful sensual heat raced around the swollen bud of her clit as he bestowed one of the hot suckling kisses to the sensitive nerve center.

A moan whispered from her lips as sensation clenched her pussy with rapid-fire pulses of agonizing pleasure sizzling through her senses. Her hips jerked with involuntary movements, the need racing through her, demanding she get closer.

"Casey." She moaned his name as she felt the edge of orgasm nearing. "Oh God, Casey. It's so good. So good and so hot."

She felt as though she were burning inside and out. The flames whipped over her body, searing through her flesh straight to her womb.

Her thighs tightened at his shoulders as she slid her hands from the mattress where she clutched the sheets to the heavy silk of his hair. Threading her fingers through the strands, Sheila gripped at it in desperation.

She loved his hair.

It was like silk, heated and soft to the touch.

She loved his tongue.

It rolled over her clit, licked along the slit of her pussy, fucked inside the tight clenching muscles and had her begging for release.

She loved his touch.

She loved, loved the way he made her feel. The sensuality, the intense attention he paid to ensuring her pleasure.

"Casey!" she cried out as the pleasure built, sensation washing through her as it began to tingle over her entire body.

Her nipples swelled tighter, becoming so sensitive that she slid one hand from his hair to use her fingers to ease the need for touch against them. Gripping, tugging at the thick strands, Sheila fought to ease the need for sensation that throbbed in them.

It wasn't enough.

It was never enough.

She couldn't get enough of each caress. She couldn't get enough sensation or ease the needs tearing through her.

The need for him, for every touch, for a deeper pleasure, for that something that drove her insane every time Casey touched her. Every time she even thought of him taking her. Moaning, she moved her fingers to the opposite nipple, desperate for the sensation that would push her over the edge of release.

His hands followed hers. Rather than only one breast, one nipple tightening in agony for that "sensual" touch. That sensation that only came for the briefest moment, for such a shatteringly short amount of time, yet for that moment, for that flash of eternity, she was complete.

She was pure energy, pure power, and Casey was there

with her, not just inside her. Not just bringing her pleasure, but bringing her such a sense of completion that she felt lost within it.

She reached for it again, desperately seeking it, willing to run headlong into complete chaos for it. Nothing else mattered.

She was becoming an addict and she freely admitted it.

Casey's addict. And she feared she could end up living only for these few precious moments.

"Please!" A broken cry left her throat, flowing around her as she lifted her hips, writhed beneath his kiss, his licks, against every luscious stroke of burgeoning ecstasy bestowed upon her.

His fingers played with her nipples, gripping and tugging, sensitizing them further when she hadn't believed they could become more sensitive. Sending pleasure streaking through them, tearing along neural pathways she had never felt before.

Casey's touch.

Each wicked little white-hot sensation detonated in her womb, clenching it, almost, just almost sending her hurtling into rapture. Just almost shooting her into the brilliant center of whatever sensation it was that had her aching every moment for one more chance to experience it again. His hands palmed her breasts, thumbs and forefingers gripped her nipples, tugged, sent fiery arcs of electrifying sensation traveling through her body and building the addiction for more.

She was grinding her pussy tighter against his lips as they surrounded her clit and sucked it inside his mouth, began to lash at it with the heat of his tongue.

"Casey—oh God, it's good. So good." Long, drawn-out, the fractured moan that left her lips and filled the air around them as she felt herself tightening, felt the pleasure whipping through her, building, threatening, pushing her to the very edge of pure, complete satisfaction.

Her hands tightened in his hair as his fingers tugged at her nipples, sending her rushing toward release.

Then he drew back.

He pulled her back from that edge. From the impending ecstasy.

"No!" Her eyes flared open, desperation and bemusement filling her cry as he came to his knees.

"You'll come around my dick first," he growled, moving over her, his hand gripping the hard shaft of his cock as he slid it against the wet folds between her thighs.

Her clit throbbed.

Sheila could feel her sex clenching, tightening, the muscles flexing instinctively as the broad, flared crest of his erection pressed against the entrance.

Fiery, throbbing, the heavy width began to stretch her flesh, forcing its way inside the slick, nerve-laden tissue as it stimulated and excited every cell that clasped it.

Sheila's back arched as she lifted her knees to clasp his hips, moving beneath him, lifting to him as the short, surging strokes thrust him further inside her, penetrating her deeper and creating flames that seared her nerve endings and intoxicated her senses. It was like being immersed in a sensual storm. In a wave of such intense pleasure she was helpless against it.

She felt drunk on his touch. The inebriation was like being enfolded in a world so rich with color and sensation that she never wanted to leave it.

Each inward impalement burned and excited to the point that she was certain more pleasure would destroy

her. Each time he pulled back she was certain she would
die from the desertion. That she couldn't bear being separated from him for even a second longer.

"Ah, babe," he groaned as he sank deeper. The sound
of the pleasure in his voice had her pussy clenching,
creaming, nearly coming from the sheer excitement and
explicit sexuality that filled that moment. His face tightened, a dark sensual appearance overtaking it as his
cock surged inside her. A harsh moan passed his lips,
pleasure filling the air as the thick, heavy flesh penetrated
to the hilt.

Her nails dug into his shoulders. She couldn't restrain
the need to hold on to him. As he filled her, all she could
do was tighten around him and lock him to her as closely
as possible.

Her head tilted to the side as his head lowered, his lips
finding her neck, caressing and nipping at the tender
flesh. Sheila swore she lost her breath. She lost control.

Her pussy milked at his dick, the feel of that burn,
that sensation that bordered pain and mixed with pleasure tearing through her as she cried out his name. It
threw her higher, tossing her into a maelstrom of nearing ecstasy and mindless pleasure.

His lips sucked and nipped at her neck.

His tongue licked.

She could feel sizzling arcs and fiery trails of rapture
tearing at her senses.

She wanted.

She ached.

Then, he began moving faster, harder.

If the pleasure was too much to bear before, it became an agony of sensation then.

Drawing back, he paused, a grimace tightening his

lips before he pushed forward, his hips leaning into her with a heavy thrust that buried him full length inside the too-sensitized flesh. Sheila gasped, crying his name as he began to ride her harder, each thrust stealing her breath.

Each time, every time, it was more intense than the last.

There was no way to hide her response or maintain her control.

She lost it the moment he touched her. She couldn't seem to find a way to regain her balance, or to regain that part of her she could feel herself losing.

And that was the terrifying part. Though not terrifying enough to make her draw back from him. Not terrifying enough to risk never having him again.

But right there, in the center of her soul, she could feel herself opening for him, crying out his name and fighting to hold him closer, deeper. She needed to hold him as close as possible or she feared there would be nothing left to hold him to her.

Her legs wrapped around his hips as he fucked her with a force that left her dizzy. Each powerful thrust was a rocking, full-length, driving motion that sent a storm of sensations whipping through her.

Her knees lifted higher, clasping his waist, opening the sensitive depths of her pussy to him and she was crying out hoarsely as new nerve endings were raked with the heated rasp of his cock.

Like iron covered with wet, rough silk, his erection caressed, stroked. Lit a flame of such intense pleasure inside her that it was all she could do to survive the exquisite agony of pleasure.

Pleasure and pain.

The muscles of her pussy rippled around the invading flesh. The natural, instinctive response to the pleasure he was giving her created another layer of sensation impossible to resist.

She couldn't bear it. She didn't believe she would survive the onslaught of sensation this time.

She swore each time she couldn't bear more. That before she found release she would simply explode from the need and cease to be.

Then, just as it always did, the world exploded around her instead.

The blinding response to the rapid-fire strokes, the burning stretch and possession of his cock never failed to take her by surprise. It never failed to open her soul to him a little bit more in the process.

Unseeing, dazed, her eyes flared wide before her lashes began drifting back over her eyes in rapture. Pulsing, incredible surges of pure white-hot energy imploded through her womb. Her pussy spasmed with the pure, rapturous pleasure. The sensations wrapped around her clit and the pleasure stole reason for long, precious seconds. It overtook her, it destroyed her, and yet it filled her with life.

It seemed never ending.

As though the release only built as it exploded again and again, drowning her in more and more ecstasy.

Then, as the pulsing waves of pleasure threatened to steal her consciousness, they began to ease. Each ripple smaller than the last until they became tremors, shuddering shivers of sensation as his own release pumped inside her and extended the heightened rapture.

Once she could function again, once time and space resumed their normal evolutions around her, Sheila found herself sprawled beneath him as he collapsed beside her, one arm pulling her to his chest as they both fought for breath. For sanity.

It was always the same.

It never mattered the position they were in. It never mattered how often she fought it or how long she went without him. Her response to his touch, to the pleasure, and to the culmination of her fiery response to him was always the same.

It was overwhelming.

It overtook her to the point that there was no way to fight it, no way to resist it. There was only the aftermath later, and the knowledge that, just as in the months past, nothing would be said of it tomorrow.

There was no relationship binding them, no promises, and no commitments. There were no discussions of the future and no mention of tomorrow.

She never knew from one night to the next where she stood with Casey or even if she stood with him.

And she was beginning to hate that feeling. She didn't believe in friends with benefits or in fuck buddies. She needed more. She needed more from Casey.

As she stared up at the ceiling, she realized their non-relationship didn't seem to be changing. She was tired of waiting on him to indicate he wanted something more, she acknowledged. She needed more. Perhaps it would be better for both of them if she found the strength to cut it off, once and for all. Otherwise her resentment could end up hurting them both.

It would definitely be better for her, because Sheila knew she was on the verge of a broken heart.

TWO

Nick Casey—just Casey to his friends—struggled to regain his senses after it seemed every one of them had pumped straight from his dick along with his come.

Sheila did more than drain the sexual tension from his body. There were times he swore she replaced that tension with something far more dangerous to his soul. And he was damned if he wanted to delve into what that "something" was. Hell, it was such an unfamiliar feeling he didn't even know how to describe it.

At the moment, the only thing he wanted to delve into was regaining his strength enough to fuck them both silly again.

At least, that would have been his first option. Instead, he found himself opening his eyes and watching as she rolled from him naked, as naked as sex itself, and padded to the bathroom.

Shower? He scratched at his naked chest as he peered through one eye at the door she had disappeared through.

Did he have the energy to follow her? Maybe wash her back? Then other areas?

He really, really liked taking a shower with Sheila.

She made it fun.

After he convinced her to let him have fun with her.

He frowned when he didn't hear the shower running. She was in there, but she was too quiet.

That wasn't a good thing. When she was that quiet she was thinking. Sheila thinking rarely added up to Casey having fun.

The last time she was that quiet— He was moving before he finished the thought, but hell, it was already too late.

The door opened and she stepped out. Dressed.

Son-of-a-bitch-dammit-to-hell! He felt like stomping his foot in childish petulance. He frowned at her. It was all he could do not to immediately demand she undress again and return to his bed.

She had even brushed the shoulder-length strands of her dark blond hair and had slid on her shoes. Somehow, she had gathered up her shoes and clothes before going into the bathroom while he'd been debating joining her.

Hell, he knew better than to drop his guard like that with her. She took advantage of it every friggin' time.

"Hey, baby?" He glanced down at the shoes again. "Why are you dressed?" Play it cool, he thought, maybe it wouldn't be so bad.

"Because I'm going home."

It was that bad, damn it to fucking hell! He should just lock her in his room with him.

She moved to the dresser, where she collected her purse.

How pissed would she get if he tied her to the bed?

It took a minute for him to process the fact that she was definitely leaving. He was a bit slow sometimes, he admitted. It had been a killer week and he was sleepy. One of those weary spells that invariably turned into full-fledged insomnia unless he managed to convince her to sleep in his arms. He slept like a baby whenever he could exhaust her enough to ensure she fell asleep just after release.

He made it to the door of the small apartment before she did, hoping there was some way to convince her not to leave. Naked, certain there had to be a way to accomplish keeping her there. Convince her to sleep with him. Just one night.

"Why?" He moved in front of her, blocking her way as he watched her eyes narrow on him. Those deep violet eyes held the faintest spark of anger, as though he had done something to offend her.

What the hell could he have done? Hell, he'd just made her come hard enough that her pussy had nearly strangled his dick as it tightened around him. He was more than willing to repeat the experience, too.

"Enough, Casey." There was an edge of steel in her voice, but those soft, soft violet eyes were filled with hurt. "I want to go home, not stand and argue with you." An edge of hurt lingered in her voice and he was damned if he could figure out why.

He lifted his hand, the backs of his knuckles brushing against the silk of her cheek as he stared down at her, confused.

Her gaze flickered. For a second, for just the briefest second, he saw the passion, the promise, and the incredible sensual depths of the woman in those pretty eyes. He also saw the same, confusing emotions he felt himself before they disappeared.

"Don't." She pulled back rather than leaning into him as he knew she wanted to do. She wanted him, ached as he ached for her. In her eyes he saw the need to stay, and that she wanted to return to that big bed with him.

He knew she wanted to. He didn't just see it in her gaze, he could feel it. Like a touch that was there, yet wasn't. Like a flame that connected them, licking over both their bodies.

And it made his dick damned hard. So damned hard that for a second he wondered if he really had fucked her. Or only imagined it?

In a heartbeat he was iron-hard, hot and ready to fuck, and he wondered how she could possibly find the inner strength to walk out on him when he knew she felt the same.

"Geez, Casey." Breathless, amazed, she glanced down at the erection attempting to stab into her lower belly. Fully engorged, the thick bulging head dark and throbbing, his cock was literally begging for attention. Weeping for it even.

"You make me crazy," he muttered, his hand dropping as he stared down at her before backing away. Hell, he wasn't going to beg her to stay. He sure as hell wasn't going to allow her to feel as though he were attempting to force her to stay.

She truly did make him crazy as hell. Completely insane like no other woman ever had. There was something about her that drew him, confused him, and made him feel things he didn't always understand. Things he didn't want to feel.

"I don't mean to make you crazy." She was breathless.

Damn, he loved that sexy little edge to her voice when she became breathless.

The sound of that edge of arousal in it had the power to make his balls tighten with the need to have her. The need to fuck her until there wasn't a chance in hell she could ever deny him again rose inside him.

"Hell, I can't get enough of you." He reached for her, and she backed away.

Sheila had never backed away from him before. What the hell was wrong with her?

His eyes narrowed. "What's going on, Sheila?"

Her chin lifted, and that little glimmer of feminine fire shifted from arousal to pure feminine determination.

Ah, hell. This wasn't a good thing. This meant he'd obviously done something completely male—and managed to either hurt her or piss her off.

He was in trouble now, and Casey damned well knew it.

"Nothing's going on, Casey." Her lips thinned and her eyes seemed to darken with the lie. Casey always knew when she was lying. And she only lied to him, according to her, when he should be able to answer his questions himself.

He'd never seen denial in her eyes when it came to him, though. At the moment, there was pure rejection gleaming there.

"Don't give me that shit," he growled. "We've never played games with each other. Not like this. I don't want to start now. I won't let you start now."

"I was never the one playing games."

Casey's eyes narrowed. Every man in the world knew that tone of voice.

Those violet eyes flashed again with the edge of anger, and Casey knew he was screwed.

"What the hell did I do?" Pushing his fingers through his hair, he wished the damned hard-on would abate just a little bit. It was hard as hell to be demanding when all he wanted to do was fuck the temperamental little minx.

She delighted in making him crazy, he decided. And she could make him crazy as hell faster than anyone he'd ever known.

"You didn't do anything." She lifted her shoulder in a shrug that warned him he sure as hell had done something. And he better find "her" way, to fix it fast.

See, this was what drove him crazy. It made him want to pull his own hair out because he couldn't figure out what the hell he had done. She was obviously expecting him to know this time what he had or hadn't done. Whichever, he probably had only moments to fix it before she walked out that door.

"Look, just tell me what your problem is, and I'll fix it." He glared back at her as he crossed his arms over his chest, certain his erection would deflate any second. Surely his dick would get a clue and just give it up.

It would have with any other woman giving him this kind of grief. Hell, it had never failed to deflate permanently with any other woman who dared to pull this shit on him.

Especially when he didn't know what he'd done to piss his soon to be ex-lover off. So why the hell hadn't it deflated yet? Why was he still standing there like a boob trying to figure out how to get her back in his bed?

"Didn't I do something right?" he demanded when that slender little hip cocked to the side and delicate fingers curved over it. The index finger tapped against her jeans silently. He'd only seen her do that a few times, and never with him. Until now.

Yep, he was in trouble. He just wished he knew why. How. Or what to do to fix it.

"You'll fix it, will you?" she asked silkily as her thick lashes fluttered over her mocking gaze. "Why, Casey, I just can't tell you how your offer makes my little heart beat faster."

Uh huh. He could tell. He really could. She was so damned sarcastic he almost winced.

He quickly ran through the night once again, just to be certain. Just to assure himself he hadn't done anything blatantly stupid. Because he really wasn't a stupid man where woman were concerned.

Had he gotten her a drink when she showed up at the bar?

Check.

He'd bought them all drinks and sent her a plate of the seasoned fries she liked as well. She and her friends sat in the corner booth and had a nice little visit. He had made certain they had everything they needed. And he'd paid for it all himself.

He'd kissed her before he got her in the car?

Check.

Fuck, he'd been so hungry for her he hadn't been able to keep from kissing her like he was dying for her.

He'd been romantic about it?

Hell yes.

He loved the feel of her hair, so he'd slid his hand into it, along the side of her face in the way he knew she liked. He knew, because it always made her eyes a little darker, and her face flush with feminine need. And he'd started that kiss slow and easy while he'd held her on the dance floor.

Once he'd gotten her to his apartment had he offered her another drink? Check there too.

He'd even offered her a snack or a meal.

He'd turned on the music, danced with her again, easing her slowly into the deepest flames of the arousal that began to burn inside them. Just because he loved the feel of her against him. Loved the way she rubbed against him.

"Look, Casey, I just want to go home," she informed him as she stepped to the door and gripped the knob. This time, he didn't try to stop her. He wasn't going to beg her. They weren't kids. They were supposed to be adults. Adults didn't play teenage games like this. At least, they shouldn't.

"Fine, when you feel in the mood to tell me what's wrong with you, then you know where to find me."

"Of course I do." He almost winced at the sound of her voice and the mockery that filled it. "Every night."

"Pretty much," he agreed with a tight nod. "I've never been hard to find. Made sure of it where you were concerned."

That only seemed to piss her off worse. Her fingers tightened on the doorknob and for a moment he thought she just might actually say whatever the hell was on her mind. He was certain the adult in her was ready to give up the game and just be honest with him.

Then her lips thinned again; she stepped through the doorway and slammed the door closed behind her.

Casey winced at the sound of metal meeting metal.

She had slammed the door on him. Hell, he couldn't believe it.

She might be more than just a little pissed.

She was pure female pissed with a healthy dose of "done had enough" when she slammed doors. Sheila wasn't normally a door slammer.

It was cute as hell actually. It was even damned arousing, though the fact that he found it arousing confused him more than he understood.

Running his fingers through his hair again, Casey did his best to try to figure out what he'd done. The funny thing was, she hadn't even hinted at being angry until she'd left the bathroom.

There was hurt in her eyes too.

He couldn't figure out how he'd hurt her.

He was damned if he could figure any of it out.

Casey rubbed at his chest before moving back to the bedroom, his gaze going over the bed critically before moving around the room as though there might be an answer there somewhere. Some way to figure out how he could have hurt her, or pissed her off.

She'd been just as hungry for him as he'd been for her when they had arrived at his apartment. Come to think of it, she had been just as eager for him as he was for her before they even left the bar.

It always amazed him how easily she matched his need. Kiss for kiss, touch for touch, pure sensual, sexual need driving them both to the brink of sanity.

Hot as fucking hell.

And it hadn't been any different than any other night. They burned each other alive.

And no matter how often he had her, it was never enough. He was always left just as hard for her as he was the first time he fucked her. And he always cursed the sunrise whenever he saw it edging through his curtains.

Because sunrise meant Sheila was going to awaken, and she was going to leave. It meant that unfamiliar warmth and the confusing yet comforting emotions he felt would disappear with her.

This time, she'd left well before sunrise, though. And there he stood, naked, hard, and rather than feeling anger he just felt . . . alone.

He heard her car start outside his window. The second floor afforded him privacy, but it also allowed him to keep his eyes and ears open.

Not that he had a lot of enemies in this new life or in this new, fairly low-key job.

He'd never seemed to make enemies as easily as he did friends, so there weren't a lot of people who wanted to hurt him, yet.

Yet, because he was involved in something that could possibly turn ugly if anyone ever figured it out. Or if they figured out exactly who Nick Casey really was.

If they did.

They hadn't yet, and it had been quite a few years since he had come to Simsburg, Texas. He'd been there for five years, ever since his days as a super-secret special operations soldier had gone to hell when an extraction had turned ugly.

He'd taken a bullet to his hip and one to his damned ankle. His reaction time was screwed then and his ability to endure the long hikes and hard runs required was forever behind him.

But he'd made enemies during those days. And once he had taken Ethan Cooper up on his job offer to handle the security at his bar, he'd learned that some men could never retire from the life of an adrenaline junkie.

Not him, not the men who worked with him at the bar, and sure as hell not his boss, Cooper.

As he threw himself back in the bed and stared up at the ceiling silently, Casey admitted that being a special operations solder had nothing on being a covert information gatherer and tattletale. The Broken Bar, Cooper's bar, was a watering hole for the dregs of society, as well as the locals and tourists. And Cooper's men were there to scoop up the scattered whispers, rumors, and gossip left behind. Posing as bouncers and bartenders, they heard it all.

Ethan's place was the only bar or nightclub coming from Corpus Christi. It was big, always busy, and drew a damned diverse crowd. A crowd that often held customers who mixed socializing with information and dropped tidbits of those secrets as they became more intoxicated through the night. More intoxicated and more self-important than they actually were.

Iron, Turk, Casey, and Jake put that information together along with Ethan for the retired army captain who headed the southern section of the Covert Information Network.

That same army captain was the father of the woman who had just left his bed. As though he had committed some horrible sin. A sin Casey had yet to realize was actually a sin.

He grimaced again and shifted on the bed to relieve the ache in his hip. The result of several nights working overtime, piecing together the information that had come in after a strike overseas on a terrorist cell. That strike had been the result of information the team had gathered the month before, making these past few nights even more important.

Sometimes, Casey wondered if they were even making headway despite the strikes the team was responsible for. Take one out, ten more slide in.

He was beginning to wonder what he had left behind as he chased the adrenaline dream. What had he given up all these years? What had he missed that he couldn't figure out the feeling Sheila made him feel? And what was he letting slip through his fingers now?

From that first night he and Sheila had come together, he'd felt he had finally found a cure to the restlessness that plagued him. He'd finally felt as though he belonged somewhere. Or to someone.

There was more to her than he'd had a chance to get to know, and more that swirled in that heart of hers than she allowed him to glimpse. Those secrets drew him. They made him hungrier by the day to know her better, to touch her more, to hold her tighter.

And he wanted to see it all.

Shockingly.

Casey had never wanted to delve into a woman's heart and soul at any other time. Not since the day his fiancée had cleaned out his apartment and his bank account when she'd heard he'd been wounded in action.

She hadn't stuck around to see how badly he had been hurt or cared if he had needed her. She sure as hell hadn't cared that he might need his furniture, his cash, hell, his bed, when he returned home.

Nope, she'd just cashed in everything she could and found greener pastures. His best friend's pasture.

That had been over seven years ago, nearly eight.

Sheila was different, though. From the moment he'd stared into those mysterious violet eyes, he'd known she was more different than any woman he'd ever touched. So unique he was determined to keep her as his own.

There was something about her eyes, something about the need he glimpsed in them whenever she gazed back at him that drew him. There was a warmth, a fire he longed for. All he wanted was to hold Sheila through the night.

Every night.

He rubbed at his jaw, a frown working over his brow again as he wondered what had happened and why she had run on him. But even more, what was that edge of hurt he'd glimpsed in her gaze?

How had he managed to hurt her when all he'd wanted to do was make love to her until they both collapsed?

Until she didn't have the strength, the will, or the desire to leave his arms again.

THREE

"Sheila, did we get those reports in from team two yet?" Captain Douglas Rutledge stepped from his office, his craggy face creased into a frown as he stared at her with that affronted, irritated look of a man who knows he should have something and knew it wasn't there.

His hair was mussed, his clothes slept in, and it looked like his socks were mismatched again.

That was her father.

Broody, impatient, and expecting perfection though he knew he wasn't going to receive it. At least, he said he knew, she thought as she watched him fondly.

"Not yet, Captain," she assured him using the title as her mother had before her. "I told you I'd let you know the minute they arrive."

Sheila hadn't called him Dad since the day her mother told her how he enjoyed the rare times she called him captain instead.

She turned back to the computer and the completion

of the final electronic copy from the past week's reports. He was her parent and she loved him, but he was as demanding as any military man could be.

Besides, things had been slow in the bars and night-clubs where the operatives under her father's command worked. He wasn't going to be happy about it either. Captain Rutledge took his job seriously and demanded results.

Reaching up to scratch at his graying head, he glared at her again, drawing her attention.

She glared right back at him. "I can't snap my fingers and get it, Captain. You're just going to have to wait for it, no matter how long it takes."

His brows lifted in surprise as she barely stopped herself from sighing in irritation. Dammit, he knew her too well, and snapping back at him never failed to start an inquisition. And that was something she really didn't need right now.

He stood staring at her, both hands buried in the pockets of his dark slacks as he continued to regard her silently. Questioningly. And she knew that look. He expected an explanation, now.

Sheila considered simply going back to the reports she was putting together. Sometimes, the best thing to do was to ignore him. She wondered if that would work today as it had in the past.

"Might as well tell me what the problem is," he grunted. "You've been out of sorts for three days and I'm tired of being your little whipping boy."

Whipping boy? Sometimes her father tended to exaggerate.

"You're not a whipping boy," she muttered. "You're a nosy old man."

She had been very, very careful not to be out of sorts. She would be damned if she would let Casey hear that she was in any way less than a terrific mood. And her father wasn't above asking everyone they knew what was wrong with her.

She simply couldn't afford it.

"Yes you have. I want to know why." Her father strode across the small office to lean against the side of her desk as he stared down at her inquisitively. He wanted an answer and she knew by the look on his face he was determined to get one.

The glare was gone, and that was an indication that the captain was now her father, and he was concerned. She could deny the captain, but it was harder to deny her father.

Besides, she didn't want him to be concerned. When he worried, he poked his nose into her life and made her crazy.

"You have reports to go over, Captain," she reminded him, barely restraining a roll of her eyes. "Not a daughter to raise. You already completed that particular mission admirably."

"You look just like your mother when you say that." Nostalgia entered his tone, his expression. "She would try to lie to me just like that too."

A wealth of love filled his voice as he spoke, as well as that ever present shadow of pain he carried. He had loved her mother, even after her death. So much so that he had never considered remarrying. He didn't even date.

"Mom never lied to you." Sheila shook her head, barely restraining her smile. Because he was right. Her mother was very good at evasion, though, not lying. And her father had always known when she was evading.

"There's no difference between an evasion and a lie," he warned her as though reading her thoughts. He simply knew her that well.

"Of course there is." She laughed back at him. "When you don't want to lie to someone, you evade. It's perfectly acceptable." That way they couldn't get angry or accuse you of deceit.

His brow arched. "So you're not lying, you're evading?" He had no idea.

"You're funny." This time, she did roll her eyes. "I'm not evading either," she promised him. "I'm trying to get this mountain of paperwork finished."

"No, dear child, you're flat-out lying."

And at that point, she had to drop her eyes, because he was right, she was lying through her teeth and she hated it.

"My business," she told him firmly.

He watched her for long, silent moments.

"Hmm, that means it's a man," he guessed.

"It means it's my business and I prefer not discuss it with you or anyone else, Captain," she informed him.

Her father could be like a dog with a bone. She never appreciated being the bone. It was highly uncomfortable.

He glared at her again. "Then that means it's a man I'd know."

There was the displeasure. How the hell had he known?

Duh! He knew everyone she knew. There was no way to be wrong.

"No, Dad, it means someone you know might know him, and I'd prefer he be unaware of the fact that I'm displeased with him."

Not exactly a lie, not exactly the truth either.

At that point, he frowned again in confusion. "But

dear, how else is your young man supposed to make the situation right and win your heart if he doesn't know why you're upset?"

Sheila leaned back in her chair, crossed her arms, and stared back at him firmly. "Dad, I don't want him to make anything right and I definitely don't want anyone else to tell him if he's done something to upset me. I prefer to take care of these things myself."

Her father reached up and scratched at his weathered cheek, and Sheila could see that he had no idea what to make of his daughter. He often lamented that she refused to fall in love and marry fast to suit him, because he had always insisted on probing into her dates' lives.

It wasn't a refusal to love, she knew how to love, it was simply a refusal to beg or to play the games she watched so many other women play. Those relationships rarely worked, she had found. It had left her friends and acquaintances with broken hearts and disillusioned lives. If a woman had to beg, plead, or hint at a need for commitment from a man, then she didn't need that man.

She didn't want that. She wanted to be like her mother. She wanted to marry once and marry a man that she not only loved, but one that loved her just as much. She didn't want to guilt Casey into loving her. Where would the satisfaction be in that?

Yet Casey had been convinced she was playing games instead.

"So, who is he?" her father asked, his tone indicating a demand for an answer.

Sheila shook her head. "Sorry, Dad, but I don't need your help in this. I'll take care of it myself. I'm rather good at that now."

She had only been young and dumb once.

His frown deepened as concern filled his eyes. "I promise to say nothing to anyone," he promised her. A huge concession from him.

"Sorry, Dad, it's not going to happen." She shook her head slowly as amusement tugged at her lips. "I know better than to tell you. You like trying to fix my life too much. And I don't need this fixed." At least, not by her father. There was nothing her father could do anyway, except make the situation worse.

He was a busybody. A loving one. A caring one. He would never do anything to hurt her. But she knew him too well. If he knew who her lover was, he would no doubt make it an order that Casey find a way to fix it.

"So why won't you let *him* fix it? Tell me that and I'll let it go," he said gently. "Otherwise, you know it will drive me crazy." Because he was her father and he felt it was his place to fix her problems. She believed differently, but she could tell him the least of what he wanted to know.

"Because, if he loved me, then he would love me enough to know what to do, Dad," she said somberly. "Like you knew with Mom."

And how many times had her father told her how he'd known the second he met her mother what she would be to him? That he had loved her from the moment he had met her and had been willing to die for her if he could have?

She wanted that kind of love as well.

Her father shook his head sadly. "Sheila, your mother led me on a merry chase. I didn't say I recognized the emotion in that first moment. It was only later I realized what I was feeling. No man that I know of recognizes love for what it is until his absolutely forced to do so."

"So will he, if that's what he feels," she told him. "Don't mess with this, Dad."

She couldn't handle it. She wouldn't tolerate it. She wouldn't be able to bear the thought that her father had somehow "ordered" Casey to love her.

She wouldn't play games with Casey, and she wasn't going to allow her father to step in to fix this for her. Only Casey could fix it and she had a feeling that wasn't going to happen either.

She had always suspected the fact that she was Captain Rutledge's daughter had kept Casey away from her for years. If her father intervened, no doubt Casey would feel that pressure to make promises he wouldn't want to make or keep.

God, she wanted him though.

She almost wanted him—no, loved him—enough to risk it. Enough to almost consider it. She was dying for him and it was all her own stubborn fault for wanting more than he had to give.

And in all the months they had been coming together, not once had Casey suggested that there was more between them than the few nights a month they spent in his bed. He hadn't asked her out, he hadn't suggested that their relationship could ever develop into anything more serious. Just as he had never indicated to anyone else that they were together in any way.

And that hurt. As though he were ashamed of her, or too frightened of her father to risk him knowing, which she knew wasn't the case. Or perhaps he just didn't want to be a couple with her.

She was tired of it. Each time he touched her, she felt

as though he had torn another part of her heart from her chest and carried it away with him. She didn't want to lose more of her heart. She didn't want to be in this relationship alone.

"You're frightened," her father finally said softly, his head tilting to the side as he regarded her with gentle admonishment.

"Frightened of what?" She couldn't believe he had said anything so ridiculous or with such fatherly chastisement.

"Of being hurt," he guessed. "You know, Sheila, I haven't heard even a whiff of a rumor that you were seeing anyone. That you were interested in anyone. You've kept him very well hidden and that makes me wonder if the problems are your fault or your unknown lover's."

Her lips thinned. "I'm not telling you who it is."

He shook his head slowly. "My dear, you wouldn't have had to tell me, if you weren't frightened of this man breaking your heart. A woman doesn't hide something so important as the man she's in love with, unless there's something holding her back. Or," his voice lowered further. "Or, she doesn't love him at all. And if that's the case, then I don't want to know who he is." He shrugged as though it didn't matter. "I only want to meet the important ones and this one obviously isn't important at all."

At that point, he straightened and moved back to his office without saying anything further, leaving Sheila to stare at his back with narrowed eyes as she wondered at what game he could be playing with her. Her father could be amazingly devious when he wanted information. That was why he made such an efficient commander for the Covert Information Network.

She only wished Casey didn't matter.

She wished she didn't miss him with everything inside her; missing him was killing her.

She wished the only thing holding her back was the fear of losing the rest of her heart.

It was the fear of losing so much more than her heart that terrified her.

Because what she was beginning to feel, she felt as though it went much deeper than her heart, went much deeper than any other emotion she had ever felt.

It went clear to her soul.

Casey sat at the bar tapping his fingers against the gleaming wood. His gaze was locked on the mirror behind the bar, giving him a clear view of the entrance.

The large, cavernous building was nearly at its limit with the threat of a line forming outside once they were forced to close the doors against additional customers. Once customers arrived at the Broken Bar, they seemed to stay until last call. Which made it hard for any additional customers arriving unless the owner, Ethan Cooper, used the one-hour limit he was often forced to set.

The band, positioned along the wall at the center of the room on the opposite side of the building, was belting out another of those sensual slow tunes they were inclined to play. Broken hearts, broken loves, and beer drinkin' nights. He was damned sick of hearing about it. Every wailing note did nothing but remind him of Sheila and the fact that he'd been waiting on her all day and half the night. He reminded himself of a lovesick teenager.

The door swung open again, but the couple that entered wasn't Sheila. She should have been here by now. It was her job to pick up the information the team had acquired over the past week. Instead, he was still here waiting on her. It felt like he had been waiting on her all his life.

He glanced at his watch before his gaze lifted to the door once more. Yep, that was him; lovesick teenager.

Sheila knew he didn't work tonight. Son of a bitch, she always showed up on Tuesday nights. Tuesday nights were theirs. Slow loving and her sensual cries as they drove each other crazy with every kiss, caress, and stroke they could bestow on each other.

Casey tapped his fingers against the wood again, his teeth clenching as a surge of hunger and anger struck at his gut. She wasn't going to show up. He could feel it. She was avoiding the bar and she was avoiding him and he was damned if he was going to let her get away with it.

His jaw bunched in irritation.

If Sheila was going to cut him off like this, the least she could have done was give him a reason why she was breaking off what they had. He didn't even know what the hell was going on, what he had done, or why she had ended the relationship the other morning as she left.

Hell, he had no idea what had happened, and it wasn't as though he could talk to her about it. He couldn't even catch up with her long enough. And now, she was late arriving to pick up the files it was her job to transport to her father.

He had asked her what he had done, something he had never asked another woman and wouldn't have bothered to even care about with anyone else.

Her reply had been "nothing."

There had been an odd tone to her voice, though. One he hadn't wanted to delve into at the time. Something about the sound of her answer had immediately had his

stomach clenching. Not in dread, but in an impending . . .
something that still didn't make sense. What did make
sense? He was dying for her.

And he had no idea how to fix any of it.

"Hey, Casey, you look down." Sarah Foxe Cooper,
God love her heart, his boss's wife. Trust her to get right
to the point and thankfully to keep her voice down while
doing so.

A charming, shy little thing, he'd once believed. Until
she came out of her shell, stole Cooper's heart, and became a regular at one of the most dangerous watering
holes in the state. She was like a breath of fresh air in a
trash dump. Pretty as a picture she was, and from the look
on her face, determined to get an answer to her question.
Determined and firm, she moved through the crowd as
though it were a family reunion.

Cooper was never far behind her, either. And if not
Cooper, then at least two of his most trusted bouncers
were planted on her ass. Cooper never, at any time, took
his wife's safety for granted.

Tonight, as on most nights, it was Cooper following
his wife. With an indulgent smile on his face, he kept a
steady eye on the woman who had stolen his heart the
summer before.

"I'm tired, Sarah," he answered. "Your husband is a
slave driver."

He was tired of waiting and watching for a woman
who hadn't arrived. She had five more minutes, then he
was going after her. Five minutes, that was it.

"Yeah, but such a damned sexy one," Sarah replied,
her smile infectious and filled with warmth as she cast
her husband a flirty look over her shoulder.

"I guess it takes a feminine eye to see the sexy part,"

Casey snorted as he glanced toward the entrance again and caught himself glaring at it.

"Hmm, that could be possible." Sarah shrugged as she lifted herself onto the bar stool beside him, drawing his gaze from the door. "But that doesn't tell me why you're looking such a grump this early in the week. I thought you reserved the bad moods for the weekend?"

Not lately he hadn't. Weekends had meant Sheila too. It had meant wild, hot, explicit sex, earthy feminine moans, and sharp little nails clawing at his back.

Fuck, he was hard. His dick pulsed and throbbed in his jeans.

That fast. His erection was all but pushing past the zipper of his jeans and drawing his balls tight against the base of the shaft. It felt as though it had been years rather than days since he had fucked her.

Damn.

He glanced at his watch again. Two minutes and he was going after her.

He couldn't handle this. He wanted her to the point his back teeth ached with it.

For three nights in a row, he'd existed in a state of miserable arousal and confused anger. There was nothing worse than caring that he'd fucked up and being unable to figure out how.

"I'm fine, Sarah," he promised as he realized she was watching him expectantly.

He glanced at the door again, then his watch.

One and a half minutes and he was going after her.

"She slipped in the back entrance about three hours ago, collected the reports, and ran," Sarah leaned forward and informed him quickly, her voice low. "Ran as though the hounds of hell were nipping at her heels."

Sarah straightened in her seat then and cast her husband a teasing look as he shook his head at her. Sarah was known to matchmake. Or at least, to attempt to. It had been making all of them crazy. They indulged her, were amused by her, but seriously, she made them crazy with it.

Well, all of them except the new guy, Morgan Keane. One of the six new bouncers Cooper had been forced to hire in the past year. He was a former special forces soldier referred by one of the U.S. Marshals who were protecting Sarah's father. A former Italian Mafia boss who had immigrated to America, now known as Giovanni Fredric.

Morgan was a brooding, grouchy son of a bitch with an attitude that managed to keep even the most aggressive jackals in the place at bay.

Nothing Sarah or anyone else did seemed to faze Keane much, though. He took it all in stride.

"Did she now?" Casey finally forced himself to mutter, irritation mixing with the lust and surging through his bloodstream with a hit of spiked adrenaline.

Yep, there it was. That shot of elixir that kept him perpetually hard whenever he thought of Sheila.

"She did." Sarah grinned. "It was all rather curious too. I thought she was running scared, but she swore she was simply in a hurry. What do you think?"

The gleam of knowledge in her eyes was highly discomforting. It meant she was matchmaking.

"Hell if I know," he muttered, deciding in that second he didn't need her help.

"Confused on that, are you?" she asked.

He leveled a suspicious glare in her direction. It only

received another of her infamous smiles. Those innocent, I've-done-nothing-wrong grins.

Bullshit. She was obviously up to something, and he
had a feeling he knew what. He was getting into trouble
just fine all by himself. He didn't need Sarah's help.

"I shouldn't be?" he asked softly.

She shrugged again as she brushed back one of the
thick, heavy brown curls that had fallen over her shoulder.

"Well, it should have been rather obvious," Sarah
sighed. "Most women of Sheila's ilk refuse to play second
fiddle to anything or anyone else, Casey. They're simply
too possessive to be placed in any position but first."

"She doesn't play second anything, period," he informed her. "Where are you going with this?"

Why was he letting her "go with it"? The "it" being
the head game she was playing.

"It would depend on where you intend on going with
things," she suggested lightly. "And perhaps that's all she's
waiting on from you, to decide if you're worth risking
her heart for. Sometimes, all a woman needs is to know
she's wanted for more than what she provides her lover
in their bed."

"Troublemaker." Cooper stepped forward, growling
the accusation in a tone filled with pure adoration. He
was damned crazy over the girl and everyone knew it. But
he did make attempts to limit her interference in other
people's lives.

"Of course I am," she admitted as she lifted her face
and accepted the quick kiss he placed against her lips.
"That's why you love me so dearly, though. I never let
you get bored."

Casey watched their byplay until Cooper helped his wife from her seat and they headed for the door behind the bar. That door led to the stairs that would take them to the office/bedroom Cooper kept upstairs. From there, Casey didn't even want to guess what they would be doing. It was better not to.

Because then, he would start thinking of all the things he could be doing with Sheila, and it would just piss him off worse.

He glanced at the mirror again and narrowed his eyes.

He knew where Sheila was. He knew where she lived and he knew how to get to her. And he knew he was really getting tired of waiting on her.

She was his, he'd made that decision a long time before and had been forced to wait far too long to claim her. But he had claimed her, and now, letting her go wasn't something he was going to do. Not now, not ever.

FOUR

For the third night in a row, sleep was a hard time coming. For the past months, Tuesday night was one of the three reserved for Casey. At any other time she would be in his bed.

Sheila rolled over to her back with a groan and stared up at the darkened ceiling morosely. What was he doing now? Was he alone in his bed or had he found someone else to share it with? Had she made a mistake? Had she let him go too quickly, before he could have realized she could mean something to him?

Was she letting the past influence the present in such a way that she could be harming the hopes she had for her future? Of course she was, wasn't that what she was good at? She had already proved it.

Seven years before, she hadn't demanded the commitment, or the words of love. She hadn't pressed the issue and she had learned the error of it. She'd been used by the man she'd thought she'd loved. Ross Mason had used her and her heart to get close to her father and to secure a military position that only Douglas Rutledge could assign.

Thankfully, her father had been smart enough to see what she hadn't, and had managed to turn Ross's game against him. When Ross had been given that position, he suddenly had no use for her. He'd even smiled at her and told her she had to have been aware of what he had wanted. She had just been a means to acquire it.

Not that she believed Casey was using her, because she couldn't imagine what he could want from her. But she hadn't imagined what Ross could want either, until the night he had broken the relationship off.

She wasn't going to allow that to happen to her again. She couldn't allow it, not with Casey. Already he meant too much to her.

She hadn't loved Ross, not really. She had liked him. He had been safe, or she had thought he had been safe. She would have never loved him to the point that losing him could destroy her. Not like she loved Casey.

Kicking the blankets from her legs and blowing out a hard, deep breath, Sheila realized she was going to end up making herself crazy. She was already aroused. That was all the crazy she needed.

Lifting her arm from the mattress beside her, she let her fingers trail along the flesh exposed between the elastic of her low-rise panties and the white silk-and-lace cami tank top she wore to sleep in.

She missed his touch, the warmth of his arms around her, and his kiss.

Her eyes drifted closed and she saw Casey watching

her. His expression heavy with lust, his gaze darkening with whatever emotion he kept hidden within his silence. The way he licked his lips the few times she had touched herself as he watched. It turned him on, made him so dominant and hungry for her that his possession stole her breath.

Innocent touches.

When she had smoothed lotion over her arms, stomach, and legs after showering, she would see his eyes narrow, his cock hardening beneath his jeans, or if he was naked, his unashamed hunger for her.

What would he have done if she had touched herself in front of him, as she did when she was alone? How intense and dominant would he become if he had seen her touching herself when she missed him?

Or even now?

Would he enjoy watching her masturbate?

The tips of her nails rasped against the sensitive flesh of her lower stomach as she remembered his touch. His kiss. The way he would use his versatile, wicked tongue to lick and taste her skin.

She wanted to moan at the excitement that suddenly rushed through her. The silent thought that she could tease him in such a way. That the next time she saw him she would have the nerve to be the seductress she always imagined being, but hadn't yet garnered the courage to be.

Or the chance. The chance to watch his gaze darken and narrow as she touched her nipples or ran her fingers through her juices before circling her clit.

His sensuality overwhelmed her. Once he touched her, all thoughts of anything but being possessed by him, taken and ridden to exhaustion, flew from her mind. She hadn't remembered to tease him by touching herself; even though she had promised herself she would.

Her fingers trailed to the band of her panties, pushed beneath slowly, then feathered over the short, soft curls at the top of her mound.

Below, the slick, waxed flesh felt flushed and swollen, her juices easing over it as arousal began to build within her. She could feel the inner flesh of her pussy heating, aching, needing him.

She knew better than to go further. The sheer frustration she had found over the months in masturbating was becoming ridiculous. She could never satisfy herself as she once had. She was always left aching, wanting, her pussy and her clit still throbbing despite the release she found.

Satisfaction could only be found with Casey and she knew it.

With his touch, his kiss, or the heavy, throbbing length of his cock pushing inside her, Penetrating her with a slow, measured surge. Each thrust would draw a cry from her lips and stretch her to her limits. It would burn. Pleasure-pain would fill her, then ecstasy would overtake her.

She bit her lip, a surge of sexual need flooding her system and tightening through her womb.

Her fingers slid lower. Any touch would be better than none, she told herself desperately. Any release better than no release at all.

Her fingers stroked over her clit as her breath caught at the wave of sensation that rushed through her senses. Swollen and slick, the little bud throbbed in desperation as she let her fingers ease through the wet, slickened folds of her pussy.

Her hips lifted to her own touch, her fingers slid lower.

"Keep that up and I'll come in my damned jeans before I can get them off."

Sheila's eyes flew open, a gasp leaving her lips as she stared at the end of the bed where Casey stood watching her. Chocolate brown eyes looked black in the darkness as he finished unbuttoning the shirt he wore, moving slowly, giving her all the time she needed to tell him to go to hell. And that was exactly what she should do. She should never let herself weaken. She should throw him out until he decided he loved her and couldn't live without her. That was what she should do.

Instead, she let her fingers reach further, one dipping into the clenched, heated entrance of her pussy. Delicate muscles gripped her fingers, spasmed, and clenched as pleasure shot through her.

His jaw tightened and a second later he was shrugging the shirt from the powerful width of his shoulders.

Muscles rippled beneath the tough, hardened flesh. Random scars, nicks, and marks covered the broad expanse, and she knew he carried even more on his left hip and ankle from the wound that had forced his discharge from the army.

Lips parting to drag in a ragged breath, Sheila pushed her finger in deeper, aware that Casey had yet to take his eyes from where her fingers worked between her thighs. Electric sensation shot through her nerve endings as a gasp left her lips. Casey tore at the metal tab and zipper of his jeans, releasing them before pushing them from his long, powerful legs. Casey didn't wear underwear. His cock sprang free, eager to join the fun.

When he straightened, his erection stood out from his body, thick and erect, the flared crest darkened and shining with moisture.

He palmed the heavy shaft. Long, broad fingers stroked his erection as he watched her with narrowed eyes, lust gleaming in naked demand.

"Take off your panties." His voice was guttural and rough, the command heavy with hungry male intent.

"Let me watch you fuck yourself with your fingers."

A chill tore up her spine before a fist clenched her womb and tightened through her pussy. A wash of juices saturated her cunt and the sizzling ache of pure sensual hunger washed through it.

Oh God, she wanted him so desperately. She needed him inside her pussy, thrusting, pushing in with the heavy thrusts she knew would throw her headfirst into ecstasy.

Feeling dazed, as though she were living in a fantasy, Sheila shed her panties, tossing them carelessly to the floor as her legs spread, giving him a clear view of her fingers sliding between the swollen lips of her pussy once again.

Sensation swept through her as he watched, sending excitement racing through her.

"Ah yes, baby," he rasped. "Let me see how pretty you are. How fucking sweet as you fuck yourself."

Stroking the hard flesh of his cock, he watched as her fingers slid once again to the snug entrance of her pussy.

She wanted him to watch. She needed him to watch. Never had her own touch filled her with such intense pleasure, such hunger.

She wanted him to ache as she ached. She wanted him as ensnared in the web created by whatever it was that flowed between them as she was. She needed him to ache, to want, to need just as badly as she needed him. In every way.

Her fingers slid back, slick and hot; her juices coating them and glistening on the curves of her pussy.

Watching him, Sheila touched, pleasured, and knew she would never be able to touch herself again without him watching. Never would she be able to find even the smallest satisfaction without Casey.

The sensations were sharper, more exciting than they had ever been without him. They sizzled through her body, burned through her clit and tightened her womb with spasms of her approaching orgasm.

Casey licked his lips, a slow, hungry movement that mesmerized her as she circled her clit with her fingers, causing the little bud to swell harder, tighter.

Her breathing was rougher now, as though she couldn't draw enough air into her lungs.

Excitement whipped through her. As though her nerve endings were live wires, exposed and spilling their energy sensation over her flesh. And if the look on Casey's face was any indication, he was feeling it as well.

His eyes were almost black. She had only seen that when he was at his most aroused. His lips were fuller, heavier, his hard chest gleaming with sweat as he stroked the length of his cock with slow, easy strokes.

The heavily veined, pulsing erection held her attention as she slid two fingers inside the gripping, saturated flesh between her thighs once more.

It wasn't her fingers she felt.

It wasn't her own touch that held her enraptured.

It was the remembered feel, the remembered pleasure of Casey's possession that made her insane. That made her come apart at the seams.

As her fingers penetrated her pussy, it was his cock she felt. It was his possession. The echoes of it. The remembered feel of him stretching her as she parted her fingers and scissored them against the clenched muscles surrounding them.

"Casey," she whispered his name, her voice rough, filled with need as she realized her eyes had closed.

They jerked open, staring back at him in surprise as she realized he was much closer. He was kneeling between her spread knees, sitting back on his heels as he stroked his cock and watched her.

"Don't stop," he growled. "Fuck yourself, Sheila. Let me see you. Let me see how much you want me to touch you."

She wanted him to touch her bad.

Her hips lifted. A moan tore from her.

His expression tightened.

Kneeling between her knees, his gaze focused on the flesh between her thighs as she penetrated herself, her fingers gleaming with her juices as she tried to hold back her release.

"I dream of you," she gasped, feeling the release racing to her.

"What do you dream, baby?"

"Of this, sometimes," she whispered desperately. "Of you taking me, making me cry out for you, because the pleasure is so intense I can barely stand it."

She wasn't going to scream in need for it. She was

going to demand he take her, that he possess her. She
was going to beg him for it.

Her fingers slid back, finding her clit as his gaze
lifted to hers once again.

"Fuck me, Casey," she whispered. "Please. I need
you. I need you inside me so bad I don't think I can
bear it."

He moved closer.

"Keep touching yourself."

He lifted her thigh, moving in, bending over her, po-
sitioning the wide head of his cock at the greedy, saturated entrance to her sex.

She caressed her clit, arching, her breasts lifting as
his lips descended to one hard, tight nipple.

Sharp, ecstatic sensation tore through the sensitive
tip, streaking through her body to slam into the respon-
sive depths of her womb, then into her pussy.

He sucked the tip into his mouth as the flared head
began to part the snug entrance of her pussy.

Sliding her fingers into the cool, thick strands of his
hair, Sheila could only gasp his name. Sensation swirled
through her senses, pleasure tore through her body.
Stretching, burning, his cock worked inside her, sepa-
rating her flesh as her fingers moved erratically on the
swollen bud of her clit.

The intensity of the pleasure whipping through her
had her senses expanding with nearing ecstasy. Sensation began to jerk through her body, to race just beneath
her flesh faster.

His cock stroked inside her in short, hard thrusts,
raking along the exquisitely sensitive nerve endings as
she began to gasp with the sensations.

His lips, tongue, and mouth caressed her nipple, drawing on the tiny bud, tormenting it. He rasped it with his teeth as she arched to him. Her muscles tightened, clenching on his cock as it slowly invaded her.

She was dying from the pleasure.

Sensation ballooned inside her, tearing through her senses until she was arching tight beneath him. Her hips writhed on the impalement as Casey sank fully inside her. He seated himself to the hilt with one firm, possessive penetration. The thrust speared through the gripping, milking muscles of her pussy, drawing a harsh cry from her lips.

No sooner than he sank inside her, he was moving.

If pleasure was a whirlwind before, it became a cyclone. The hard, rapid motions of his hips, the heavy, deep thrusts inside her, the caress of the velvet over iron flesh impaling her was like riding a starburst.

Sensations swelled and detonated through her nerve endings, yet the release that seemed so near never seemed so far away. Moving her fingers over her clit in short, rapid motions as he shafted inside her, Sheila only increased the torturous pleasure. She couldn't stop. She was so close.

"Casey," she cried out, panting for air. "Oh God, it's killing me. Please."

His head lifted from her nipple.

"Please what, baby?" he groaned, his lips moving against the mound of her breast, his tongue licking over the damp skin he found. "Tell me what you want. I'll give it to you. You only have to ask."

"I need to come," she gasped, staring up at him, dazed, watching as a trail of sweat ran slowly down the side of his hard face. "Make me come, Casey. Make me come all over your cock. It's so thick and hard inside me . . ." she moaned.

As though she had struck a match to fuel, Casey gave a tortured moan before he began moving harder, faster.

Thrusting, shafting inside her with hard, quick strokes, his cock shuttling in and out of the tight confines of her sex, he gave her what she begged for.

Within seconds Sheila was exploding. Tossed headlong into a rapture she couldn't control and had no desire to rein in. It began in the very depths of her pussy, radiating outward to attack her clit as she stroked it in time to the hard strokes filling her cunt, and the brutal shudders that began tearing through her.

The little bud swelled quickly, harder, more sensitive than ever as she gave a wild, fractured moan and let it fling her into an ecstasy she was certain Casey had never given her before.

This one was brighter, hotter, it tore past her mind, completely obliterated thought or any belief that she could ever be the same once reality returned.

Because as that explosion ripped through her, it did more than fill her body with the most exquisite rapture she had ever known. It did more than simply satisfy that feminine ache as no other man had ever been able to do. As she exploded around the hard, fiery erection filling her, she felt him bury in deep once again, then felt his release tear through him as well.

She felt the hard, heavy spurts of his release filling her.

She felt his arms wrapping around her.

She felt his wide, muscular chest scraping against her nipples, his powerful thighs tightening.

She felt the white-hot center of her release tear a hole through the defenses she had built against him as well.

As his release jetted inside her, she swore she felt a part of *him* sink inside her soul.

He had finally possessed her.

And she knew she hadn't managed the same with him.

She knew. And she swore she felt it breaking her heart.

FIVE

Sheila remembered what it felt like when she was nineteen and she learned the man she thought she loved had only been using her to get to her father. That it hadn't been her he wanted, it had been a position that her father controlled. One that, once he'd acquired it, Douglas Rutledge couldn't take from him.

But, as her father had said, it wasn't worth taking back. It had been worth it to know he'd wanted the job rather than the daughter. And better she'd known before Sheila had messed up her life and married the man.

At the time, she hadn't seen it that way. She understood the reason he had tested the relationship by assigning the position before the proposal, but the knowledge that she'd been wanted for anything more than what her father could provide still managed to hurt.

She had never taken a love interest to meet her father since. Dates picked her up at her house, a small cottage a half mile from her father's main house. She never told her father who she was seeing, or when she was seeing them.

It was easier that way.

If anyone mentioned wanting to meet her father, it spelled the end of whatever relationship they had.

She never dated anyone her father knew.

Until Casey.

But, she excused herself, she wasn't exactly dating Casey. She was only sleeping with him, wasn't she?

Still, she was breaking one of her own rules and she knew it.

Then she had compounded that error by falling in love with him.

Yes, she was in love with him, and she knew it.

Sitting in her car outside the bar two nights later, she knew she had made that drastic mistake. A horrendous mistake. One guaranteed to break her heart in half.

Breathing out roughly, she tested the feel of the boots she wore before opening the door of her small car and stepping out.

The hollow heel still felt a little strange.

Casey had brought her the boots the night before, claiming he felt the newly designed heel would be more secure than her purse for hiding the flash drives she carried to her father twice a week.

The tiny chamber was waterproof and it would be impossible to detect the drive using any electronic means, he assured her.

He'd acted positively protective, and for a second, just a second, she'd wondered if she had been wrong, if he felt something more for her than simply lust.

"Can't have those drives getting lost or stolen if some yahoo decides to grab your purse." He'd shrugged then. "I hate wasting my time."

And her hopes had plummeted.

Dammit.

She'd thought by now he would have at least shown a few emotions besides worry over the damned flash drives.

The information on them was imperative, she knew. The tracking of terrorists, both homeland and overseas was imperative. Drug and weapons runners and any other criminal element that walked through the doors of the bar was fair game.

Every customer was photographed the second they entered and, using hidden remote cameras, additional pictures could be taken.

Who they met with, who they danced with, what they did in the parking lot. Rumors, gossip, and drunken bragging were recorded, saved, and then placed on the flash drive to be given to the captain. He then delivered it to the homeland security team assigned to break down the information and investigate as needed.

It was done quietly, effectively, and it had worked for eight years. Since the day Ethan Cooper had reopened the Broken Bar and brought the proposal to the captain, after he'd learned about the clientele he wouldn't be able to keep out of it.

Since that day, the bar had reigned as the only alcoholic establishment allowed within the county limits. The Broken Bar was a favorite among the locals as well as the criminal element. And Ethan Cooper ran the establishment with an iron hand.

No dealing, drugs or otherwise, was the rule, though they'd recorded it happening often enough.

The bouncers watched out for the women first, innocent men second, and they were all friends of Cooper's. Tough, hard-eyed bastards who had been discharged from the army for one reason or another.

Some honorably.

Some not so honorably.

Smoothing the skirt of her short dress, Sheila made her way from the parking spot she'd managed to snag at the side of the building and stepped up to the wood walkway that stretched around the bar.

The entrance was manned that night by Turk.

One of those hard-eyed bastards who had been not so honorably discharged.

"Miss Rutledge." He nodded as he opened the door for her.

"Thanks, Turk." She threw him a quick smile as she moved past him.

"Casey will be out in a bit, he's in a meeting with Coop."

She almost paused at the bouncer's announcement. She almost turned around and asked him why she should care. But she knew these men.

Number one, he wouldn't tell her what he knew, and there was no doubt he knew something; otherwise, he'd never have said anything.

Holding her irritation for Casey until later, she moved into the building and headed for the long, gleaming teak bar at the side of the room.

A band was belting a country-western tune on the other end. The sound of the steel guitar, the lazy sensuality in the singer's voice, and the sight of the customers swaying on the dance floor was enough to assure her she'd arrived late.

Everyone had had just enough booze to loosen inhibitions, if any existed, and lead them to the dance floor where they could rub and grind and in some cases even complete the sexual act in the dimmer areas as the sexually charged music seemed to infect them.

Her father had always warned her to beware of alcohol and slow dancing.

And he was right.

She almost grinned at the thought.

The first night she and Casey had been together, they had danced to a slow, lazy tune after the bar had closed and after they had shared more than one drink.

Her stomach clenched at the memory of that night.

There on the bar. He'd turned the cameras off and he'd taken her like a man starved for a woman.

"Hey, Sheila, you're blushing." Sarah Cooper's brows were arched as she made the accusation teasingly. "What are you thinking about that has your face all red?"

Hell.

She was half tempted to turn around and walk out rather than face the warmhearted teasing. She hoped that Casey wasn't around.

"Secrets," Sheila informed her as she took the bar stool one of the bouncers vacated.

The new guy, Morgan Keane.

Six feet four and a half inches of power and well-honed muscles. Dark blue eyes and black hair, sun-bronzed skin, and a hardened expression.

Wearing jeans and a black "Broken Bar" T-shirt, he

looked like a man most men would be scared to run into in a back alley, let alone a woman.

The background check her father had done on him had pretty much confirmed that impression. He wasn't a criminal, and never had been, as far as Captain Rutledge could tell. He was just a man that had treaded a thin line a little close to that element.

Even worse, and a bigger sin in the captain's eyes, Morgan Keane hadn't joined one of the military forces and served his country either.

He was a hell of a bouncer, and one Sheila knew Cooper was coming to depend upon after less than six months.

"You are not answering me." Sarah leaned forward, a shy dimple peeking out from her rounded cheeks as she brushed back the incredibly long curls that fell around her.

"That's because I don't want to," Sheila answered as she leaned forward as well, ignoring the other girl's playful pout. "Where's Cooper? He's supposed to be keeping you out of trouble."

"In a meeting with your bed warmer," Sarah all but whispered as her grin widened. "Tell me, Sheila, how long did you think you would keep it quiet if you dared to challenge Casey as you did?"

Sheila's brows lifted. What in the world had Casey told Sarah? It wasn't like him to tell anyone *anything* about his private life.

To say she was shocked he had even let on that they were sleeping together was an understatement.

Sarah rolled her eyes, almost laughing back at her.

"His truck has been parked at your house the past two mornings and several of the bar's customers just happen to be working on your father's landscaping."

Sheila grimaced. She had forgotten about that. She should have thought. There were very few members of the community who hadn't been in the Broken Bar at one time or another.

"Oh well, he can deal with it then." She shrugged as though it didn't matter when she knew very well it did. She detested being gossiped about. But even worse, she knew for a fact that Casey had broken off relationships with other women for no more reason than the fact that his personal business with them had become public knowledge.

She didn't need this.

She didn't need to be forced to grapple with her own emotions and fears while wondering who in her father's employ would dare to gossip about his daughter. Because she knew every damned one of them would. It was the reason why her father employed them.

How better to stay below suspicion where the wrong men were concerned than by employing the worst gossips in the county? Men and women who knew or worked with the very men that Ethan Cooper and his bouncers watched on a nightly basis.

"So when did all this begin?" Sarah propped her cheek in her hand as she stared back at Sheila. "Come on. Give deets. Ethan so refuses to allow me to take an interest in his bouncers' buff bodies."

Sheila winced as the bouncer behind the bar, Morgan, stared at his boss's wife in amazement. He was only seconds from blushing, and Sheila had a feeling he rarely, if ever, blushed.

"I'm not giving you deets, Sarah," Sheila informed her, well aware of the fact that the other woman would be horrified if she did attempt to do so.

Sarah pretended to pout before giving Sheila a subtle wink and turning to Morgan once more. "Perhaps Morgan will satisfy our curiosity then."

Morgan lifted his gaze from where he was cleaning a whiskey glass and stared back at Sarah with an expression of baffled concern. And for the smallest second, Sheila could have sworn she saw something more there.

Did Ethan Cooper's new bouncer have a crush on Mrs. Cooper?

"Curiosity regarding what?" Morgan asked warily.

Sheila almost laughed. That wasn't concern. Morgan was bordering on fear. It was one of those rare times anything managed to bother him.

He was saved at the last second, though, as Casey and Cooper stepped from the office. Cooper took one look at Morgan's face, then at Sarah's, and shook his head with a chuckle.

"Is she causing trouble, Morgan?" Cooper drawled with an edge of laughter

Morgan grunted. "She's dangerous, Coop. You should lock her up for our safety."

Sarah smiled back at him sweetly, but Sheila was aware that the other woman had noticed where Casey stopped. And she was very, very curious indeed.

Because Casey had stopped right behind Sheila.

Then his arms slid around her and a small kiss was pressed to the top of her head.

"Evening, sweetheart," he drawled. "Are you having fun out here with Sarah?"

She barely managed to hide her shock at the public display of possession. She had never, ever known of Nick Casey to show such attachment to any other woman. Neither in public nor a hint of it having been shown in private.

"Observing Sarah is always fun," she assured him as she fought to ignore both Sarah and Cooper's curiosity.

"I live to entertain," Sarah sighed, her dimples peeking out again.

"Then you will live a very long, happy life," Sheila informed the other woman as she held back her own laugh.

It was hard to pay attention to the conversation, though, as Casey stood behind her. His hands rested low on her stomach; placed flat, they drew her closer to him, holding her firmly as her back pressed against his torso.

She could feel the strength and the warmth of him, as well as the sensuality that seemed to wrap around her. Against the small of her back she could feel the jutting arousal contained by his jeans, and in his hands, the firm strength that anchored her to him.

She had never felt that before with Casey. As though he were trying to seduce her with more than the pleasure he gave her body.

"Oh yes, Sheila—Cooper and I received our invitations to your father's barbeque this month. I can't wait. I hear the Rutledge party is the event of the year," Sarah stated happily as a glimmer of excitement filled her vivacious brown eyes.

And Sheila felt a twinge of remorse that she had been unaware Sarah had lived in the county for more than a year before Ethan had finally claimed her. Everyone in the county was invited to the Rutledge barbeque. Catered, rousing, and filled with food and laughter, the yearly party was Douglas Rutledge's way of giving back to the community his wife had loved.

It had been their hometown, but it had been Eleanor Rutledge who had wanted to come home when Douglas retired. She had died six months before that retirement of a heart attack.

"Well, it's an event, anyway," Sheila agreed, her smile almost shaking as she felt Casey settle his chin at her shoulder.

"Do you have a partner for the Rutledge party yet?" he murmured at her ear. "Or the ball?"

Sheila swallowed tightly.

The barbeque was her mother's dream, but the ball a week later was the captain's baby. Inviting officers of all the military branches as well as political and private sector law enforcement officials. The ball was the captain's excuse to be more than the stern, supposedly disillusioned army captain whose friends were generals, admirals, and senators.

It was also his chance to revel, even if privately, in the fact that the job he had accepted while in his prime, the one that had required he remain a captain rather than advancing, was succeeding.

The position of head of the National Covert Information Network.

"I don't have a date yet," she answered quietly. She had never had a date for her father's balls unless she did the inviting. She had stopped doing the inviting the summer she turned nineteen. And she'd gone alone ever since.

"You do now," Casey informed her as her eyes narrowed on him in the mirror behind the bar.

He stared back at her, his gaze heavy-lidded, his expression reminding her of the night he had taken her on the bar. That memory was seriously messing with her ability to stay angry with him.

"Do I really?" she murmured, aware of the fact that Sarah, Ethan, and Morgan were attempting to carry on another conversation despite their rabid curiosity.

"What do you think?" The look in his eyes dared her to refuse.

"I think I don't recall giving the invitation," she replied smoothly, careful to keep her voice low.

Casey smiled, his lips curving with cool warning.

"I don't wait on an invitation," he informed her, his tone warning now. "I was informing you, Sheila. You have a date. Period."

Oh, now that just wasn't going to do.

Sheila turned to him slowly.

"Choose your fights, sweetheart." If she wasn't mistaken, there was a sudden edge of anticipation in his voice. "And choose them wisely."

Her mother had warned her of that once as well. She'd told her that one day she would come across a man who didn't give a damn who her father was, or how strong she had become. He would sweep into her life and leave her heart, her mind, in disarray.

"Choose your fights, sweetheart, and choose them wisely," Eleanor had warned her. *"Otherwise, you'll destroy yourself, as well as him, fighting against him."*

But her mother hadn't known Nick Casey.

She was almost anticipating a fight with him, as much as he seemed to be anticipating one with her.

She could see it in his eyes, hear it in his voice.

Hell, she could feel it radiating in the sexual intensity that suddenly seemed to consume them both.

"They need to get a room," Cooper grunted behind Sheila.

"You are becoming such a fuddy-duddy," Sarah laughed. "Tell him, Morgan, he's becoming a prude. Nothing like the wild man I married."

Morgan was turning away as she spoke, his expression somber as he poured drinks, his eyes downcast.

"Sarah, sweetheart, you're too nosy," Casey warned her as he laughed back at her, though he didn't release Sheila, and it seemed he had no intentions of doing so.

"And you are being way too intense, Casey." Sarah shook her head.

"And this conversation is beginning to bore me," Sheila informed them all, though the look she shot Sarah was filled with an apology.

She wasn't bored, but she could definitely feel the fear beginning to travel up her spine.

Not a fear of harm. Or at least, not a fear of personal harm.

A fear of having her heart broken was another matter entirely.

"Bore you?" Casey growled. "I rather doubt it."

"Dance with me or shut the hell up, Casey," she finally demanded in exasperation. "If you're going to stand around holding on to me like a damned junkyard dog, then the least you could do is make it worth my while."

It was her mother's advice to choose her battles wisely that rang through her head as Casey led her to the dance floor. A slow, sensual beat began to fill the air, drawing couples to the floor and heating the building with the power of human lust.

At least, that was what she tried to tell herself as she felt Casey's arms wrap around her and allowed him to draw her to him. Possessively.

"What is with you and the ball-and-chain attitude?"

she asked, genuinely bemused with the way he was acting.

"Trying to become a ball and chain?" he asked.

She almost stopped in the middle of the dance floor.

"Are you proposing, Casey?" She could feel her heart beginning to race in her throat. "Because if you are, then this is a lousy way to go about it."

He snorted back at her, pulling her closer once again as he bent his head against hers and swayed to the lazy, sexually charged music filling the building.

"You'll know when I'm proposing, Sheila. There will be no question about it."

Son of a bitch.

Casey was cursing silently with every four-letter word he could come up with and a few he knew were illegal in several parts of the world. Probably in the States as well.

Yeah, it was sort of a proposal.

Casey was a man who accepted what he knew he didn't have a chance in hell of changing. And the feelings burning inside him for Sheila weren't going to change.

Fidelity being the key. In the months he had been slipping in and out of her bed, not even once had he found another woman attractive. It purely, simply sucked, though, that she seemed to think he was so horrible at the whole proposal thing.

What did he have to do, anyway? Get on one knee?

He scowled back at Cooper as they swayed around the floor. This had to be his fault. That big lug had gone down on his knee to Sarah and presented her with a diamond the size of a tennis ball.

Okay, so maybe it had been slightly smaller, but that had to be where she had come up with these ideas. Sarah had to have told her.

"You're acting strange, Casey," Sheila informed him. "Like a man making a claim, and I'm not some pretty doll you can claim and expect me to fall into line with it."

"Darlin', I wouldn't expect you to fall into line with anything. We'll just keep on keepin' on till you see things my way, is all. I didn't say I expected you to agree with me overnight."

"Until I see things your way, huh?" He could hear the amusement in her tone, along with a rather vague confusion. As though she weren't entirely certain how to deal with him.

That was a good thing. Keeping Sheila off balance was always a damned good thing if a man could manage it.

"Yep," he agreed, hiding his smile in her hair. "We'll get along better that way, you'll see."

"You know, I can't decide if you're truly insane, or if you're just trying to make me crazy."

And if it were the latter, he wondered, was it working?

Of course, it could be the former as well, because God knew she had managed to turn his life upside down.

"Does it matter which?" he asked softly against her ear, feeling that little shiver of response as it raced down her back. "Tell me you really want me out of your life, Sheila. Go ahead, lie to me and I'll walk away."

Could he walk away? He didn't think it was possible. Not as long as he could feel her body heating for his, as long as he could feel that response for him in her kiss.

"No, you wouldn't, Casey," she denied as he finally felt her softening in his arms. "You'd just try to find another way to convince me."

Hell, she knew him too well.

He hadn't expected that.

"Why don't you just tell me what you want from me, Casey."

They both came to a stop as the music faded away.

His head lifted as she turned her gaze up to him, those deep violet eyes nearly drowning him in the knowledge, the sadness that filled them.

"Tell you what?" he asked her softly. "How much I want you? How hard you make me? Hell, Sheila, you already know all that."

She shook her head softly. "No, Casey. Why don't you just go ahead and tell me what you want from me, or from my father. Don't you know I still want you so desperately that I'd probably give it to you, or convince Dad to do it? You don't have to play these games with me. You never did have to play these games with me."

You never leave a lady standing on the dance floor.

Never curse a lady.

A lady was a lady even when she wasn't behaving like a lady.

Never embarrass a lady in front of friends and co-workers. Especially if she holds a position of power.

Those lessons had been drummed into him as a child before his parents' deaths.

He could remember lazy summer mornings as a young boy spent fishing on the banks of the river that eventually killed his parents and listening to the amusing assortment of rules his father had attempted to teach him where women were concerned.

Those lessons came in handy now.

He allowed his fingers to deliberately curl around her upper arm as he led her from the floor and back to the bar. He should have left her at the bar. Hell, he should have parked her right at the bar with Sarah and Cooper and left himself.

Hanging around was the worst thing he could have done. And allowing himself this confrontation with Sheila was sure a real bad decision.

He just couldn't seem to help himself.

Anger, resentment, and pure male pride had him by the throat while lust still had him by the balls.

It was a hell of a combination.

And even as he pulled her past a watchful Morgan and shouldered open the swinging door that led to the kitchen and offices, he knew he was making a damned mistake.

It might even be the biggest mistake of his life.

SIX

This was what she got for being honest, Sheila thought as she allowed Casey to pull her into one of the small offices. This was what she got for trying to lay to rest the doubts that filled her own mind, and to get whatever relationship they had on an equal footing.

He was pissed.

She could feel that anger vibrating through his body and threatening his control.

She didn't know whether to be frightened or turned on, because she had never seen Casey like this. She had never seen him so angry that his eyes glowed like burning chocolate, backlit with a tobacco flame.

She had a glimpse of those eyes as he swung her around at the desk, placed his hands on both sides of her and leaned into her until they were nose to nose.

"Do I look like a fucking man whore to you?" he snarled into her face, causing her to flinch with the rage in his voice. "Do I look like someone who would fuck a woman to gain anything other than both their damned pleasure?"

His words seemed to pierce a part of her that instantly latched on to the end of his statement.

"Their pleasure," he said. As though it was a lover's pleasure and satisfaction that caused his own.

"Casey, I never meant—" She hadn't meant it to sound that way.

But the rest of the words were cut off.

"The fucking hell you didn't." His nose was touching hers.

His eyes were so dark they were nearly black, body heat pouring from him in waves as rage seemed to burn through his system. "That's exactly what you meant, Sheila. Was I a fucking man whore willing to climb between your legs for a favor from you where your damned father is concerned? Do you want to know what I think of any favors your father could fucking give me? Do you, Sheila?" he all but yelled in her face.

"Not really." Weak, more submissive than she liked, her voice trembled as her gaze held his.

Not in fear, but in a variety of other emotions. Emotions she wasn't certain she knew how to adapt to.

She only wished her response to this new, volcanic Casey was fear. Fear would have been easier to handle. It would have been far easier to understand than the other emotions she felt.

Especially the lust. The hunger.

The angrier he became, the more she wanted him.

She could feel her nipples hardening and tightening, growing more sensitive by the second as he glared into her eyes.

"Not really?" he snarled back at her. "Maybe I want to tell you anyway. Just for the fucking hell of it."

"If you feel you have to." She shrugged, almost catching her breath at the feel of her nipples raking against the material of her bra.

And she wasn't the only one who felt the lust. Amid his anger, that hunger was there as well. The feel of his erection pressing wide and hard against her belly assured her of that. He wanted her just as fiercely as he wanted to rage at her.

"Then tell me, Casey," she retorted, albeit breathlessly.

Her clit was aching with a swollen intensity she didn't know if she could bear much longer. In turn, she could feel the clench and flushed arousal tightening her pussy as well as the heated, slick warmth easing through it.

Had she ever been this aroused by him?

She was certain she had never been this aroused in her life. For him or any other man. For anything or at any time.

His eyes were still blazing with fury, his expression twisted with it when she lifted her leg and let it slide up the outside of his.

The silk of her skirt slid back along her thighs, the rasp of his jeans against her sensitive inner thigh had her breath catching.

His gaze jerked down, locked on the pale flesh as her skirt slid back.

When his eyes came back to her, that rage was diluted, the smallest bit, with another fire. One of hunger and of lust.

"There's not nothing, not a single friggin' thing your

father has that I want with the exception of his stubborn, wayward, completely intractable daughter."

"Completely intractable?" Her hands pushed beneath the soft cotton of his shirt and touched the iron-hard abs beneath.

With just her nails, she stroked up his abdomen, being certain to find the flat, hard points of his male nipples.

His fingers wrapped immediately around her wrists, holding her in place.

"What the hell are you up to?"

Had she ever made the first move when it came to their sexual encounters? Casey knew she hadn't. She'd always left that first step to him.

Until tonight.

Until this confrontation.

And now, she was simply hotter than hell. Hot enough to burn through his senses and make him almost, almost, forget the anger surging through him.

It was his pride. That sheer male core of the man that she had stabbed that dagger into. To dare to suggest that he wanted more than the woman he was holding in his arms was more than he could countenance.

How could anything she or her father possessed or had access to be more important?

"I could get up to many things," she whispered. "But at the moment, I'm more interested in what you're up to."

Her hips tilted upward, causing her lower stomach to press and rub against the erection barely contained by his jeans.

Releasing her wrists he allowed one hand to slide along her arm until he reach her underarm. From there, his hand skimmed down her side, to her lifted leg. Curving his fingers beneath her thigh, he reached around until he could rub the silk of her panties against her sensitive pussy.

There, he found her hot and wet, the juices of her pussy dampening her panties as he rubbed against the sensitive bare lips beneath the material.

Her head tilted back. Dark, violet eyes became drowsy, heavy-lidded as her hand smoothed back down his abs to the heavy arousal beneath his jeans.

"You make me want to bite nails." His tone was between a growl and a hungry groan. A sound he had never made before with a woman he couldn't stop wanting, no matter how often he had her.

"Is that what you want to do?" she asked softly, her fingers curving around the hard shaft pounding beneath them.

"That, among other things." Narrowing his eyes, he watched her closely, wondering how far she would go.

It was the first time she had made the first move; was she willing to continue that path? At least, for as long as he could allow it.

He was all for Sheila making her mark on him. Hell, there were nights he dreamed of it, fantasized about it.

Then, her hand slid away as disappointment began to tighten his body. But only as long as it took for him to realize those slender, delicate hands were gripping the hem of her camisole top and slowly easing it upward until she drew it over her head.

His breath caught, then he completely lost the ability to breathe as the sheer lace of her bra revealed the spiked, dark pink of her nipples as they begged so prettily for attention.

They were pert and eager for his touch, and he couldn't

resist lifting his hands and framing the generous mounds that cushioned the candied perfection.

Raking his thumbs over them, he watched as her breathing roughened, a flush rushed across her face, and the drowsy sensuality in her expression increased.

Busy, industrious, and determined, her fingers hadn't forgotten their task, either.

They loosened his belt, sliding one end free of the other before they moved to each of the metal buttons. They slipped free easily, the heavy denim parting to reveal the engorged, iron-hard length of his cock.

His teeth clenched as her fingers, cool and slender, inquisitive and filled with eager pleasure, wrapped partially around the shaft and began to caress it.

"Fuck. Sheila, love, I don't know if I can stand this for long."

"Ah, poor baby," she whispered as his lips moved over hers, then brushed over them.

"I bet you think this is all the courage I have in me too." She was laughing. Casey could hear the amusement in her voice and it only spurred his determination that tonight, in this office, he would damned well own her when they were finished.

He was sick of this damned cat-and-mouse game they kept playing. Sick of chasing after her, knowing damned good and well she wanted him clear to her soul, and yet she still refused to admit it.

"You belong to me." It was a warning, and one he hoped she took seriously.

But as he made the claim, he made certain she couldn't fight against it too hard.

As the words slipped from his lips, he slid two fingers past the elastic leg of her panties and speared into the slick, heated depths of her pussy.

A cry tore from her lips as her back arched and her head fell back weakly.

Pleasure suffused her expression, tightened her nipples further, and sent a rush of juices flowing over his fingers.

Soft, slick; he knew the taste of it, and ached for it.

He could spread her out, right there on his desk, and taste her as he craved.

But Sheila had other plans.

Surprise raced through him once again as one small hand speared into his hair, her fingers gripping the strands and pulling until his lips met hers.

And there, control became only a distant memory.

He had heard kisses described as many great and varied things over the years, but no description could come close to the sweet nectar and sensual spice that filled his senses as her lips parted beneath his.

As though starving for feminine touch, addicted and hopelessly lost to it, Casey felt his senses focus on it entirely. Her kiss, her tongue stroking back against his as he devoured her.

She devoured him in return.

The fingers of one hand tightened even more in his hair as the other stroked and caressed the violently sensitive head of his dick. He could feel himself beginning to break apart for her. His balls were tightening, the head of his cock thickening further, throbbing in an impending release when she suddenly stopped.

His head jerked back, his eyes opening, lips parting to demand an explanation when his gaze moved down again and he watched those lush, hungry lips descend to his stomach.

Like silk against roughened iron, her lips parted, and her tongue licked out to allow herself a taste. Running down the tightening muscles, Casey could only watch, suspended in disbelief at the incredibly erotic sight of Sheila going down on him.

Without urging, without that desperation on his part, or that first moment of shyness or uncertainty on hers, she was taking what she considered hers.

Her lips covered the broad, engorged head of his cock. Curious and destructive, her tongue licked over it, learning his dick as though it were the first time for her and she wanted nothing more than to experience each sensation, each stroke of pleasure.

She was taking every part of him and loving every damned minute of it.

The furiously pounding crest was tucked against the roof of her mouth, her tongue moving against that sensitive spot just beneath the head.

A moan of feminine pleasure vibrated against the hard crest as heat began to burn his already overloaded senses. Delicate fingers moved between his thighs as one hand tugged at his jeans. He helped her push the denim down his legs, so fucking eager for her touch he would have torn them off if he needed to.

Anything to feel her palming the tight, tortured sack of his balls as his thighs tightened with the need to come. He could feel his seed beginning to heat, to boil through his system. There was no way to hold it back. There was no way to hold on to his control.

His fingers tightened in her hair, his attempt to pull her back impossible to complete. He was holding her to him instead. Staring down, watching as he fucked her swollen lips and watching her eyes darken with anticipation.

Her cheeks hollowed. Her mouth worked him with burning sensuality.

Ah God. Not yet. If he came now there wasn't a chance in hell he'd have the control to touch and taste her as well. To drive her as insane, make her as desperate for him as he was becoming for her.

And there was only one way to stop her. Only one way to ensure that his satisfaction wasn't the only one attained.

A second before it was too late, just as his balls gave that final convulsive squeeze and sent his release spurting between her lips, Casey pulled back.

In a single move he had his dick out of her mouth, bent, gripped her arms, and pulled her to her feet before laying her back on the desk.

The soft material of the skirt fell back along her thighs as he pushed his hands beneath, gripped the elastic of her panties, and tore them from her slender body.

In the next heartbeat, he had his head buried between her legs, his lips circling her clit, his tongue tasting the soft spice and feminine pleasure that welled from her.

There was no time for seduction, no control left to tease. There was only the hunger for her and the need to taste her sweet release spilling to his lips.

He should have been used to it by now, he thought. The taste of her, the heat of her. The incredible pleasure that whipped through his body at the knowledge that she was losing herself in the intensity and in the sensations just as he was losing himself in the giving of them.

Pushing his tongue deep inside the tight depths of her pussy as her fingers moved to his hair, Casey licked and probed at the sweetness. Fucking her with his tongue, his body clenching, need raging inside him as she writhed beneath him.

Sheila fought to breathe through the wild, chaotic pleasure beginning to zip through her.

She couldn't help clenching her thighs, her legs lifting, gripping his shoulders as a cry escaped her lips. She couldn't fight against it. She didn't want to fight against it. She just wanted to feel him against her, over every inch of her body.

Inside her—

A harsh, unbidden moan passed her lips as his tongue thrust inside the clenched, snug depths of her pussy again. The rasp of his tongue against the sensitive nerve endings sent her spiraling closer to release. Spasms of sensation shot to her womb, drawing it tight as she arched and felt the warning tremors of her orgasm as they began to vibrate inside her.

So close. She was so close to coming, the need for it pounded painfully in her clit and the tormented depths of her pussy.

She was burning out of control.

Her hands clenched in his hair to hold him closer. Her hips lifted further, desperate to force his tongue deeper inside her. To increase the strokes, to make him fuck her deeper, to give her that last teasing thrust that would propel her over the edge.

And she was so close. So very close . . . when he pulled back.

SEVEN

"Casey, don't stop." Sheila reached desperately for him, confused, aching with a sensual hunger that went so deep she knew it went far beyond the physical.

"I want to feel you coming on my dick, not my tongue," he groaned, as he gripped the heavy shaft and tucked it between the swollen folds of her sex.

Flames, sharp and intense, shot through her pussy, then the rest of her body as the electrical sensations continued to build between them.

Gripping her hips with his hands, his gaze locked with hers, Casey began to move, slowly at first, stretching her, working his way inside her. The heated burn of the penetration had her gasping, fighting for breath as pleasure began to build inside her with a strength she hadn't experienced with Casey so far.

It was always better than the time before.

It was always hotter.

"Good, baby?" he asked, his voice strained, the

muscles standing out in his neck with his obvious fight to hold back his release.

"Oh God, Casey, it's so good," she whispered. "You know it's always so good."

"Like being wrapped in pleasure, Sheila," he agreed. "You wrap more than my dick in pleasure, baby."

Every muscle in her body seemed to clench and spasm at the explicit pleasure his words sent tearing through her body.

He pushed in deeper, an inch at a time, wedging between the tightening muscles of her clenched sex as his hips worked slow and easy, his muscles tense and powerfully restrained.

It was all she could do to keep her eyes open. Sensuality and building ecstasy had her fighting to stare up at him, to watch his expression.

At times like this, she could glimpse emotion on his face. She wasn't always certain what that emotion was, but it was there, and it fascinated her.

Just glimpses, just small hints of the emotions he might feel. Emotions she craved, feelings she needed so desperately to know he felt.

"Casey," she moaned as his cock slid into her pussy to the hilt. It sent fire raging through every cell of her body. It had her flying through sensations she didn't know how to describe or how to handle.

"Tell me, baby." Leaning closer, his head lowered, his lips moving to her neck, to her ear. "Tell me, Sheila. Do you love it? Do you love feeling me inside you? Fucking you until we both feel as though we're going to die?"

"I love it." She loved him. "It's so good, Casey." It was so past good. It was incredible.

It was flying without wings.

Moving beneath him, hips rising and writhing, grinding against his pelvis as his cock sank deep inside her, Sheila let that pleasure—let the man—have her in ways she never had before.

She was barely able to hold her eyes open, but she did, to hold his gaze. To stare into the swirls of emotion that filled them. To become ensnared in him as the heavy strokes began to quicken, lengthen.

Ecstasy began to build, to tighten and stimulate until Sheila couldn't hold back the moans and pleasure-filled cries that rose in her throat.

She couldn't bear the sharpened pleasure much longer, she knew. She couldn't get close enough to him. She couldn't move fast enough, he wasn't moving hard enough.

"Casey, please," she cried out as her legs wrapped around his hips, her arms tightening around his neck.

She had to come soon. She couldn't bear this much sensation much longer. She couldn't survive the pleasure, the building pressure that swelled the muscles of her pussy, clenching it, tightening it as Casey fucked her with ever faster strokes.

Their moans filled the air. Her nails dug into his shoulders as his teeth rasped over a torturously hard nipple. That additional stimulation sent her exploding, careening as ecstasy detonated inside her with a force that obliterated reality.

She felt the rush of her juices as Casey buried himself deep inside her. The heavy, fierce spurts of his come filling her destroyed her senses.

The fierce throb and jetting heat amplified her ecstasy, throwing her higher, racing through her system and increasing the rapturous surges of intensity that exploded over and over and rushed through her body.

Shaking, trembling, she could only lie beneath him shuddering as Casey came above her, their bodies locked in pleasure, and in something she knew went far beyond the physical.

In a blinding second of insight, Sheila knew she had finally fallen irrevocably and totally in love.

She loved Casey in ways she had never loved when she was younger. She loved him past her heart, and into her soul. And she loved him with a power she knew she would never escape.

And she knew that as of yet, there hadn't been so much as hint that Casey cared more for her than for any other woman he'd taken as a lover.

She could very well be lost in this maze of emotions alone. And being there alone was a very frightening thought.

EIGHT

There was a small bathroom and shower to the side of the office that they used. The pelting water cascaded over them, washing away the perspiration that had accumulated along their bodies.

They shared the shower. Casey's larger body should have made the small space seem cramped; instead, there was a distinct feeling of comfort—perhaps protection—that Sheila welcomed.

But she was damned if she knew how *he* felt.

The past few days without him hadn't been her best, either. For some reason, she'd been more on edge than usual, nervous, almost panicky each night as she drove home from the bar with the flash drive of information collected the night before tucked in her boot.

It had never bothered her before if she saw headlights in her rearview mirror, but the last few days—it bothered her.

And it shouldn't. Other than the fact that it seemed to

be too frequent, and those lights seemed to be the same ones nightly.

"You look worried." Rubbing a towel over his hair to get the last of the water from it, Casey watched her questioningly, his head tilted to the side as Sheila pulled her clothes back on.

She gave a quick shake of her head. "You worry me."

Pulling her shirt over her head and adjusting it over the hem of the soft skirt she had worn that night, she glanced back at Casey.

"And why do I worry you?" Tossing the towel to the counter, he turned, braced his very nicely rounded, towel-wrapped rear against the counter and crossed his arms over his broad chest as he regarded her.

"You never do what I expect, I guess." She shrugged. "I wouldn't have expected sex in exchange for your anger earlier."

He scowled, a darkened lowering of his brows as his gaze narrowed on her. "Reminding me of that accusation you made isn't a good idea, sweetheart. We don't want to revisit that place just after we made each other feel so good."

Pushing away from the counter and dropping the towel, Casey reached for his clothing and began dressing.

Sheila watched for a moment before forcing herself to draw her gaze back from the definite eye candy he represented.

Damn, this was her problem when it came to Casey. He was simply luscious. Even the scars along his lower back and left leg didn't detract from the bronzed flesh that covered iron-hard muscles.

That always got her in trouble. Whenever she allowed herself to be distracted by that incredible body, she seemed to lose her mind, her control, and her common sense. And now, she'd gone and lost her heart.

Not a good thing.

"Of course, not a good place to revisit," she agreed softly as she turned away and headed back to the bedroom.

"Tell me, Sheila." He followed her, of course. "Why the hell do you keep fighting this relationship every step of the way? Aren't you afraid I'm going to get tired of chasing you?"

She turned to see him behind her, his hands on his hips, just above the waistband of his low-riding jeans.

Honesty. It had gotten her in trouble earlier. It wasn't going to help her now either.

"Because," she finally answered. "I haven't figured out why you want a relationship with me, Casey. Perhaps when you tell me why, I'll stop fighting it."

Hope began to fill her. She could feel it, no matter how hard she tried to fight it back. Could there be more to the sex than he was letting on? Was there more there than just a game he could be playing?

She'd heard multiple times how Casey liked to play with his lovers. He'd laugh, push them, tease them, insist on drawing them out when they wanted to remain secretive or hidden.

It was one of his gifts to his lovers. But it was a curse once he left.

"The obvious answer isn't reason enough?"

Sheila stared back at Casey silently for long moments as she tried to figure that one out.

There was an obvious answer?

She bit her lower lip, trying to figure it out. Because she knew Casey—if she asked, just out-and-out asked what that answer was, then there wasn't a chance in hell he was going to tell her.

He would turn it into a puzzle and into a game and he would make her completely insane with it. She didn't need that. Her heart had enough weight on it already.

She cared for her father.

She helped him.

She covered for him.

She scheduled for him.

She carried information for him.

And she had given up her own dreams of love the day she had learned that she was no more than a conduit to her father.

It wasn't Captain Rutledge's fault. It was her own.

But now, it was backfiring on her.

"There's an obvious answer, Casey?" She finally asked the one question she knew he wouldn't answer.

She wondered what game he would turn it into now.

"Why yes, there is, and if you haven't figured it out yet, then perhaps there's nothing left for us to talk about."

There was no anger in his tone, there was no anger in his expression or in his eyes. There was something that went beyond anger and sent her stomach clenching with dread.

"What do you mean by that?" she asked cautiously.

"When you figure out the obvious answer, Sheila, let me know," he told her with that icy calm that had come over him. "Until then, I'm tired of trying to move the mountain and I'm sure as hell tired of chasing after a woman who doesn't want me." He headed for the door. "I'm sure you can see your way out."

"I knew you would turn this into a game," she cried out as his fingers curled around the doorknob. "I know a trick question when I hear one, Casey. Is this how you break it off with all your women once you're tired of the pity fucks and the lessons in life?"

He stopped.

For a moment, Sheila wondered if perhaps she had gone too far. She had definitely exaggerated slightly, but it was *just* slightly.

Casey had a tendency to take lovers who needed to awaken, whether they wanted to or not.

"No, Sheila, I just thought this time, I'd found a woman who didn't need to be dragged kicking and screaming into life." He turned back and glanced at her for just a second. A very short, very disappointed second. "I guess I was wrong."

He opened the door and walked straight out of the room. The door closed behind him, an almost silent click that for some odd reason had Sheila flinching involuntarily.

She felt her stomach drop, then clench. Tears sprang to her eyes and she didn't understand why. She couldn't explain the dampness or the sense of agony that tore through her.

Her father had told her once, well, really, he'd told her several times that her habit of honesty was going to end up hurting her more than she was going to be able to heal.

That might have just happened, and she couldn't explain to herself why it had. All she wanted was the truth. She just wanted to know if there was a chance that he loved her. That he could love her.

Pulling her boots, on, she pushed her toes forward as she jerked the expensive leather over first one foot, then the other.

She felt the heel that contained the flash drive she had

collected earlier that night. Before she had danced with Casey. Before she had asked him what he wanted for her and before she had experienced the most incredible sex of her life.

What had she done?

Shaking her head at the frustration caused by that question, Sheila moved slowly to the door and left the room as well. Rather than leaving by the public exit, Sheila moved through the dimly lit hallway to the door in the back.

Pressing the code to the back door, Sheila slipped from the building and made her way to her car. She hit the remote to unlock it and managed to get inside before the first tear fell.

How had this happened?

Call him when she figured out the obvious answer as to why he wanted a relationship with her?

What was the obvious answer?

Laying her head against the steering wheel, she let the tears fall, though she tried to hold back the sobs.

There was no obvious answer. Casey wasn't a man who held a whole lot back in that way. He threw himself into whatever endeavor he took on. Whether he was laughing, drinking, fighting, or fucking, he gave it everything he had. If the obvious answer was "love," he would have never allowed her to push him away. He would have never left the words unsaid between them.

He would have told her he loved her. Wouldn't he?

A sob shook her shoulders, surprising her. The sound had her jerking her head up, wiping the tears away, and fighting back fresh ones.

Crying didn't help, she told herself. Feeling sorry for herself sure as hell wasn't going to improve the situation.

Pushing the key into the ignition, she started her car and pulled out of the parking space. She didn't know if she could bear coming in night after night now, without Casey's touch, without his determined seduction.

How was she supposed to live without it now? How was she supposed to live without him?

Nick Casey's woman left the parking lot, but it had taken her awhile to get going. And there was the suspicion she had been crying in her car.

What had Casey done to make her cry?

If Nick Casey was truly Beauregard Fredrico, then it could be any number of things. He wasn't likely to break a tender heart, or to throw away a precious female he had seduced so effectively.

He had been much sought after in Italy before the Fredrico empire had crumbled.

Beauregard Fredrico, so handsome, so charming, and so disapproving of the families and the rules that had sustained them for so many generations.

Making his woman cry wouldn't change how he felt about her, though. And Nick Casey, despite the gossip that he cared for no woman, treated this woman far differently than any other he had taken to his bed.

Yes, there was love here, and that was surprising. He wasn't known for allowing his heart to become so involved with a woman. And neither was Beauregard Fredrico. Yet, all men loved eventually, didn't they?

And this man's heart was well and truly involved with his woman. It was proven by the fact that he stood in the shadows watching as she left, his expression heavy—was that sadness lining it as well?

It seemed this man felt much more for this woman

than even he was comfortable with. How surprising. Judging by the look on his face, perhaps he and the woman had argued. Or was there a split? Because that was grief twisting his expression, and anger. Casey was not happy with his woman, or with himself. Perhaps some help was needed to draw them back together. After all, when a man and woman loved so fiercely, such separation should not be allowed. Nothing short of, well, death, should keep them apart.

Unfortunately, despite the subtle moves that had been made to frighten his woman, Casey still appeared unconcerned, and had not made the phone call that would bring in reinforcements for only one man. Beauregard had an army at his disposal. He had only to make a single call to cash in on the vows made to him.

And yet, he had not made that call. Perhaps he needed to be convinced.

With a deft turn of the wrist, the ignition of the four-by-four pickup sprang to life.

Pulling out of the shadowed parking spot and following Miss Rutledge took only seconds. Options began to come into focus and play out. Beau wasn't getting a clue. He hadn't yet realized his woman was in danger. A danger Beau couldn't resolve on his own, and there was no chance he would tell the men he worked with about his past.

That past was too rife with blood, the sins of a family, and the choices Beau himself had made, which hadn't been exactly wise. No, his friends wouldn't know who he was, or what he had been. And he would trust only one person to protect the woman who could be endangered because of that past.

A few changes would have to be made to force that

call, unfortunately. Actually striking out at Casey's woman would have to be the next move.

With that move, the danger of actually harming her was increased. And it was a danger that would have to be faced. Faced and accepted. It was one that preference would have dictated unnecessary; unfortunately preference wasn't an option any longer.

Beauregard Fredrico couldn't be allowed to escape so easily.

He had to pay.

And, just as in the past, a woman would have to pay for his crimes. Hopefully, this Nick Casey was the identity Beau had chosen. It meant no other woman would have to be endangered.

With any luck, it would end very soon.

NINE

One week later

Sheila stood at the large picture window in the center wall of her father's office and stared out at the tall, evergreen border of trees that separated her small bungalow-style house from her father's front flower gardens.

Her mother had planted those flowers. Hundreds upon hundreds of perennials that filled the exquisite English garden her mother had created several years before her death. A garden her father worked in daily to keep it in the same pristine condition her mother had so enjoyed. Just as he kept the maid busy creating the dozens of flower arrangements that filled the house.

Cutting through the immaculate acre of fragrant blooms was a stone path that led from the evergreen wall to the side of the house. The blossoms waved in the breeze, their soft fragrance wafting through the heated Texas air and filling the office through the AC unit positioned outside.

Her father had tinkered with that unit for years to allow the fragrance from the air outside to fill the office.

The office was the bedroom her mother had been confined to in the year before she had died. That bouquet from the flower gardens she worked so hard on had been her father's last gift to the woman he had loved.

The garden had once been a source of comfort, but now, Sheila watched them with a frown, wondering if they could hold something more sinister than the precious memories she'd always had of them.

Memories of working with her mother to plant the fragrant blooms. Memories of gathering the ones her father had used to create the arrangement atop her mother's casket.

And with those memories was the one created last night. The one where she had slipped along that stone path, a feeling of trepidation breathing at her neck as panic had tightened her chest.

Someone had been in her house.

Crossing her arms over her breasts, Sheila closed her eyes and fought to control the fear.

Who would have dared to have broken into her home? And even if they had dared, how had they managed to break the locks her father had had installed on both the front and back doors?

She couldn't think of anyone but Casey who could do such a thing; he was simply extraordinarily well-trained in such things.

"Sheila, dammit, I can't find my glasses."

Sheila nearly jumped out of her own skin.

A squeak slipped past her lips as she jerked and turned around, facing her father breathlessly, her heart nearly choking her as it pounded out of control.

Her father paused, a scowl tightening his expression. "Are you okay, dear?"

For a moment, Sheila considered telling him about her suspicion of a break-in.

He would lose his mind, though. Protective, overly so, and filled with fatherly concern, Douglas Rutledge would put one of his guards on her twenty-four/seven and she'd never have a moment's peace.

Which wouldn't be so bad if someone had definitely broken into the house. The problem was, she just couldn't be sure. She hated worrying her father without some sort of proof, or at least her own certainty that it had happened.

Had she really walked away from her house and left the doors unlocked? Had she been so deep into her anger and need for Casey that she could have done such a thing?

"Sheila, girl, you're not answering me." There was a hint of true concern beginning to edge into his tone.

"I'm fine, Dad, just distracted."

She had just lied to her father. Sheila almost winced at the thought. Of course, it wasn't the first time. There had been the time she had slipped out to go to that party with a college boy during her senior year. She'd told her father she was staying all night with her friend Cara Cartwright. And there had been the night a few weeks ago when her father had called and asked her at the last minute to accompany him to a dinner in Corpus Christi with the city's mayor.

Sheila had told him she wasn't feeling well. At that exact moment, Casey had been undressing.

"And what has you so distracted?" He moved into the office, obviously thoughtful as he began searching the room.

Sheila walked over to him, tapped his shoulder with

a smile, and then, as he turned to her, lifted the glasses from his graying hair and handed them to him.

"Hmm." He held the glasses and glared at them accusingly before looking up and giving her a sheepish smile. "I should remember to look here, huh? Your mother was always doing the same thing. She'd find them and hand them right to me."

Sheila nodded wistfully. "I remember, Dad."

"You look just like her," he sighed. "Some days, I can almost swear she's home again as I watch you move around those gardens."

She could hear the loss in his voice. For all his full and busy life, she knew her father desperately missed the woman he had called his wife. Just as she knew that he had felt no woman would ever compare to her.

He patted her on her shoulder, a gesture of affection, before dropping a kiss to the top of her head and going to his desk.

"I had a call from Cooper earlier," he told her as he slipped his glasses back on his face, sat down, and looked up at her.

"What does he need?" Sitting on the side of the desk as she had even as a young girl, she pulled her jean-clad legs up to the top of the side of the desk, crossed them, and watched her father expectantly.

"The network is doing very well." Her father sat back in his chair as his face creased thoughtfully. "Cooper's group is one of our best, and the information he's been pulling in has been damned important."

Sheila nodded. The Broken Bar wasn't the only operational location set up to gather intel on criminal and terroristic activities, and it wasn't the only location under her father's command, but as he said, it was one of the best.

"So why did he call?" she asked.

"According to Cooper, you've been slipping in, getting the intel, and slipping back out. You're not coming in at your usual time, and you're acting nervous."

Sheila looked beyond his shoulder to the gardens outside. Rather than facing the question in her father's gaze, she avoided it.

"I've been busy."

"Yeah, that heavy social life you have," he grunted with what she called his loving sarcasm. He had a way of saying things to her that let her know he was clearly disapproving, and/or disappointed. Sometimes just plain disbelieving.

In this case, perhaps it was all three.

"Yeah, my social life is just all that," she agreed with the same tone.

"Yep, it's matching Casey's if my suspicions are correct."

And there it was. Sheila had wondered how long it would take her father to say something if he was aware of the relationship. Or the non-relationship. Whatever the hell it was. Or had been.

A wave of pain swept through her as she fought to keep from dragging in a ragged breath.

God, she missed him. She missed his touch, the sound of his voice, the amusement in his gaze, and that crooked smile he often carried.

"I wouldn't know," she finally said faintly.

"Yeah, avoiding him will do that." She watched him nod from the corner of her eye as he continued to watch her. "Is it working?"

She shook her head, not bothering to lie any longer.

It wasn't working.

"How did you know?" she finally asked without meeting his gaze.

"Ah yes, how did your father find out you were sleeping with one of his agents when you were so very careful to hide it?" That disappointment was there. "I've known since the first night you didn't come home because you were at his apartment," he revealed. "I swore to your mother I'd watch out for you, Sheila. I almost messed up with Ross Mason, but I haven't messed up since."

"You didn't mess up, Daddy," she sighed as she lifted her hands and began to pick at her nails rather than letting her gaze meet her father's.

If her father saw how much it hurt, he might blame himself. She didn't want that.

"I almost messed up," he reiterated. "I almost didn't introduce Mason to the general out of pride. I knew what he wanted, what he was, but seeing how it hurt you would have broken your mother's heart. I couldn't have that, you know."

A sad smile pulled at her lips as she nodded again. That was her father's way of saying it had hurt him to see her hurt.

"I got over it, Dad," she promised him.

"Not all the way," he guessed softly. "You weren't in love with him, so you got over the man, but you didn't get over the lesson, did you, baby girl?"

"Dad—" she began to protest.

He lifted his hand, silencing her immediately. As always, she clenched her teeth, irritated with herself because that one moment could immediately remind her that if she didn't quieten, then her father could refuse to speak to her for days.

It had happened once, and only once, when she had been no more than five.

"Now, look at me."

She lifted her gaze slowly, emotion clogging her throat as she met the concern and affection in her father's eyes.

He'd been a stern disciplinarian when she had been a child, but he had been a friend after she'd passed that unruly teenage stage. He was her boss and, sometimes, her sounding board, but he was always her father.

"Daddy, I don't want to talk about Casey," she stated, her tone respectful but determined. "This is my fight, not yours."

"And why is it a fight?" he asked softly. "What is it, Sheila, that has you watching the road expecting him, and yet refusing to make that first move?"

"Because I don't know what he wants from me." Frustration filled her voice now. "He wants me to guess, or to beg, I don't know," she bit out furiously. "And I can't stand not knowing."

"Maybe he just wants you," her father suggested gently.

Sheila turned her gaze back to the flowers as she shook her head. "He wants more. He has to."

"What do you want from him?"

Her gaze swung back to him in surprise. "I just want him, Dad," she whispered. "That was all I ever wanted."

"His love?"

She nodded slowly. "Just his love."

"Maybe, Sheila, you're wrong. Maybe that really is all Casey wants from you."

Her lips parted to argue the suggestion. There had to be more. Casey had to want more. No one had ever wanted just her love, and she couldn't imagine Casey did either.

"Cooper has intel ready to come in," he told her before she could argue his opinion of Casey. "He'll be waiting on you in the office tonight at nine sharp. Don't be early, Sheila, and don't be late."

She wanted to roll her eyes at the order. Her father was a stickler for punctuality.

"And what time should I be home, Daddy?" Unfolding herself from the top of the desk, she slid from the seat until she was standing beside his chair, looking down at where he pushed his glasses back atop his head.

"Getting back isn't the problem," he told her. "Cooper and his wife Sarah are leaving town tonight and want to get on the road early. Cooper knows how I am about chain of evidence."

Anyone who worked with her father knew that. Cooper was always present if he wasn't the one to turn over the flash drive.

"I'll be there at nine sharp," she promised as she turned to leave the office.

"By the way, Annie said you were at the house looking for me last night?"

Sheila composed her expression quickly before turning back to her father with a quick smile. "I was just bored."

Or scared. One or the other.

Scared, she decided. "I'm heading home, Dad. If I'm going to be there at ten sharp, then I have some things to do before I leave."

"Of course, dear. I'll see you tomorrow." He waved her away as he turned his attention to the files on his desk. "Afternoon if you don't mind. I'll be leaving in a few hours myself for Corpus Christi. A meeting with the other network commanders."

"In the morning then," she agreed, lifting her hand in a farewell wave as she left the office and headed for the front door.

If she was going to chance seeing Casey, then she was going to do what she did every night before picking up the flash drive. Shower. Choose just the right outfit. The right perfume. The right shoes.

Just in case she saw Casey.

TEN

Was it good luck or bad luck? Fate or karma? Whichever it was, when Sheila slipped into Ethan Cooper's office, Casey was there as well, waiting.

His arms were crossed over his broad chest, his expression stoic, his gaze swirling with dark emotion. It seemed as though his emotions reached out to her, wrapped around her. Her chest tightened and the tears she had shed only in the darkest part of the night for the past week threatened to fill her eyes as their gazes met.

"Hey, Cooper, Sarah." Shoving her hands into the pockets of the light blazer she wore over the sleeveless top, she glanced toward Casey again. Clearing her throat she said, "Hello, Casey."

"Sheila." His expression didn't change, but something in his eyes did.

Dropping her gaze for a second, she turned back to Cooper and Sarah as they watched both her and Casey silently. She could see confusion in their expressions.

And she understood why they felt it. After all, the last time she and Casey had been in the same room together, it was all they could do to keep their hands off each other.

They weren't having that problem now, though.

Sheila couldn't tear her eyes off his broad chest, covered by the short-sleeved denim shirt, or the powerful cut of his thighs encased in jeans and framing the hard, heavy length of his erection.

He was aroused, and the proof of it had her womb clenching, her pussy tightening, and her juices spilling to the silk of her panties.

Perhaps she shouldn't have worn the skirt. It was short, gauzy, frilly, and intensely feminine. The camisole tank and light silk blazer she wore emphasized her feeling of femininity.

The four-inch heels only topped it off.

Sitting down in the chair next to her, Sheila slid the left shoe off, pressed the small indention at the side of the heel, and watched as the tiny spring-loaded opening slid to the side to reveal the compartment just big enough to hold the tiny flash drive.

Taking the black stick that held the information gathered the night before, she tucked it into the small recess before activating the mechanism once again, closing the small hollow.

Her gaze lifted to Casey once again. He had been the one who had come up with the idea for the hiding place. It had been a hell of a decision for her to make, to allow him to cut into several pairs of her favorite shoes.

His excuse for using more than one pair of old boots was that it would throw suspicion further away from her if she altered her dress often. Any electronics created to scan her purse or clothing would miss the tiny drive nestled just beneath her heel.

He was staring at her feet, his gaze narrowing as he lifted his eyes back to her.

She felt lost in his look.

Sarah was talking, and though Sheila heard her, answered her, nothing really existed for her except Casey. Except the pure hunger and latent anger that burned in his eyes.

"Okay, that's it then," Cooper announced as Sheila signed off on the acceptance of the small card.

She used the code name her father had assigned her, just as Cooper used his.

"Yeah, that's it," she repeated, her gaze sliding to Casey once more as she rose to her feet. "Good night, Cooper. Sarah." Her lips trembled as she glanced back at Casey again. "Good night, Casey."

He inclined his head slowly and Sheila felt as though her heart had been ripped in two.

Dragging in a hard breath, she turned and strode quickly to the door, desperate to get away from him now, to find the privacy she needed to release the tears building in her eyes.

She hadn't known it would hurt this bad. She hadn't known that being without him would slice through her soul like a jagged knife, ripping past her defenses and leaving her so very vulnerable.

Holding back the tears was impossible.

By time she reached the dimly lit shadows of the building's side parking lot, the first one had escaped. Cupping her hand over her mouth, she fought to hold back the cry that would have spilled free with it. Allowing it to escape would only lead to more tears, to the pain erupting inside her like a tightly capped volcano spewing free.

She was unaware she had been followed. Unaware that the man who caused the tears was no more than a step behind her.

Casey heard the hitch of her voice, and as though the knowledge of her tears was borne in the air following a storm, he knew the pain suddenly raging inside her.

He'd never felt another person's tears or another person's emotions as he felt hers now. As though they reached out to him and pierced his chest like an arrow, shooting straight to his soul.

"Sheila." He reached for her as the door slammed behind them, the shadows of the night wrapping around them.

He gripped her shoulders, turning her, overcoming the instinctive struggle, the pride that had her stiffening against him as he pressed her body between his and the side of the building.

"God, baby, you're killing me." The words, whispered at her ear, seemed to break something inside her.

Her body slumped, her shoulders trembling as he felt the silent sobs that suddenly escaped and the tears that spilled to the thin white dress shirt he wore.

She cried silently, which was all the more heartbreaking as her fingers tightened and fisted in the shirt over his chest. Wrapping his arms around her, Casey held her as closely, as tightly to him as he could, and still, it didn't seem to be enough. He wanted her under his skin, to be a part of him, locked so tight to him that neither of them could escape.

Bending his head to her shoulder, the soft flesh bared

by the thin straps of her camisole top, he let his lips press to her flesh, his tongue ease out to taste the soft, feminine taste of her.

As though that small hint of her essence only intensified the need, he allowed his lips to part further, his tongue to take more of her taste as he kissed the fragrant flesh.

"Fuck. Roses," he growled as that hint of a taste penetrated his senses.

God, he loved the taste of roses against her flesh.

His hand smoothed up her arm, lifting until he was cupping her neck, his thumb pressing beneath her chin to lift her face to where the moonlight gleamed on the damp trails of her tears.

Her eyes glittered in the darkness, filled with pain. And God knew he understood how she hurt. How the hunger and the need beat inside her soul, because it beat inside his own.

As her lips parted on a ragged breath, he couldn't resist the taste, the soft, crushed-silk feel of them.

His head lowered and he took instant advantage of the parted curves, the damp, tear-drenched saltiness, and the heat and pleasure he'd found only with his Sheila.

Her breathing hitched, but this time in response to his kiss rather than in response to the pain.

Lifting her closer as his knees bent, one hard thigh pressing in between hers, Casey pulled her to the furiously hard flesh pounding beneath his jeans.

Her skirt slid back, revealing tempting, creamy thighs in the dim light as her legs lifted, her knees bending to grip his hips and ride the cloth-covered erection raging beneath the denim.

Damn her. His body craved her like air. She was as

natural to him as breathing, and he couldn't seem to exist without finding a way to see her, to touch and hold her.

He let his palm slide up her thigh, beneath the skirt. His fingers tucked beneath the tiny square of material that barely covered her sex to find her hot and wet, the silken folds drenched in sweet, feminine honey.

He was so damned hungry for her it was all he could do to keep from ripping the zipper of his jeans and impaling her with the stiff flesh of his dick.

He wanted inside her so bad he could barely think for it, barely concentrate on anything but the remembered feel of her pussy milking the come from his dick.

As he snarled his head jerked back, his hips grinding between her thighs as a soft, desperate little moan escaped her lips.

"Tell me, Sheila." He had to hear the words. "What do you want from me? Tell me, baby, and I'll give you what we're both dying for."

He left his fingers tucked between the folds of her pussy, to rub against the snug, clenched entrance in a sensual promise to fill her if she gave him what he needed.

"Casey, just tell me."

He froze. Staring down at her he could see the confusion in her gaze, the desperation, and he could see how much she loved him.

A love so strong, so deep was what he felt for her.

No, his was stronger, deeper he decided, because he knew it for what it was, felt it for what it was, and she continued to hide from it. From him.

His fingers eased back.

"Casey, please," she cried out, her voice hoarse with tears. "What do you want from me?"

What did he want from her?

Hell.

"As strange as it may seem, baby, I want you to see without being shown." He sighed as he eased her back to her feet and steadied her until she was standing on her own. "Come on, I'll take you to your car."

Before he ended up fucking her against the wall.

That was a serious danger if he didn't get her the fuck away from him. He would end up taking her there in the shadows and he wouldn't give a damn who caught him.

"Wait." The fingers of both hands wrapped around his wrist. "Were you at the house last night? Did you come to see me?"

He could hear the need in her voice, the same desperation that he had. What the hell did she want? To ensure he made the first move?

"No, I wasn't." But he knew it wouldn't be long. He would break, and the thought of that sent a wave of anger rushing through him.

She had to know what he felt for her. She had to have realized it. No woman could be so fuckin' obtuse that they couldn't see when a man was so engulfed in her that he would gladly die for her. Or worse, kill for her.

He'd wondered several times, and prayed he was only being facetious, when he'd wondered who he had to kill to convince her he loved her?

"Oh." She released him slowly.

Catching her hand, he drew her to her car.

"Where's your key?" He couldn't keep the anger from his tone.

Pushing her fingers into the side pocket of her skirt, she pulled out the small electronic key and the snick of the door locks filled the silence.

Jerking the door open, he held it for her, watching as she moved around him to slide into the driver's seat.

"Why are you doing this?" she whispered as she stared back at him. "What kind of game are you playing with my heart, Casey?"

And that only pissed him off more. If she thought he was playing a game, then it could only be because she was playing one herself. And the thought of that lit a fuse to his temper that went straight to his lusts.

He'd find out the game she was playing.

He hadn't been at her home last night, but tonight? Oh baby, he promised her silently, he'd be there tonight.

"Go home, Sheila," he told her gently as he stepped back, gripping the edge of the door. "And think about it. I'll give you one more chance to figure it out on your own."

He closed the door before she could argue and stepped back, his gaze still connected with hers, his expression, harder than she may have ever seen it.

She had him ready to explode. Not so much in anger as in pure dominant male lust. A dominance and a lust that went far beyond anything he had ever wanted to give another woman.

He wouldn't allow her to play games with what he knew existed between them. He'd be damned if he'd ever seen the love a woman felt for him in her eyes. But he'd seen it in Sheila's. Just as he'd felt her pain, her longing, her fucking confusion.

The vehicle started, and as he watched, she backed out of the parking space and turned, heading to the exit.

He watched until her taillights faded around the curve ahead and several other vehicles pulled out behind her.

And he promised himself, he silently swore to her,

that before the night was over, she would know to the soles of her feet who the fuck she belonged to, and why she belonged to him.

After tonight, she'd know better than to ever again ask him what game he was playing with her heart.

ELEVEN

By all accounts and research, Sheila Rutledge was a good girl.

Her heart had been broken once by Ross Mason, a young man who had used her to further his own ends. He had, at a very vulnerable time in her life, used her to get to her father and to gain an important government position within the financial sector.

The knowledge of Ross Mason deception had caused Miss Rutledge to retreat behind a wall of frigid unconcern where men were involved. Until a man named Nick Casey had arrived in town five years before to work for Ethan Cooper at the Broken Bar.

Gossip, it appeared, had been focused on Miss Rutledge and her bouncer since the day she had met him.

And in the past nine or ten months, it had only become stronger.

Since the night Miss Rutledge had left the bar with her bouncer and spent the night at his apartment.

They were an item, despite the fact that it seemed the young miss was determined to hold on to the man whose past was shrouded in shadows.

Strange, the fact that Captain Rutledge seemed blissfully ignorant of the fact that Nick Casey wasn't who he said he was.

Of course, Rutledge himself had a rather shady past as well. A man in his fifties and he'd never risen above captain? For all his connections and political friends, his rank should have been far higher. Which meant somewhere, in some way, Rutledge had compromised his position and his values.

Ahh, such tangled webs.

A sigh filled the pickup. Following Miss Rutledge, knowing the task ahead, weighed heavily on the shoulders.

It wouldn't be easy, terrifying her, harming her. She was a gentle person, a kind person, and forcing her to pay the price for a past she had nothing to do with would be a haunting act. It would be a memory that would haunt not just the present, but the future as well.

Hands tightened on the steering wheel. The vehicle began to accelerate. No, harming her wouldn't be easy, but what other choice was there?

Beau refused to make the call.

There was no gossip that his woman was in danger, Miss Rutledge had kept her suspicions to herself. No one else knew her home had been broken into. No one knew a vehicle followed her a little closer each night.

No one else knew about the phone message she had on her recorder.

Beau had no idea his lover had been targeted and had not yet made that all important phone call.

It was time to ensure that all knew Miss Rutledge had a stalker. One willing to kill her to achieve whatever ideal she represented.

The vehicle accelerated further, moving steadily closer to the small car ahead and the future Sheila Rutledge might well pay the ultimate price for.

TWELVE

Sheila watched in her rearview mirror as the headlights behind her accelerated at an unusual speed. They were moving faster, coming up on her at a speed that was rarely used on the back road that led to the exclusive estates outside Simsburg.

The mostly retired residents didn't drive like bats out of hell. Like the vehicle behind her and the one that had ridden her ass for the past several trips to the bar. For some reason, she never failed to miss the driver who came up on her like an Indy Car driver and, after a few seconds, zipped around her as though she weren't even there.

Tonight, though, it wasn't zipping around her.

This time, it wasn't a car but a monster four-by-four. The powerful sedan that had come up and gone around her at such high speed was absent. The chrome grill of the pickup filled her rearview mirror, the lights almost blinding as they speared into the back window.

And it wasn't trying to pull around her.

Sheila slowed down, and the truck slowed.

She sped up, and the truck sped up.

She didn't take any more chances.

With her heart in her throat, she hit the call button on the steering wheel.

"Casey." She had to fight to steady her tone for the voice-recognition software that powered the automatic calling feature of the Bluetooth connection.

The sound of the phone's ring was overly loud in the car as the truck's motor revved behind her. And it came closer. Impossibly closer.

A second ring as her gaze jerked back to the rearview mirror.

"Sheila, you okay?" Casey's voice came across the line, concern filling it.

Yeah, that was right, she never called anyone as she drove home. It was an agreement made when she first began carrying the flash drives from the bar to her father.

"I have a tail." Her voice was trembling now. "A close one, Casey."

The sound of the truck's powerful motor giving a hard, dark growl behind her sent fear pumping through her system.

"Stay on the line," he ordered. "Turk, Jake, Iron, and I are on our way. How far away are you, baby?"

She swallowed tightly at the threatening rumble of the vehicle behind her as it advanced, slowed, then advanced on her once more.

"I'm about fifteen minutes from home, Casey. I'm passing through Gator Bay now."

Gator Bay was the locals' nickname for the road she

was on because of the increasing number of alligators seen on the road and along the edges of the swampy marsh further out.

"We're coming after you, sweetheart—"

At that second, the sound of the engine behind her revving and the harsh, shocking impact of the truck's grille on her bumper caused a shocked scream to escape her lips.

Her foot hit the gas harder as she fought to control the little car and edge away from the truck as it nearly rammed her again.

Casey barked out her name, the sound of loud voices and harsh orders being called out on his side of the connection echoing around her.

"Oh my God, Casey, he just hit me," she cried out as she clenched the steering wheel and fought to get more speed out of the car. "I can't outrun him, Casey. Oh God, I can't outrun him."

She was trying, but the car wasn't built for speed. They were doing seventy down the little country road and Sheila could feel the tires' grip on the road lessening with each curve she took at that speed. They threatened to skid, to throw her sideways; at one point, the back end almost fishtailed as she hit a particularly tight curve.

A curse exploded from her lips as the headlights behind her gained on her once again. A second later the impact of the truck's grille on her already abused bumper had her cheek hitting the steering wheel as she nearly lost control once again.

Sheila screamed as the car was thrown forward, the tires screaming as she fought to control the vehicle, to employ the driving lessons Casey had given her when she had first taken the job as courier from the bar to her father's office.

"Casey!" she cried out as the truck suddenly rammed the back of the car again. "Casey, I can't stay ahead of him!" she screamed.

"By God you will!" he screamed back at her. "I didn't spend those months teaching you to drive to let some asshole defeat you."

Fear was a cold, hard lump in her throat as she pressed her foot harder to the gas, barely managing to keep from being rammed again as both car and truck tires squealed going around another curve.

The car was jerked sideways as the tires lost precious traction. Fighting the steering wheel, Sheila finally managed to straighten the vehicle when another hard nudge from the back nearly had her crashing into the guardrail protecting motorists from the deep, still waters that ran alongside the road in that area.

She could feel the terror lashing at her. There were alligators in that water. They'd been driven into the area after the last tropical storms had swept through. As though they were tired of playing in the Everglades and decided to come to Texas and play there instead.

And Sheila was terrified of them.

"Casey!" she gasped as she finally sped past that danger, only to have the next heavy nudge throw the car onto the wide graveled shoulder of the road before she managed to fight the car back onto the blacktop.

The headlights stayed behind her. No matter how hard she tried, how fast she went.

"I can't take much more!" she screamed as the next

nudge nearly jerked the steering wheel out of her hand. "Casey, where are you?" she cried out desperately.

"I'm coming, baby. We're passing Gator Bay. I'm almost there."

"Oh God." She pressed the gas harder.

The truck was trying to come around her.

She was afraid of what that meant, terrified of allowing the huge vehicle to come around her. It had been years since Casey had taught her the defensive driving techniques, and then, they hadn't had someone actually trying to knock them off the road.

"Casey, I can't keep him behind me," she said, feeling the tears, the terror threatening to choke her. "Oh God, Casey, I'm sorry," she sobbed. "I'm sorry I didn't understand. Casey, I'm so sorry—"

"Sheila, don't you dare let that bastard win." Casey felt his guts clenching with pure, unimagined terror as he pushed the truck as hard as he dared, speeding around the curves at a speed he had never dared before as he raced to get to her.

Beside him, Turk grabbed hold of the handgrip above him and continued to report through the Bluetooth he wore to Cooper and the others behind them.

Casey and Turk had managed to tear out of the bar well ahead of the others when the call had come through.

He heard her scream again, then swore insanity was only seconds away as he heard the horrifying explosion of a weapon and Sheila's agonized scream of his name as glass shattered around her.

"Fuck! Fuck! Sheila!" He was screaming her name as he pushed the truck harder, his foot landing heavily on the gas and sending the truck careening around the curves.

He listened to Turk yelling out a report to Cooper as he jerked the Glock from the holster beneath the jacket he wore and checked the clip despite the wild ride Casey had him on.

"Sheila!" Casey screamed her name again as he heard an impact and the sound of what he knew was the driver's side air bag inflating. "Sheila. *Answer* me, damn you. You will not leave me like this. I won't let you."

She wasn't answering.

Casey felt such an insane rage overcoming him that he didn't know if he could control it. God help whoever, whatever had struck out at her. If she was harmed, if anything had happened to her, the pain he would deal out to the culprit once he found him would be unimaginable. No mercy.

"I have her." Mechanical, cold, the voice came over the line. "The past has come to collect, and the future no longer has a defense. I have taken her, and there is nothing you can do to stop me."

Casey heard the weapon cock as he slid around the curve to see the vehicles in the small clearing off the road just ahead.

A black-garbed, shadowed form took off running as Casey raced for the location.

He let it run.

The truck sped away just as Casey swung into the clearing and came to a bone-jarring stop next to Sheila's car.

He was aware of Turk sliding over and the truck racing off after Sheila's attacker as he jumped out and ran to the car.

The driver's side door was open and his woman, his life, was slumped over the air bag, blood smearing the inflated pillow as he searched desperately for a sign of movement.

"God no! Sheila. Baby." He was terrified to touch her, fear unlike anything he had ever known in his life gripped him, took him by the throat and strangled the sanity from him as he reached in for her.

Terrified of what he might see, Casey gripped her shoulders and eased her back carefully.

She was breathing.

Tears, honest to God moisture that hadn't touched his eyes in longer than he could remember, as her eyes slowly blinked open and he watched her take a shaky, confused breath.

"Casey." The tears she held back slowly fell from her dazed, confused eyes as he lifted her from the car only to collapse to the ground beside it as he held her tight to his chest.

His head bent over hers as he shook, trembled, and felt the first rivulet of saltwater ease from one eye to her hair as he rocked her, held her, and let himself believe she was alive.

"No more games." Ragged, torn, he whispered the words against her ear as he let his head lower further against her. "No more games, baby. I love you. I love you clear to my soul and beyond, Sheila. Oh God, baby." His hands stroked over her, and he found himself terrified that feeling her alive and breathing against him was only a dream. "Sweet, sweet Sheila. How I love you."

"What? Casey. What?" She forced him to pull back, to lift his head as she stared back at him blinking, her gaze confused, filled with disbelief. "Me?" She shook her head, clearly confused. "But why?"

He touched her face, desperate to feel her warmth, to feel her alive. "Why do I love you?" he laughed raggedly, cherishing her tears, her confusion, even her disbelief. Cherishing her and the fact that he could hold her, that she was in his arms where he intended to keep her. Safe, as he intended to ensure she stayed. "Because you make me warm in a place where I think I've been cold all my life, Sheila. Because the first day I saw you, I began to live. God help me, Sheila, because you're my fucking life and I think I died listening to that bastard try to kill you."

He framed her face with one hand, his thumb brushing over her tear-drenched lips as they parted in shock— and was that hope in her gaze?

"You love me?" Her hand gripped his wrist. "You love me?"

"With everything in my soul."

Her lips trembled. The scratches on her face still seeped blood, tears still filled her eyes, and she was the most beautiful thing in the world to him.

"I've always loved you," she whispered. "I thought I'd never see you again, Casey," she suddenly sobbed. "I thought I'd never get to tell you I love you. That I didn't understand until I didn't think I'd ever see you again, that the only reason was because you loved me." Her breathing hitched as his lips touched her. "I wanted to tell you, and then there was glass exploding around me."

He laid his finger against her lips. The horror of hearing that gunshot would live in his nightmares the rest of his life.

"I have you," he swore. "I have you, Sheila, and I'll never let you go. That son of a bitch will never get the chance to touch you again."

Because Casey was determined to kill him.

His lips touched hers. Tears, a hint of blood, and the overwhelming knowledge of love filled his senses as her lips parted for him, her hands moving to his neck, his hair, as her lips met his.

"I love you," he swore again before he kissed her deeply, licked her, tasted her. He let the knowledge that she was alive seep inside him. Let the truth of it wrap around him.

Because Casey knew, he couldn't have survived otherwise.

THIRTEEN

One week later

Ross Mason was led from his hotel room in Corpus Christi in handcuffs.

Once, years before, he might have been a handsome man, the man Sheila Rutledge had once believed she loved, though it was rather doubtful.

A weak chin, plain brown eyes, shaggy hair, and a plump midsection—it was hard to imagine he had ever drawn the gaze of a woman as lovely as Miss Rutledge.

Though, perhaps her once-deep shyness and the loss of her mother had caused her to look beyond the surface to that weakness beneath and unconsciously believe he would be the one who would not leave her, would not betray her.

That had nothing to do with looks. Betrayal came in all shapes, sizes, races, and creeds. Betrayal came when one least expected it, when one could be destroyed by it the most.

It was a lesson that only the strong survived.

Miss Rutledge had survived that lesson and lived to find a man who might or might not know honor. Who seemed to understand it, live by it.

There was no doubt now Nick Casey wasn't Beauregard Fredrico.

Beau knew nothing of trust, honor, or true love. He knew nothing of holding a woman tight or of risking his own life to save hers, as Nick Casey had done.

No, Nick was not Beau.

The call had not been made before Ross Mason had been revealed as the attempted murderer of the young and lovely Miss Rutledge. There had been no reinforcements called out, no waiting army of loyal men willing to give their lives for the one their fathers had pledged to defend. And those sons would readily pick up arms now and travel across the seas if it meant the heir to the past would return and retake the legacy that had been meant to be his.

The past was truly dead and gone, though. There was no way to convince those men that there was no way to resurrect that past, that glory, or that wealth.

Not that the Fredricos had understood the business anyway.

Giovanni Fredrico, once known as Gio the Giant, hadn't ruled the families as he should have. There had been no blood shed for infractions, just as the whores had not been punished when they fell in love and defected, and the drug dealers had not been murdered, painfully, when they stole the product that was the lifeblood of the organization that had once ruled with a steel fist.

Once, before Giovanni had taken the mantle of leadership.

Once, before his son Beauregard had turned his nose up at the legacy that he had been honor bound to claim.

The bastard.

A fist clenched, jaw tightened, and the familiar rage began to burn like a wildfire within a chest that had been ripped open, the very heart extracted so long ago.

No, Nick Casey was no Beauregard.

That suspicion had been there before Sheila had left the bar the night Ross Mason had followed her.

It was the reason only Ross had been following at first.

Realizing there was trouble following Miss Rutledge hadn't been easy. Diverting suspicion had been even harder.

Casey had nearly caught sight of the shadowed figure moving through the darkness to take the pictures needed.

The one of Ross Mason pointing that gun at the girl's head just seconds after firing into the car and causing the wreck would be a haunting memory.

But it was over now. The authorities had the pictures that proved Ross had been behind the assault on the woman Nick Casey now guarded so diligently.

Not that she seemed to mind. There was a smile on her face that hadn't been there before, and a joy and youth to her that would stay with her for many years to come. Because the man she loved, the man who loved her, refused to let her out of his sight.

Just as Ethan Cooper loved his Sarah, Nick Casey loved his Sheila.

That left three: Jake Murphy, Iron Donovan, and Turk Rogan.

A weary sigh filled the inside of the truck that held the eyes of the past. A tired, disillusioned sigh. It wasn't over yet. Not yet.

And there could be no peace until it was.

FOURTEEN

There was a heat surrounding him that Casey knew he would never escape. One he never wanted to escape.

As he lay with the woman he loved more than life itself and pulled his lips from the kiss that was pulling him headlong into a complete meltdown, he realized how he was looking forward to that final surrender to her.

Until then— He looked down at her kiss-swollen lips, the drowsy sensuality in her gaze and her flushed cheeks, and he reminded himself that getting there was just as heated, just as incredible.

Beneath him, Sheila arched closer, her lithe, naked body twisting beneath his as the blunt, heavily engorged head of his dick prodded at the swollen lips of her pussy.

Slick silk. Damn, that was what her bare, satiny pussy felt like. Like the softest, hottest syrup saturating a silk so pure and fine it could only be made in paradise.

"Casey, please," she whispered as his lips descended

to her breasts. "Oh yes, lick my nipples." She arched closer yet, whimpering as his lips closed over them and he let her feel a hint of his teeth. "Suck them," she moaned. "Suck my nipples. Make me come."

Taking one of the hardened tips between his lips, Casey sucked it hungrily, the taste of her, the passion that flowed from her, making him desperate for more as her fingers fisted in his hair to hold him closer.

That slick, wet silk surrounding the head of his cock, his hips moving as he ate at the tender tip of her nipple. Slowly, with precise gentleness, he began working his cock inside her, feeling the snug muscle and tissue as it parted beneath each slow, easy thrust.

Oh, God. It was like being buried, like being wrapped in pure, wild heat. Her juices eased between her flesh and his, another caress that made him ready to growl with pleasure. To snarl with the demand to come.

He'd be damned if he would let himself go that easily. If he would allow Sheila to go that easily.

He didn't want to leave the hot, milking grasp of her pussy until he had no other choice. Pushing inside the liquid heat, slowly, working his cock inside the tender portal, he had to clench his teeth to keep from riding her hard and heavy and spilling his seed inside her.

His balls were drawn tight beneath the iron-hard shaft, his muscles locked tight against the ecstasy threatening to claim him.

With his dick encased inside her, his tongue playing erotic games with her nipples, Casey knew his control wouldn't last much longer.

Her silken inner thighs caressed his flanks as her legs bent and clasped his hips. Her hips rolled against him with each thrust of his dick inside the searing depths of her pussy; each time he had to work his way past the tight muscles rather than slamming inside her.

Fuck, he wanted to ride her hard. He wanted to thrust fast and work inside her and feel her clenching on his cock, sucking his seed straight from his balls.

He wanted to fuck her with the inborn passion that he knew had only come when he touched Sheila. A hunger he'd never known before, and he knew it was a hunger he would never know for any other woman.

Giving a final lick to a cherry red nipple, Casey lifted his gaze to stare down at her.

Her head was thrown back, her hair spread around her like a dark blond halo. Small hands were clenched into fists, holding on to the sheets beneath her, her eyes staring up at him with a hunger that matched his own.

"Fuck me harder." The words slipped past kiss-swollen lips. "I dare you, Casey. Fuck me like you mean it."

For all the challenge in her voice, he also heard the love. A love Casey knew would last him until he took his final breath.

Sheila wanted to scream in pleasure. She wanted to beg, demand, and cry out with the sensations building inside the exquisitely sensitive muscles of her pussy.

Casey stretched her until he was certain she could take no more. He filled her, heated her pussy, and stroked inside it with a rhythm that was driving her insane.

She wanted more.

"Harder," she gasped, her hands lifting from the sheets to grip his shoulders, her nails biting into the hard flesh and iron-hard muscles as his hips ground against hers.

He was teasing her. Pushing her higher. He was filling her with such incredible pleasure, sensations that sizzled across her nerve endings before speeding through her system and tightening every muscle in her body with the need to orgasm.

"It's so good," she moaned, nearly incoherent with the pleasure that burned inside her. "Oh God, Casey, I love you. I love you so much." It was a plea. "Please let me come. Please, I can't stand it any longer."

Flames were building inside her, spreading outward, threatening to set the world ablaze if she didn't find her release soon. She could feel the clenching around the flesh penetrating her, tightening and spasming as the swollen bud of her clit began to throb warningly.

"Yes," she moaned. "Oh yes, Casey." Neck arching, she felt it begin, felt it rushing through her, over her, tearing into her with a force that had her trying to scream as her orgasm began to detonate inside her.

Casey wasn't but a second longer.

As he buried his cock to the hilt, Sheila felt the hard, fierce throb, the feel of the brief expansion, then the fierce, jetting spurts of his come shooting inside her.

His release mixed with hers, burned and melded until there was no longer just Casey, no longer just Sheila. Until the two of them were suddenly joined and made whole. Made one.

"I love you," she cried out desperately. "Oh God, Casey, I love you."

With his head buried at her neck, his arms wrapped around her, his very life pumping inside her, Casey whispered, "You're my soul, Sheila. My home."

His home.

As he was hers.

And together they were creating the dream Sheila had believed she would never know.

That dream of belonging.

DEADLY DANCE

CHEYENNE McCRAY

ONE

"Detective Adam Boyd, NYPD." He held up his shield so that the woman could get a good look at it through her screen door. Her porch light was bright enough that she should be able to see it. He heard a dog barking at the back of the house.

She studied him for a moment. "What do you need, Detective?"

"Ms. Holliday," he said. "I'd like a few words with you about Edward Carter."

Through the mesh screen he saw Keri Holliday's shadowy expression freeze. Given his intimate knowledge of this case, he was sure she wasn't going to like what he had to tell her.

Hell, the news had hit him like a truck slamming into a concrete barrier. The instant burn in Adam's gut had come with a wash of memories that could turn him into a killing machine rather than a levelheaded cop. The desire for revenge was so strong that it was all he could do not to hunt Carter down and empty his Glock into the sonofabitch's chest.

During the pause between telling Keri he wanted to speak to her about Carter and when she finally opened the screen door, the March night wind picked up. The month was going out like a lion and the icy wind cut through the opening in his jacket, through his T-shirt, straight to his skin like claws.

In a good impression of chalk screeching across a blackboard, the screen door squeaked as she pushed it open, and he barely kept from wincing at the sound.

"Come in." Keri stood aside so that he could enter the modest-looking Brooklyn Heights carriage home.

Like other carriage houses on the street, hers didn't begin to look like it would go for the astronomical prices that were being asked for the homes. Adam lived in Brooklyn, too, but had a much less pricey Victorian in Kensington. Much less pricey.

As Adam started to take a step inside, his gaze met hers. For a moment he forgot why he was there. Something stirred in him, something beyond anything he'd ever felt before.

Seven years ago, the severity of an injury had kept him from interviewing her with his partner, Jerry. Adam would never have forgotten how beautiful Keri Holliday was. He could never forget a face like hers.

The room's soft lighting touched her. Eyes the color of dark green jade. Long auburn hair drawn back in a ponytail, accenting her cheekbones. Lips that looked soft and warm.

The simple ponytail and the youthful freckles across

the bridge of her nose didn't take away from her natural elegance. She wore no makeup, her skin slightly pink as if she'd just washed her face.

He'd read in the file a couple of hours ago that she was a former ballerina, but he didn't need that knowledge to see she was an athlete. Despite the early end to her career, she was slender and fit, her arms toned, her body lithe. It was easy to see that she had a dancer's body beneath the simple jeans and black sweater with little pearl buttons.

According to Jerry's notes, she'd been referred to as the "Angel of New York" and had been at the height of her career when things had gone very wrong for her.

At the same time he assessed her, thoughts hit him, crazy thoughts. Of kissing this angel's soft lips . . . of his hands caressing the sensual lines of her body.

Well, damn. It was too soon after his breakup with Nyx to start feeling this way about another woman. Not to mention the fact he wasn't there for any kind of social reason.

Tension crowded the air around them. The movement of her throat caught his attention as she swallowed. When he met her gaze again he saw recognition—recognition that something was passing between them and it wasn't one-sided.

"This way, Detective." Keri's voice was low, throaty, like Kathleen Turner's in that old movie, *Romancing the Stone*. Sexy as hell.

Adam gave a nod and shoved his hands into the pockets of his worn brown leather bomber jacket as she shut the door and led him past a set of stairs, down a short hallway, and into a living room.

The view he had as he walked behind her was spectacular. The most graceful walk he'd ever seen accompanied by gentle, elegant movements. Not to mention one hell of a nice ass.

She turned to face him. "Have a seat."

He took the few steps necessary to make it to the love seat that she'd gestured to.

Cream-and-burgundy fabric covered the seat as well as the rest of the Queen Anne furnishings in the comfortable living room. He recognized the style of furniture thanks to his mother, who'd owned an antique shop. From the time he was just a kid until college, he'd worked at the shop during the summers as well as after school.

Adam sat on the edge of the love seat and waited for Keri to take the armchair across from him. When she was settled, he leaned forward, his forearms braced on his thighs.

"How did you find me?" she asked before he had a chance to speak.

"Through a friend who is former NYPD and now a private detective," Adam said. "I would have eventually tracked you down, but she's much faster than anyone on the police force."

She nodded.

"Ms. Holliday—" he said.

"Keri." She offered him a smile. "I'm a dance instructor and I get called Ms. Holliday all day as it is."

He went straight for the bad news. He wasn't into screwing around when it came to giving information like this. "I stopped by to let you know that this afternoon Edward Carter was released from prison."

* * *

Keri stared at Detective Boyd, her mind and heart having come to a complete standstill. She couldn't possibly have heard right.

"Edward was released from prison?" Each word she repeated was painful.

"Due to a technicality." The detective's expression was hard as he studied her. "Worst decision I have ever heard," he continued. "Letter of the law police work wasn't followed according to the judge, so he released Carter, saying he regrets the decision but he has to apply the law."

He continued, "There was talk of a new trial, but the DA said the case was smashed with the ruling, suppressing evidence and essential testimony. So Carter is back on the streets."

Keri heard Fred give several short barks from the back courtyard, as if expressing what she couldn't get out. A denial that what the detective had just told her was true.

The detective gave a single nod. "Do you have someplace you can go for a while?"

"What?" Confusion followed the shock of hearing of Edward's release and she felt her forehead wrinkle. "Why would I need someplace to go?"

"Your testimony is, in part, what helped lock the key on Carter's prison door." The detective dragged his hand down his face. "Considering his violent history toward you, as soon as I got word I thought I should let you know."

For a moment Keri just stared at him. The memory of Edward's threats years ago seemed to reverberate in her ears. *"You'll pay for this, bitch. One way or another you'll pay."*

Sharp pain shot through her knee and she flinched. After what Edward had done to end her career, she had thought that was what he had meant by what he'd said— that he would hurt her again.

Detective Boyd flexed his hand and a muscle ticked in his jaw. He looked like he was getting ready to punch his fist through a wall. "Not only did he hurt you, but Carter had my partner, Jerry Marks, gunned down seven years ago. He was never tried for that, but we know he did it."

Kerri sucked in her breath. "I remember Detective Marks. He spoke with me before the FBI did."

Detective Boyd's next words came out in a growl. "Jerry had a wife and three kids."

The words hit as hard as learning of Edward's release. Detective Boyd's partner. A wife and three children left behind. More lives that Edward had ruined.

Fury burned her skin. Fury over what he had done to her. What he had done to this detective's partner and his family. What he had done to countless people, including all the lives he had affected just by running drugs and pushing them. He had been the cause of ruined lives and probably more deaths than she had ever wanted to know about.

"It's best if you get out of the house and find someplace to stay until we know you're safe," Detective Boyd was saying.

Keri struggled to move her thoughts from violence against Edward to attempting to regain focus on what the detective was saying and what steps she should take next.

Keri met the detective's warm brown eyes. Eyes that just moments before his news had drawn her to him.

"Detective—" she started.

"Adam," he said.

She nodded. "Adam, if I start running now, I'm letting Edward control my life," she said. "It's also unlikely he'll find me. I moved after he went to jail and I get my mail at the post office. I don't have anything delivered here."

"If he wants to bad enough, he'll be able to find you." Adam was frowning. "Don't forget that I had someone track you down."

Keri frowned too. "I have my dance studio and my students, and I need to be available to my parents, especially my mom, who is in poor health," she said. "What am I supposed to do about them?"

"We'll figure that out," Adam said. "Right now what we need to do is get you away from here."

She paused for a moment. "I appreciate you taking the time, but I'll be fine. I don't think Edward is going to want to jeopardize his freedom."

"I hope you'll reconsider." He stood and offered his hand.

She reached up and allowed him to help her to her feet. When he grasped her hand, Keri caught her breath. Incredible currents traveled between them. A zinging sensation went through her abdomen and her heart rate picked up.

His fingers were warm and callused, his grip strong. She had to look up at him to meet his eyes. At five-six, she was a little over average height and the detective had a good eight inches on her.

She drew her hand away and focused on not abandoning the important things in her life. "I can't just leave." She shook her head. "I can't." She straightened and took a deep breath. "I'll let you know if anything comes up."

"Be careful, Ms. Holliday—Keri," he said. "We don't know what to expect. He's a dangerous man and you shouldn't take any chances with him around."

Keri tried not to think of her firsthand experiences as she gestured to the back door that led to the courtyard. "I carry Mace and I'll keep Fred inside with me."

Adam glanced in the direction she was pointing. "Your dog?"

She nodded. "Golden retriever. He's a great watchdog." She waited for him to say something else, but he didn't. "How can I reach you?" she asked.

Adam brought out his wallet, with his detective's shield on the top, and from it he withdrew a card. Keri reached for it, but it slipped from her fingers and fluttered to the floor.

At the same time, they both crouched to grab the card and bumped heads so hard that Keri fell back and landed on her butt.

With a laugh she rubbed her forehead. "So much for grace."

He grinned as he stood and took her hand to help her up. "You okay?"

She nodded and he gave the card to her. It had the NYPD logo along with his badge number and contact information. "You can count on me keeping an eye on Carter," Adam said. "As a precaution, lock every door and window. Pay attention to see if you're being followed or watched. Call me if you notice anything that doesn't seem right."

She cocked her head. "Are you that concerned he'll come after me?"

With a thoughtful look, Adam said, "I don't think you should take chances."

"I won't." She waved the business card at him. "I know how to reach you if I need to."

Adam gave a short nod, then went down the hall to the front door. He paused, his hand on the doorknob. "Good night, Keri," he said before he let himself out and closed the door and the screen door behind him.

TWO

Thirty seconds later a knock on the door startled Keri. She'd had one drop-in guest tonight, who could be here now? She looked through the peephole. *Safe*, she thought.

When she opened the door, Detective Boyd was standing on her doorstep. This time he looked a little shy. Almost embarrassed.

Keri tilted her head. "Did you forget something?"

Adam shook his head. Cleared his throat. "I'm off duty now," he said. "By any chance would you like to have dinner with me at Pete's?"

Keri blinked in surprise. "Um, well. I don't know. We just met. I really don't even know you."

"It's a good way to get to know me." His eyebrows rose and the corner of his mouth turned up in a slight, pleading grin.

Charming and persistent. A dangerous combination.

Keri shook her head. "It's probably not a good night.

But it was very nice of you to ask. Thank you, but I should really say good night."

She closed the door, leaving him on her doorstep.

With a sigh she leaned against the door and tilted her head back so it thumped on the wood.

Truth was, she really did want to go out with him. But she never did things like that, went out with men she just met.

Hers was a simple life that included a nice routine with her dance studio and her parents, and not a whole lot else.

She really, really wanted to go out with Detective Boyd.

Keri turned and hurried to jerk the door open. "Adam. On second thought I'd love to go to dinner," she called out before he reached his SUV.

He smiled as he returned and the cutest dimple appeared in one of his cheeks. "Grab something warm, it's chilly outside."

Damn he was hot. "I'll meet you there," she said. "You can snag a table for us."

"See you," he said and headed outside, and she locked the door behind him.

The coat closet was right by the front door and she picked out a short black leather coat and slipped her arms into it. She scooped up her wallet, keys, and cell phone from the stand in the entryway and stuffed them into her coat pockets.

Kinda crazy that she was going out with a man she had known for a few minutes at most, but she had the feeling that the detective was a genuinely nice guy. Not to mention really, really sexy. Besides, this had a little more excitement to it than sitting home eating leftover Chinese and reading a book.

After going through the kitchen door to the garage and raising the garage door, she climbed into her red VW Bug and backed out into the narrow street. She made sure her garage door closed behind her before driving downtown to Pete's on Water Street.

When she arrived, Adam was seated at a small table near the bar. The buzz of voices, the clink of dishes, and music was a pleasant hum in the background. The restaurant had the warm smells of Italian food that made her mouth water.

He stood when she reached the table. "Nice to have an excuse to get out of the house," Keri said as he assisted her in getting out of her coat. "Other than going to the studio to teach classes or visiting my parents in Forest Hills, I don't get out much these days."

"I'm glad you said yes." Adam helped her with her chair and she caught his scent of coffee and leather. "It's great to have good company to enjoy dinner with."

"How do you know I'll be good company?" Keri gave him a teasing smile as he took his own seat.

Again that dimple that made her sigh as he said, "It was worth a shot."

The server appeared with glasses of water and a basket of garlic bread. After glancing at the menu and asking Keri what she liked for an appetizer, Adam ordered her favorite, the fresh mozzarella and red peppers.

When the server walked away, Keri met Adam's gaze. "So, Detective, you said you live in Kensington?"

"A two-story Victoria." He pushed his hand through his thick brown hair and she watched the play of muscles beneath his snug T-shirt. "Been there a couple of years," he was saying and she just nodded. She would have been happy to watch him all night. He was the picture of masculine grace despite the rough edges.

As he spoke, Adam reached for the bread at the center of the table. At the same time he was going for the basket, his gaze dropped to Keri's breasts. His hand shot too far and hit Keri's glass of ice water.

The water glass tipped over and a wave of ice water covered Keri's lap.

Keri gasped from the icy cold of the water that drenched her jeans and the belly of her sweater.

"Sh—damn," Adam said as he rushed up from his seat to hand her a napkin. His arm hit his own glass of ice water and it tumbled over and sent another splash of cold over Keri.

At the look of utter embarrassment on the detective's face, Keri started giggling and within a moment she couldn't stop.

While the server brought napkins to help clean up the water, Keri laughed so hard that her eyes watered and her stomach hurt.

As she laughed, she saw Adam's embarrassed smile turn into a grin. "It's a special woman who can laugh at some guy dumping two glasses of ice water on her their first night out."

"The first night out?" Keri said as she caught her breath and sopped up as much of the water as she could with napkins the server handed her. "So when's the second night?"

"I get a second chance?" Adam said.

"Sure, maybe, if you stop with the water fights." Keri dried herself about as much as she was going to be able to and handed the soaked napkins to the server. "But first tell me what distracted you to begin with."

Adam cleared his throat. "The top two buttons of your sweater are undone."

"Oh." Keri glanced down and heat rushed to her cheeks. Her sweater gaped wide enough to get a good look at her black lace bra. "Uh, thanks," she said as she fastened the pearl buttons.

"Well, I didn't mean that you had to button it back up. I've dumped all the water we have on the table." Adam gave her a teasing look. "It's not like I can cause more damage,"

Keri gave her best serious act. "Yes, but I still have a glass of wine, and we'll probably end the evening with a cappuccino. When you dump that on me it will cause a bit more of a problem than ice water. Better to keep them buttoned for you, Adam, you apparently get easily distracted."

"Easily distracted?" Adam said. "What healthy red-blooded American boy wouldn't be?"

The server came with fresh glasses of water, along with their appetizer.

"I feel like I know you well enough now after knocking heads and you sharing your water with me to say yes to another night out," she said in between bites of fresh mozzarella and peppers on bread garnished with basil.

"Good," Adam said. "Let's hope you feel the same way by the end of dinner."

Their conversation was easy and fun. Adam made her smile and laugh and she had no problem forgetting the fact she was still damp.

"How long were you a ballerina?" he asked over shrimp

scampi and white wine, after they discussed the Knicks' last game against the Celtics.

"My mother put me in dance as soon as I learned how to walk." Keri smiled. "I had an aptitude for ballet at an early age," she said. "I loved it and worked hard at it, dreaming that one day it would be my career. And it was. In another way it still is."

"I read in your file that you were about to go on an extended world tour before your career ended," he said.

Keri liked how he didn't baby her by "dancing" around the subject. "We were scheduled to dance for the Queen of England to start our tour." Keri tilted her head as she thought wistfully about the excitement she had felt during those days. "But Edward put an end to that dream."

"You don't seem bitter about it," he said.

Keri shrugged. "I was at first, but not long. There's no use in wallowing in self-pity. Now I have another career I love, one that would not have happened for a long time. Who knows how insane my life would have been if I'd continued dancing for another three to five years."

"How did you get involved with someone like Edward Carter?" Adam looked genuinely interested.

With his bad boy grin, blond hair, and blue eyes so bright it almost hurt to look at them, Edward had been drop-dead sexy and sought after in the social circles. Most females, from young women to cougar age, had found the charismatic man charming, well-spoken, and completely hot.

If they'd only known the real Edward Carter. If *she* had only known.

"I saw him at a party," she said. "He had everyone

fooled and ran with the same groups that I did." Keri looked at her wine glass, swirled it, and studied the gold liquid. "He was fun to be around and he seemed so level-headed, intelligent, confident. He had his business front that fooled so many people, including me."

She paused before she went on. "He actually treated me well then. I fell for the man I thought he was." Keri sighed. "Then I starting seeing and hearing certain things around him. I asked him about what I'd overheard on occasion and he finally got comfortable enough with me to tell me details, thinking I would go along with it.

"Things went bad when I didn't accept it." She tapped her finger on the glass, making small tinking sounds. "I began to see his violent temper. He was a different man—almost like he was possessed. It shocked me that someone could fool me like he had.

"When I realized the truth," she said, "it was like someone I cared about died." She lowered her eyes before looking at Adam again. "It's hard to think about right now."

Adam saw the topic was starting to change the good mood of the evening. "You mentioned that you teach," he said.

Thankfully his question pulled her mind away from thoughts of Edward. "All ages, and I love it." She tilted her head to the side. "What about you, Detective? What made you go into law enforcement?"

Adam gave her his adorable boyish grin. "Batman."

Keri laughed. "Batman?"

"I really wanted to be Batman when I was growing up," he said. "I didn't grow up as rich as Bruce Wayne and my parents said a Batmobile was too expensive. I figured the next best thing was to be a cop."

"So now you're a superhero police officer," she said.

Adam shook his head. "Believe me, I know super-heroes and I'm no superhero."

Keri gave him a mischievous grin. "I'll be the judge of that. There is something about a man in a mask."

"What about Catwoman?" Adam had an amused expression. "Any young male who watched that show had to have had a thing about Catwoman and her mask."

"I have one," she said.

"You seriously own a Catwoman mask?" Adam said. "Okay, that's it. We need to get this take-out and I need to see that on you."

Keri laughed. "I was Catwoman at a Halloween party and I still have the outfit."

"True confessions," Adam said. "Now you know one of my weaknesses—a Catwoman look."

She gave him a devious smile. "I just might have to model it for you someday, Detective."

Keri shivered, thanks to her damp jeans, as she stood outside the door of her home. They had driven separately to the restaurant, but Adam had wanted to see her home.

"Better hurry and get inside," he said, obviously noticing that she was shivering.

She unlocked the door, then faced him. "Thanks for dinner, Adam."

"I'm glad you took me up on it." He shoved his hands into his leather bomber jacket. "I have to say, you're a fun person to spill water on."

On impulse she reached up and kissed his cheek. "Good night."

His voice was husky as he caught her hand and rubbed

her knuckles. Again the crazy sensations traveled from his hand to hers. "You still game to do this again?"

She tried to catch her breath. "Absolutely."

"What's your phone number?" he asked and she gave him the number for her cell.

He gripped her hand for a long moment, as if he was frozen, too. His brown eyes were so warm, so inviting. She had the urge to reach up and touch his lightly stubbled jaw, to caress his cheek with her fingertips.

His throat worked. He finally released her and she let out her breath as she let her hand fall away from his.

"Good night, Keri." The way he said her name made her stomach flip. "Guess I don't get to see how that Catwoman mask looks on you, do I?"

"Maybe if you're good and let me win the next water fight, Detective, I just might show it to you," she said.

"I'll hold you to that." His voice was deep and rumbly and oh-so-sexy.

"Good night, Batman." Telling him good night had been hard to say, but she got it out.

He winked, then turned and walked away.

It was almost unnerving how he made her feel, and she barely knew him. She had never felt this way with someone she just met. It was something about the way he looked at her, the depth of caring she saw in his eyes. And maybe more than that.

Keri rubbed her temples and stared at the door for a long moment before locking it. The bolt lock *thunked* and the chain rattled as she slid it into place. After she set her car keys, cell phone, and wallet on the stand by the front door, she turned away and went toward the kitchen.

So many thoughts went through her mind, but the primary one was Adam. How much she had enjoyed his company, the fun they'd had, including getting dowsed with ice water. She had felt so comfortable with him and never felt any awkward moments the whole night, including, surprisingly the incident with her sweater buttons.

As she began to straighten up the kitchen, her thoughts turned to Edward. The fact that he was out of prison and the possibility that he might be searching for her right now was constantly at the back of her mind. She did her best to keep it there. Edward wouldn't come after her or have one of his men hurt her, would he? He wouldn't be that stupid.

But then it was Edward. And he lived by his own set of rules.

Thinking of Adam was far more fun. She rubbed her palms on her jeans. "You're like a schoolgirl, Keri," she said to herself. "With a crush on the cutest boy around."

She finished up a little cleaning, then headed up to get ready for bed, skipping the squeaky step. At the top of the stairs she flipped on the light switch in the hall and then went into her bedroom and turned on the Tiffany lamp beside her bed. She went into the bathroom and washed her face and brushed her teeth before heading back into her bedroom.

She unbuttoned the sweater and smiled as she thought about Adam and the mini chaos that had come from a couple of undone buttons. After she tossed it aside, she pulled on a white T-shirt to sleep in, then started to take off her damp jeans. A sound from downstairs caused her to halt.

Heart pounding, she paused, her hands at the hem of her T-shirt, and waited to see if she heard the noise again.

Nothing.

Fred started barking like crazy in the rear courtyard.

She'd forgotten to bring him in for the night. But what was wrong with the golden retriever? No doubt she should let him in before the neighbors decided to call or come knocking at her door.

She skipped the squeaky step as she silently walked down the staircase to go let Fred in. She reached the foyer and went into her living room—

The lights went out.

THREE

Keri clapped her hand over her mouth, holding back a cry. Was it Edward? Had he or one of his hit men come for her?

She was being stupid.

Keri sucked in her breath, her heart pounding, and wondered why she was so jumpy. The power must have gone out on her block.

It was now so dark in the living room that she couldn't see anything. She blinked rapidly, trying to get accustomed to almost pure darkness.

A squeak and the brush of the door from the garage opening came from the kitchen.

Panic crawled its way up her throat. That door couldn't possibly squeak unless someone had pushed it open, and she knew she had left it closed.

She had to call 911, but she had left her phone on the stand by the door like she always did. If someone was there she would never make it. She would call from the landline.

Silvery light came in through the curtains from the full moon. It wasn't much, but she could see well enough. Keri glanced over her shoulder.

Her breath stuck in her throat as she saw a shadowy figure pass from the kitchen toward the stairs.

Oh, my God. Someone was really in here.

She watched as the dark form moved up the stairs.

Keri remained frozen until she couldn't see the figure anymore.

Heart pounding, she worked her way through the living room, cursing herself for the clutter that decorated the place, afraid she was going to knock something down.

The stair that she always avoided gave a loud squeak.

Whoever it was had reached the top of the stairs.

Fear tore through her like a jagged knife ripping her belly open from side to side. What was she going to do?

She had to hide. First she would call for help and then get to the cellar door.

When she picked up the phone, she started to press the number for emergency—the phone was dead.

She needed to run outside *now.*

She glanced over her shoulder again.

Someone rushed toward her.

Fear closed off her throat before she could scream.

"Down!" Adam said in a harsh whisper as he grabbed Keri's arm and jerked her to the floor. "Don't move."

Keri's heart thundered as her knees hit the hardwood. "How did you—"

He whispered, "I'll explain everything later."

Fred's barking became more frantic.

Relief that it was Adam poured through her, but that relief was followed again by terror.

"There's someone upstairs," she said. "I saw him go up." The words came out in a rush.

Adam didn't answer. She realized he had drawn out a cell phone when he started talking to the police. He identified himself, asked for backup, gave the address of her home, then folded the phone and slipped it inside his jacket.

"It might be Carter or one of his men. We need to get out of here now."

Fred hadn't stopped barking. All of this time he had been trying to tell her something was desperately wrong and she hadn't listened. All she had been worried about was the neighbors hearing him and complaining about it.

The silence inside the house was almost painful. Only Fred's barking made it truly clear that something was wrong.

The stair squeaked again from above.

Keri's heart launched into her throat.

"Someone's at the top of the stairs," she said in a strangled whisper.

Adam stayed in a crouch. "What does the back door lead to?"

She tried to control her breathing. "The courtyard. There's a gate to the street from there."

Keri glanced over her shoulder. Through the darkness she saw a shadow across the room, behind them.

Adam shoved her down flat.

Whoever it was had probably heard him make the call.

"Police!" Adam shouted as he turned and aimed in the direction of the intruder. "come downstairs with your hands up."

The sound of a shot, and a vase exploded near where her head had been.

Keri nearly choked on a scream. Her shoulder hit the end table and she knocked the phone off. It clattered to the floor with a thump and rattle.

Another shot.

Adam lunged toward the door, her hand still in his, taking her with him.

He let go of her hand and twisted. He fired several shots in the direction the gunfire had come from.

The sound of Adam's gunshots made her ears ring. She crawled through debris as bullets shattered more of her things and scattered pieces across the floor.

She reached the back door, next to floor-to-ceiling windows.

Adam had his back to it and was still firing off shots where the shooter had been.

Keri stumbled and fell against the door. With shaking hands she found the knob and turned it.

Pain pierced her arm and she cried out. The doorframe splintered beside her.

Adam yanked the door open and shoved her through it.

With a ferocious growl, Fred bounded past her and into the house.

"No!" she screamed as she heard more shots. "Fred!"

A loud snarl and more growls from Fred.

Shots.

Keri's heart felt like it was going to explode like the vase had done so close to her head.

Faintly she heard sirens. The police. They had to get here before Adam or Fred was killed.

Something sticky trickled down her arm and pain burned it like fire.

"Come on!" Adam jerked her away from the doorway. "Run!"

Keri tried to get away from him. "But Fred—"

"Dammit, Keri." Adam caught her by her T-shirt and dragged her toward the back gate.

Keri held back a cry as she barely avoided tripping over Adam. She had the bizarre thought that she had never been so clumsy in her life as she was tonight.

"We've got to get you out of here," he was saying. "There's nothing you can do for your dog."

More barking, more snarls. A man's cry.

More shots.

"Like hell—" she started, but Adam yanked her hard and forced her toward the gate. She felt and heard her T-shirt rip at the collar.

"Fred is giving us the distraction we need," Adam said. Instead of taking her to the gate he brought her up to the wall. "Climb over this wall. If it is Carter, he may have someone watching the back. Go to your neighbors and wait there for me."

"They're not here," she said. "They're in Texas."

"Just get over," Adam growled.

"What about you?" she said.

Adam pointed up, indicating she needed to get over the wall. "I'm going after the suspect."

Adrenaline pumped through her body as if she was getting ready for a performance. The wall was high, but she didn't need Adam's help to jump, grab the top block, and pull herself up with her upper body strength. Her injured arm screamed with pain. Her dance training and her continuous efforts to maintain perfect shape made it possible for her to get over the wall. She went down the other side with the intention of ending up in a crouch beside the wall.

Branches jabbed into her body as she came down. Thorns scraped her arms and face, and snagged her clothing. Her skin stung.

She had landed in a huge rosebush, but she didn't care about that. All she cared about was Fred and Adam.

Keri stumbled away from the rosebush and leaned up against the wall. She dragged in ragged breath after ragged breath. It wasn't from exertion, but from fear.

Burning pain increased in her arm and she glanced down to see that the short sleeve of the formerly white T-shirt was dark with blood.

It took effort, but she managed to rip off the bottom of her T-shirt and wrap it around her upper arm. She put pressure on the wound and bit her lower lip to hold back a moan of pain.

The gunshots had stopped. She couldn't hear Fred.

She hadn't noticed the biting cold of the March night until now. Her damp jeans and half T-shirt didn't help at all. Shivers wracked her body as the cold and shock set in.

Sirens shrieked through the night. Tires screeched outside the carriage homes on her street. Lights flashed, highlighting the house in front of her in an eerie wash of blue.

Keri tilted her head back and looked up at the sky.

And she prayed.

Backup had arrived and now they just had to get the shooter.

Sounds of shots and Fred's barking had stopped abruptly after Keri had climbed the northern side of the block wall surrounding the small courtyard. Adam hoped like hell that Fred was okay. The dog might have saved their lives.

The shooter's no pro, Adam thought. Too sloppy. *He wants to take out a single woman, alone, but he comes in, shuts the lights off, and has guns blazing.* It didn't seem to have the mark of Edward. But it was just too coincidental.

The night was cold, but Adam didn't feel it as he dug his cell phone out of his jacket pocket. He dialed in and had the dispatcher patch him through to the captain in charge of the force outside the home.

"Holder here."

"Detective Adam Boyd, NYPD," Adam said as he worked his way toward Keri's back door, his Glock in both hands. The house was still dark. "I called it in and I'm onsite."

"What's the situation, Boyd?" came the captain's voice over the line.

Light from outside Keri's home would make him an easy target if he wasn't careful. "I'm in the back court-yard," Adam told the captain. "One shooter, last seen inside the house on the first floor."

The captain informed Adam he'd have officers joining him in the courtyard as well as surrounding the block.

With the line still open to Captain Holder, Adam kept his body close to the house. He paused when he came to the floor-to-ceiling windows that separated him and the back door. If he went forward he put himself at risk of being seen and shot.

When he'd checked out the layout of the living room,

one of the things he'd noticed was a couch along the wall of glass. Hopefully it would be enough cover.

Adam got down on the ground and worked his way forward. The ground was soft and damp.

He still didn't hear anything from inside the house. Was the shooter holed up somewhere inside? Or had he—

The sound of barking from above caused Adam to tilt his head up to look at the roof of the carriage house.

Fred's deep barks and growls echoed through the night. As Adam stared upward he saw a figure outlined by moonlight.

Damn.

"Suspect is on the roof," Adam said into the phone as he eased to his knees. "I'm going in."

"Got it," Holder said and Adam heard him shouting orders to officers.

Adam stuffed the phone into his jacket pocket. Fred was still barking as Adam hurried into the house and rushed up the stairs. Adrenaline pumped through him as he bolted past the second level and up toward the door that led to the roof. The door was already wide open.

Growls and snarls echoed through the night.

A shot, then a dog's yelp.

Adam paused at the door, still holding his Glock in a two-fisted grip. He peeked around the doorframe, saw nothing but the rooftop garden. On the other side of what looked like a little greenhouse, he saw the shadowy figures of a man and a dog.

Heart pounding, he swung around and out the door, sweeping the area with his gun.

A man came from around the greenhouse, his gun pointed at Adam.

"Drop your weapon!" Adam shouted.

The suspect shot at Adam.

Adam fired.

The man dropped. His gun flew out from his hand and landed several feet away from him.

Eyes focused on the suspect, Adam scooped up the other gun and stuffed it into the back of his jeans. He approached the man, keeping his gun steady and on him the entire time.

The suspect didn't move. Still wary, Adam crouched down and felt for the man's pulse.

Nothing.

Adam pushed the body over and a man's sightless eyes stared up at the heavens.

He looked up and saw a dog limp from around the small greenhouse. Fred's golden coat glistened black on his right haunch. That, and the way he favored it, told Adam that the retriever had been shot.

Fred looked at Adam with thoughtful, intelligent eyes.

Adam gestured in the direction of the neighbor's home. "Keri climbed over that wall."

Despite his injury, Fred turned and shot toward the doorway into the house and disappeared through it.

Adam quickly checked the suspect for ID but found none on the man. However, he did locate a cell phone. Rather than turning it in, he shoved it in his pocket.

Responding officers came onto the rooftop and Adam set his gun down and raised his hands. "Detective Adam Boyd," he said.

After the routine of identifying himself and showing his credentials to responding officers, Adam rushed to find Keri.

By the time Adam got to the courtyard, Fred was barking on the other side of the wall where Keri had climbed over.

Adam jumped up, grabbed the top block of the fence, and pulled himself up.

Before he jumped down he said, "Keri?" He saw her next to a rosebush, propped against the wall.

Fred sat beside her with his head tilted up to look at Adam. He seemed to be saying with his eyes, "Please help her. And hurry." How the hell did the dog get over the fence? Must have been another way there.

Adam's heart beat faster when he didn't see Keri move and she didn't respond. He jumped down and landed in a crouch beside her.

To his relief she raised her eyes and looked at him. She tried to give a smile, but her entire body was shaking and her lips were blue. It was obvious she was going into shock. Fred whimpered and started licking her face.

Fred backed away as Adam tore off his jacket. He prepared to put it around her shoulders, but he paused. He saw that Keri's belly was now bare. She was holding one arm with a free hand. Cloth wrapped around her arm was soaked with blood and her hand was covered with it.

"Whoever it was shot me in my arm," she said, and he heard the clicking of her teeth chattering.

"I'm calling in for an ambulance." He dialed in to the captain again and told him what he needed.

When he was done, Adam tried to keep his professional calm as he eased his jacket around her shoulders.

She gritted her teeth, holding back a whimper, before she said, "I don't think it's serious. Just hurts like a beast."

"We'll let a doctor determine whether or not it's serious." Adam cursed beneath his breath. "I'm going to carry you," he said as he eased his arms around her. She nodded and he scooped her up. "You okay?" he asked.

Keri nodded again, looking pale in what light was offered in the night. "Just a little cold and sleepy."

She felt too light, too limp in his arms. "Stay awake for me, okay, angel?"

"Okay." Her voice was just a whisper as he charged out of the backyard and toward a waiting ambulance, Fred limping alongside.

"It's a flesh wound," Adam said to Olivia DeSantos over his cell phone, a few steps away from Keri's hospital bed. "The bullet went through clean. Just wanted to say thanks. If it wasn't for you tracking her down for me, she would probably be dead."

"Glad I could help." Olivia didn't give a smartass remark like she would have normally. "Get some sleep, Boyd."

Adam snapped his cell phone shut. Anger burned in his belly as he looked at Keri and thought about the fact that she could have died tonight.

It had been a busy night for the ER, which meant they'd been there for what felt like forever. Eight hours after being taken to the hospital, she sat up on the hospital bed as the nurse gave her release instructions, including how to care for the wound in her arm.

Adam studied Keri as she responded to the nurse. In the bright fluorescent lights of the emergency room, she looked pale, her auburn hair falling out of the now loose ponytail. She held her arm close to her chest in a sling.

Her rosebush landing had scratched and scraped her face and arms, leaving angry-looking marks across her fair skin. Other than that, according to the doctor, she was fine and could go home.

Of course there was no way in hell Adam was going to let her near her house. He'd take her to his own place in Kensington, where he was certain she'd be safe from Carter and anyone he might send.

"Sure you're okay?" Adam said to Keri after the nurse left.

Keri gave him a little smile. "My arm just throbs and burns a bit. Other than that I'm fine." Her eyelids drooped and she appeared tired, but he had to admit she did look better than could be expected for what she'd been through.

Adam took her hand and helped her off the bed. "You look like you just got in a fight with a rosebush and lost."

With a quick grin she said, "I guess I do."

After he draped his leather jacket over her shoulders and she grabbed her small purse, they walked through the hospital and out into the chilly early morning. It was still dead dark, but it wouldn't be long until sunrise.

Her smile faded as she said, "Did you find out any information about the shooter?"

"Not yet." Adam did his best to keep his concern as well as his anger out of his voice. "But we will."

"How did you know to come back?" she asked.

"A car drove past me on my way out of your neighborhood; it was driving at a crawl. It stopped, then turned around," Adam said. "I continued heading home, but something about the car kept bugging me. Something didn't feel right." He frowned as he remembered seeing the beat-up Corolla make its way down Keri's street.

"I drove for another minute or so and then turned around to swing by and check on you," he said. "I saw the Corolla parked up the street and I called in the license plate. A prior record on the owner—a small-time punk. Just after that I saw your house go completely dark. It didn't make sense to have all the lights go out at once."

He'd known in his gut that it had something to do with Carter.

"I checked around the house," he said, "and the door off the garage was open, so I entered there."

Keri came to a stop before they headed into the parking lot. The night air chilled his bare arms and the breeze stirred her loose hair. "So you're positive Fred is going to be all right?"

Adam couldn't resist touching the side of her face and brushing a few strands of hair from her eyes. "The vet said he should be able to go home within twenty-four hours."

He kissed her forehead like he'd known her forever, then wondered why he'd done it. Her surprised expression told him she was wondering the same thing. But then the look of surprise melted into a smile. She didn't mind, it appeared, she didn't mind it at all.

"You and Fred have matching injuries." Adam cupped the elbow of her good arm and guided her into the parking lot toward his new black Ford Explorer. "Now we just need to keep you both out of trouble."

Keri asked about her house and Adam assured her that everything was being taken care of.

When they reached his SUV, Keri brought them to a stop again. "Thank you." Her voice was soft as she touched his arm. "For everything."

It was his turn to be surprised when she reached up, touched the side of his jaw with her free hand, and kissed the corner of his mouth.

Adam brought his hand to her face and brushed his fingers along her cheek. "You need to rest," he said. "Let's get you out of here."

FOUR

"They failed?" Rage seared Edward's gut like boiling oil, heat expanding through him in a growing fire. He slowly rose from his chair in the living room of his penthouse.

He'd grown up with nothing, but here he was now, easily one of the richest men in the city and one of the most powerful in the drug trade.

Johnny, his first in command, stood to the side as they both stared at Hector and waited for the dickhead to answer.

Hector's eyes shifted from Edward to Johnny and back. "Larry went in alone, Mike waited in the car."

Fury burned so hot in Edward's chest that he found it difficult to breathe. "Who killed him?"

"Mike said some guy showed up. Mike thought he might have been a cop." Hector's leg bounced, betraying his nervousness.

Don't shoot the fucking messenger, Carter. Edward ground his teeth. "Where was Mike?"

Hector licked his lips. "When he heard sirens, he thought he should get the car outta there before the cops arrived."

"And he left Larry." Edward clenched his fists so hard his arms shook. "Where is Mike?"

With a nod Hector indicated the doorway. "In the other room."

"Get him in here," Edward said in a snarl.

Hector turned and scuttled out the door. His shoes left impressions in the plush burgundy carpeting.

Edward sucked in his breath and reached for a round paperweight on an end table. It was one of his favorites. Inside the clear weight was a scorpion with its tail curled over its head, poised to strike.

Edward tossed the ball up, then caught it. Up. Down. Up. Down. The ball made a loud smacking sound every time it hit his palm. The sting of it striking his palm again and again and again made everything seem more real.

Mike came in, his eyes downcast.

Edward approached Mike. "You left Larry when the cops showed up." Still tossing the paperweight up and down, Edward walked around Mike.

"I thought I should get the car out of there." Mike continued to stare at the carpet. "Knew you wouldn't want the cops to get a hold of it."

"Why would I give a shit about a car that can't be traced back to me?" Edward's arm shook from the rage building inside him. He stopped tossing the paperweight and gripped it in his fist. "You were Larry's backup. Your job was to kill her and get out. You sat in the car and left when you should have made sure the target was dead."

"I figured he'd take her out. Just a woman." Mike's chest rose and fell with the rapidness of his breathing. "I didn't know he'd get nailed. Figured he'd kill the bitch and get out."

"You're a fucking coward, Mike." Edward clenched the paperweight tighter. "You will die a coward. I told you I wanted it handled right.

"How do you fuck something like this up?" Edward went on. "I can't trust you. And you wanted to be in with us full time? We had a way of communicating so it wouldn't be traced back to me. It was a simple job to prove yourself and you screw up the job. Then you came right over here to my home. You want to lead the cops right here? What the fuck were you thinking? I don't want anything leading back to me, you moron."

"Please—" Mike started.

Edward brought the paperweight down hard on the back of Mike's head. A satisfying *crack* and Mike went down.

With the strike he pictured that bitch, Keri. She'd ruined his life for the past seven years. If it hadn't been for her testimony, he wouldn't have been in the joint like some animal.

Edward tossed the paperweight onto the carpet as he stood. "He's that sloppy on this simple job, the cops would trace the car back to him and the coward would spill everything. That won't happen now, will it?" He stared at Hector, the desire to beat the punk to death raging inside him. But Hector hadn't been the one to screw up. "Clean up the mess."

"Yes, sir." Hector's voice shook. "Right away."

Edward looked at Johnny. "Figure out a way to take that bitch and the cop out. I want them found and I want them to be history. I want to hear the plan before you do it. I don't want mistakes next time. You see how well I handle people making mistakes that can ruin me."

FIVE

YOU'RE JUST JEALOUS
BECAUSE THE VOICES ONLY TALK TO ME.

Adam shook his head and leaned back in his chair in the Brooklyn Bagel Café as he looked at the saying on Olivia DeSantos's black T-shirt. "And what voices are those?" he said to the former NYPD-officer-turned-private-investigator as she sat down in the chair opposite him.

"Wouldn't you like to know." Olivia handed him a sheet of paper. "Here's a list of Edward Carter's known hangouts; his three places of residence, including his new apartment in the city; and some of the key players in his drug business."

She pointed to the name of a bar in Manhattan, Triumph. "That's always been his favorite place, since the days before his jail stay, and where you can likely find him during the day. My source told me today's a good day to do just that."

Before Adam could get a word out, she extended another sheet. "As you know, the phone you found on the shooter was a prepaid job." Adam took the paper as she continued talking. "The phone numbers you gave me—the last number called was to another prepaid cell phone in Manhattan." She pointed to the information. "My sources show the phone call was taken while the receiver was in the vicinity of Carter's penthouse."

Adam nodded, impressed. Olivia went on before he could tell her so.

"Here's the icing." Olivia handed him the third and final piece of paper she'd been holding. "The shooter you identified this morning as Larry Cruz, a small-time drug dealer in Manhattan, has some distant ties to Carter, but ties nonetheless. Those links weren't easy to find, but I tracked him down through another drug dealer and a snitch."

Adam gave a low whistle of appreciation. "Olivia, I love you," he said and Olivia raised her brows with an amused expression on her face. "I'm not even going to ask how you got all of this so fast." Adam held the page and studied the information. "I gave the info to you, what, eight hours ago?"

"Seven," Olivia said. "You owe me."

He glanced at the sheet and back at her. "Big time. Maybe we can work out a payment plan. Just tell me what it will be."

Olivia let her gaze drift over him. "Hmmm. Now that we don't work together, Mr. Stud, maybe I have some ideas."

Adam laughed. "Okay, okay, down girl."

"I'm a little out there for you. Probably a lot more than you could or would want to handle anyway," Olivia said with a teasing grin.

Adam leaned back in his chair. "I don't know what that means and I think it's safer not to ask."

"Ya wimp," Olivia said. "Okay, back to business. What's this information for?" She gestured to the page. "Whatever it is that I'm busting my ass on."

Adam gave her a quick rundown on the case and on all the zeroes he'd come up with until now.

"You and a ballerina?" Olivia smirked. You've got the hots for little twinkle toes?"

He cleared his throat as he thought about Keri and hoped his face hadn't just turned red. "It's just a case, DeSantos."

With another smirk she leaned back in her chair. "Riiiiiight."

Adam hesitated, then went for it. "How's Nyx?" He was surprised it didn't hurt like it usually did to ask about her.

"She's all right." Olivia tapped her fingers on the table-top. "Business is picking up, but it was a little slow for a couple of months after the last big case. Thank God."

"Tell her I said hello," he said quietly.

Olivia studied Adam with her dark eyes. Eyes that were far more insightful than anyone would realize before getting to know her. "You doing okay, Boyd?"

He nodded and realized he meant it when he said, "Yeah. I am."

"Good." She gave him a look that was completely serious, totally Olivia. She had a model's good looks but a cop's bulletproof attitude and mouth to go along with it. "I'd have to kick your ass if you were doing nothing but moping around."

This time he held back a smile. "Oh, is that what you meant by a little out there? I'll keep that in mind."

Olivia pushed back her chair and got to her feet. "There are some odd things going on that I need to get back to at the office. No big deal, just strange."

Adam stood. He was a full foot taller than Olivia. "Anything you need help with?"

"Nah." Olivia zipped up her New York Mets sweat jacket. "Anything we deal with at the agency is strange. I'll let Nyx know you said hi."

"Thanks." He knew Olivia was just teasing on the payment plan. She was too close to Nyx to cross that line with Adam, and Adam with her. Olivia was a harmless flirt, he thought, a fun harmless flirt. Adam watched Olivia weave her way through the café and through the door before he looked back down at the papers in his hand. He had a little more to go on now.

Adam folded the papers and tucked them into the inside pocket of his jacket.

At the thought of last night, he ground his teeth. He intended to have a talk with Carter.

After paying the tab, Adam headed over the Brooklyn Bridge to Manhattan. He used his NYPD placard to park in front of the Triumph bar.

Carter was a thug, but he was a "high class" thug. He had picked a relatively classy place to hang out in here. But then Carter had mingled with high society before. Everyone who knew him had been knocked on their asses that he had been tried for running a drug smuggling ring and had gone to prison.

It still amazed Adam that they were never able to nail

Carter on a murder rap. The fifteen-year drug sentence without the possibility of parole had been at least some consolation, as he was to be gone for a long time. But now he was back on the streets. The thought made Adam's gut tighten with anger.

Adam left behind the chill March breeze and entered the comfortable warmth of Triumph. Light was dim inside and he had to take a moment for his eyes to adjust.

With a cop's trained eye, he ran his gaze over the room, cataloguing the layout and where the exits were. He evaluated every person in the bar with a glance, including one server, as well as one woman sitting alone while two men were side-by-side at the bar.

His interest was right there in the corner. Carter sat with three other men. And they were staring at him.

Adam strode over to where Carter was seated. The man acted nonchalant as he reclined in the booth. The way he toyed with his drink was the only indication that Adam could see that he might be agitated by Adam showing up in his favorite hangout.

Carter was nearing forty, had a head of thick blond hair and blue eyes. He was full of charm and charisma.

And as far as Adam was concerned, the man was an evil sonofabitch.

The weight of the Glock he carried was comfortable and welcome in Adam's side holster as he reached Carter's table. He kept his fingers relaxed, his arms limber and ready. There was no telling what a loose cannon like Carter might do.

"Detective Boyd." Carter put one arm along the back of his booth. "Nice to see you after all this time. What's it been, seven years? How've you been?"

Carter knew exactly how long it had been. He was just toying with Adam.

"I have a message for you." Adam braced one hand on the booth's cushioned back and leaned in to get into Carter's personal space. "Stay away from Keri Holliday. And you'd better keep your distance from me if you don't want to find your head stuffed up your ass."

The other three men at the table stirred like they were ready to jump to Carter's defense.

"Threats." Carter raised his hand, motioning to his men to stay down. "I get out of prison where I was wrongly incarcerated, and now I get threats from the dick who helped put me there. Incredible."

Adam had so much he wanted to say to Carter, but he bit his tongue. Literally.

"Anything else, Detective?" Carter asked with a smirk. "You enjoying threatening an innocent man?"

"Innocent my ass." Adam straightened, his glare fixed on Carter. He was entirely aware of the other men at the booth, judging whether or not they would be a problem as he spoke. "You sent someone after Keri last night and the bastard shot her."

"Me?" Carter frowned and gave a pretty good expression of innocence. "Keri was shot? And you're accusing me of being responsible?"

Adam had to fight to keep from showing his tension, his anger. Instead he kept loose and ready for any move any one of the four men might make.

"The man you sent after Ms. Holliday had a phone on him," Adam said.

"So?" Carter shrugged. "Everyone and their mother carries a phone."

"A call was placed to that phone from near your location last night shortly before the attempt was made on Ms. Holliday's life." Adam studied Carter, watching him for some telltale twitch or micro expression that would confirm Adam's statement.

"Yeah, sure it was, Detective. I don't need your harassment," Carter said. "If you had something on me you would be taking me in. You have nothing because I've done nothing." Carter gestured toward the door. "Why don't you go back out there and do something you're good at, like arresting a jaywalker. Isn't that what you're in charge of these days? The jaywalker patrol."

"I'm warning you, Carter," Adam said as he thought about how satisfying it would be to take out the bastard. "Don't touch Keri. Don't call her. Don't go near her."

The man got to his feet and Adam squared off with him. Maybe Carter would lose control, give Adam an excuse to take him down.

Carter's expression had gone dark. Adam had definitely pushed him to the point that he might actually do something that Carter would regret and Adam would enjoy.

"You fucking her, Detective?" Carter said. "Sounds to me like you are."

Anger flashed inside Adam and he had to hold himself from going for Carter's throat. "Better watch it, Carter." Adam spoke in a low voice, keeping it controlled.

"Eddie." One of the other men stood, this one pale with light brown hair and eyes. "You should get out of here. This dick isn't worth it. You don't want to end up back in the joint."

"Don't tell me what I should or shouldn't do, Johnny," Carter said without looking at the man.

Come on, Adam thought almost recklessly. *Give me an excuse.*

Carter's scowl melted away into a laugh and he sat down. "Thanks for the afternoon entertainment, Detective. I bet we'll see each other around."

"You'd better hope not," Adam said, then turned and headed back to the door and out into the chilly day. He climbed into his SUV, tossed the placard on the floorboard, then pulled his vehicle into traffic when there was an opening.

Adam knew what he'd done wasn't the right approach. In fact, his boss would be pissed at what had just happened, but Adam didn't care at the moment. He wanted this lowlife bastard to know the police were on him.

Time to check in on the ballerina.

SIX

Edward watched Detective Boyd leave the bar. The bastard didn't seem to be worried that someone might gun him down from behind. Because that was exactly what he wanted to do. He felt it in every fiber of his being. With everything he had.

There was no doubt in his mind that the detective was fucking Keri. That thought alone sent heavy, hot, hard rage through every bone in his body.

Keri had been *his*.

"Not worth it," Johnny repeated as the detective walked out of the bar. "Later."

A growl climbed up Edward's throat. Fury at the detective rose inside him like a storm. A storm that was about to turn into a hurricane that would destroy the detective.

He liked that analogy. Yes, he was a storm that would tear the detective apart. A little planning and the prick would be his.

"Shut up." Edward glared at Johnny.

Everyone at his table shut their traps. Edward leaned back in his seat and closed his eyes as he started to plan. Heard it before. Don't kill a cop 'cause they won't stop until they get you. Well, he had gotten away with it before. It really didn't concern him. He'd screw with their minds first . . . then figure a way to kill them both.

SEVEN

Keri woke, groggy, having a hard time raising her eyelids and focusing. Her head ached and her arm throbbed. Her face and arms stung as if a cat had scratched her in multiple places.

She opened her eyes. It was dim, but she knew at once that she wasn't in her own room. Nothing around her was familiar. Not the rustic-looking dresser or framed print on the wall at the foot of the bed. If she squinted, she could see a red fox in the middle of a snow-covered forest in the picture. She thought she caught a glimpse of a pair of Native Americans on horseback slipping through the forest.

Confusion made her head spin. Where was she? She tried to push herself up in bed, then cried out from pain that exploded in her arm and she flopped back down onto the pillow. Why did her arm hurt so badly?

She forced herself to calm down and she closed her eyes.

Like a slap, memories rushed at her.

A man. Chasing her. Shooting at her.

Pain erupting in her arm when one of his bullets hit home.

Fred going after the man.

Fred, shot.

She opened her eyes again and realized her heart rate had kicked up. Her skin prickled and she slowly drew in a breath and let it out.

Everything came back to her. Starting with Detective Adam Boyd giving her the news that Edward was out of jail. Her memories ended with the detective driving her to his home, taking her straight to his spare bedroom, and tucking her into the twin bed before turning off the light. She had been asleep before the door had fully closed.

She stared up at the plain white ceiling. Her arm hurt, but it was nothing like what she had been through with her knee all those years ago. The constant pain, the hours and hours of physical therapy.

A knock at the door jerked her attention toward it. The door was slightly ajar and Adam pushed it open.

"You look beautiful for someone who was just shot and in a fight with a rosebush," he said as he smiled and crouched beside the bed.

When he smiled, his dimple made him even more sexy, more desirable.

"Thank you." She struggled to sit up in bed as she spoke.

Adam's hands felt warm on her good arm and her shoulder as he helped her. She winced from the pain due to the wound, but she managed not to cry out.

"The doc prescribed some pain meds," he said when she was sitting up. "Want me to get you a couple?"

She shook her head. "No thanks."

"You're tough," he said. "I know some pretty tough cops who've had lesser wounds but happily popped the drugs while they needed them."

"I have a fairly high pain tolerance," Keri said as she rubbed sleep from her eyes. "And I want nothing to do with any kind of drug that can be addictive."

"Smart girl." Adam got up from where he knelt beside the bed and grabbed a straight-back chair that was up against one wall. He brought it around and sat facing her.

He braced his forearms on his thighs as he leaned forward, his warm brown eyes focused on her. His position was so familiar it was as if she had seen him do it a thousand times, even though she had only met him last night.

The same feelings that had come over her when she had first met him returned as she studied him. On some deep, primitive level she not only wanted him, she needed him.

A crazy thought.

But as she looked at him, he had an intensity to his brown eyes that was mesmerizing. His short brown hair looked permanently tousled as if he had just woken and he had a day's growth of stubble on his jaw.

Today Adam wore a white T-shirt that was taut across his chest and his biceps stretched the sleeves. He wasn't a large man, but he was tall and extremely fit, with an athletic build.

And he had that adorable dimple when he smiled.

"Fred is fine," he said before she could ask. "The vet is keeping him for another night. He was afraid that Fred wouldn't take it easy."

"The vet is right." Keri smiled. "He wouldn't take it easy at all." Then she added, "Thank you. For being there last night. For everything you did for me and for Fred."

"I'm just glad I was there." His voice was low, serious. "And very glad Fred was, too." He pushed back his chair and stood. "Ready for dinner?"

"Dinner?" Keri looked at him in surprise. "What time is it?"

"Six." He moved the chair away from the side of the bed. "Would you rather have me bring dinner up or would you prefer to eat downstairs?"

"I can't believe it's so late." Keri pushed down the covers. "I'll eat downstairs. No reason at all to serve me in bed."

She swung her legs over the side. "But I do need to check on my parents. I usually call them every day and I obviously haven't called yet."

"You can use my phone." Adam helped her out of bed and she held her arm to her chest in its sling. She realized she was only in her panties and one of his T-shirts and it was bunched around her waist. She had forgotten that he had helped her out of her dirty and bloody T-shirt and jeans last night. Her face burned as she tugged the shirt down from her waist and it fell to her thighs.

When they'd arrived at his house early this morning, she had cleaned up the best she could with a washcloth, warm water, and soap, but she really needed a shower. Or rather a bath, since she couldn't get her bandages wet.

"I'll pick up some clothes from your house in the morning," he said. "After dinner you can take a bath in the hall bathroom if you'd like."

The man was a mind reader.

She nodded and let him guide her out of the room. The moment she stepped onto the landing she took a deep breath of delicious smells coming from below. Her stomach growled, reminding her that she hadn't had anything to eat for almost twenty-four hours.

"Something smells wonnnnnderful," she said as Adam helped her down the steep stairs that led to a small but very cozy kitchen.

"Tacos." He pulled out a chair and she took the seat, being careful not to bump her arm. "Along with salad and a nice cabernet I've been saving for the right time."

Keri's stomach growled again and she grinned. "I love tacos."

Well, her stomach certainly was fine. She had always had a good appetite and she worked out hard enough every day that she could pretty much eat what she wanted without worrying about her weight.

When she was seated, Adam handed her his phone and she dialed her parents while he brought dinner to the table. Her mother was in bed early, but her father talked with her for a few minutes until he said he was going to get some sleep.

After she disconnected the call she said, "I need to check in on them tomorrow."

Adam nodded. "I'll give you a hand with anything you need help with."

While they ate they talked about everything from the weather, the Yankees and Mets—he was born a Mets fan and she had been a lifetime Yankees fan—to current politics and the hottest Broadway play. Adam's interest in cultural events delighted her and she found she enjoyed talking with him.

* * *

Adam started gathering the dishes from the table and motioned for her to remain in her seat. "You. Sit," he said as he took the dishes to the sink and rinsed them before putting them in the dishwasher.

As he sat back down at the table, he looked serious. "Do you mind if I ask you about how you ended up getting injured? I read the file about it, but tell me yourself."

The memories came over her, harsh and unwanted. "I think Edward got to the point where he felt he had enough control over me that he didn't have to worry about me seeing something I shouldn't."

She shook her head as she went on. "I started seeing him fly into rages with his employees, rages that were almost frightening. But then he would turn to me and be sweet and attentive. I started to become confused.

"Then I found out what Edward really did for a living—that he was a big time drug dealer—and I told him it was over between us."

Keri tried not to flinch from the memory but it was hard. "He was furious—so full of the same incredible rage I'd seen in him at other times. He said I belonged to him and he threatened to make my life miserable if I tried to leave or if I went to the police."

She went on, "It was then that I realized how blinded I'd been. I hadn't realized how controlling and possessive, how obsessed he was. It became really obvious from that point on."

Adam studied her with a police officer's patience, but also with the understanding of a man who cared for her and her welfare. Really cared.

A sick sensation that she hadn't felt in a long time filled her belly as she went on. "One night he became enraged at me for nothing—for looking at another man wrong. He was so jealous, he would not quit. He actually hit me and I just lost it emotionally.

"I started screaming," she continued, "that I was going to go to the police with the information I had written out and documented. I told him I had what I needed to ruin him. It was so foolish to say, but I had lost it."

Her throat worked as she swallowed. "He went crazy on me. Just insane. He had a metal bar and swung it at my knee and completely blew it out. Said it was only my knee then. It would be my life if I talked about what I had seen or that he was responsible for the knee."

She swallowed. "I was in fear for my life, at that point. I couldn't even tell anyone what actually happened to the knee. I had to make up a story."

Growing anger crossed Adam's strong features as she continued. "The doctors said that with the type of injury . . . there was no way my knee would ever be the same to dance. That was almost seven years ago, when I was twenty. I can expect to have a replacement someday."

Adam dried off his hands on a dish towel, then came back to the table and helped her to her feet. "Sorry to dredge up bad memories," he said quietly.

"It's good to talk about it to someone who understands." Keri was keenly aware that Adam was still holding her good hand after helping her stand. "Most people act like I might fall apart if the subject is even brought up."

Adam brushed strands of hair away from her face, catching her off guard and sending zinging sensations through her abdomen. "You're a strong woman, Keri," he said.

Seeing the conviction in his eyes almost made her believe he was right.

* * *

Keri waited as Adam filled the tub with warm water and bubbles. She loved watching him. He had fluid, easy movements, and she could see and feel the controlled power in his body. She liked looking at the muscles flex in his forearms and beneath the T-shirt that stretched across his back.

When he turned he saw she was watching him. He winked and heat rose to her cheeks. She had probably been staring at him like some schoolgirl with a crush.

He smiled and gave Keri a couple of thick, fluffy towels and a washcloth. While keeping the towel between them, affording her some modesty, he helped her out of her T-shirt.

"Make sure you don't get your bandages wet," he said and Keri nodded. "I'll be in my office across from the bathroom," he said. "Just call me if you need me. I'll check in on you and help you out when you're finished."

Keri nodded. "Thank you."

"Do you need help getting into the tub?" he asked.

"Getting in is the easy part." She shook her head. "I think getting out will be the challenge."

"Like I said, I'll help you out." Adam walked to the bathroom door and rested his hand on the doorknob. "Wait for me, okay? I don't want you slipping and falling."

Adam closed the door behind him. Keri eased into the wonderfully warm water and sighed. This was exactly what she needed.

Keri propped her bandaged arm on the rim of the tub while she bathed. She took her time, enjoying the feel of the warm water lapping her tired body. The cuts and scratches stung at first, but then gradually it all faded to a warm burn, like she had sunburned skin. She gently washed her body, doing her best without moving her arm too much.

When she was finished she let the water out of the tub. A knock at the bathroom door was followed by Adam's voice. "Okay in there, Keri?" He seemed to have a sixth sense for knowing what she was thinking and what she needed. "Ready to get out?"

She reached for the towel on the bar to hide her naked body. As she was drawing it toward her it slipped out of her grasp at the moment she was already saying, "Ready."

The door opened and Keri's face flushed as Adam walked in. He didn't say anything, just took the towel off of the floor and covered her with it as if seeing her with nothing on wasn't a big deal at all.

"Thank you." She clenched her jaw as Adam helped her to stand and climb out of the tub. "This looks just too strange with me dropping the towel as I told you to come in. I wasn't trying . . ."

"It's all fine." Adam smiled gently.

As she arranged the towel around herself, Adam grabbed a second towel and began to dry her hair with it from behind. He didn't say anything as he worked. The fog-shrouded mirror didn't show their reflections, just a misty hint of an outline.

When he finished towel-drying her hair, he tossed the towel onto the rim of the tub so that it hung half on, half off.

"We need to change your bandage," he said as he reached into a medicine cabinet and began taking out first-aid supplies.

Adam removed the bandages carefully, but she still found herself gritting her teeth from the pain. Blood had seeped onto the bandage—a lot more than she had expected.

With gentle hands he cleaned the wound. The entire time she tried to ignore how badly it hurt and to keep from flinching. After it was clean and he had applied antiseptic, he put a fresh bandage on it. She let her breath out in relief when he was finished.

She started to move away from him, but he caught her by her good arm. "I'm not finished with you yet." His tone was teasing and she smiled as he reached into a cabinet and brought out a comb.

He had her sit on the vanity chair in front of the mirror, then began combing the tangles out of her hair. He was gentle with her, not tugging too hard, and falling into a rhythm as he combed.

The feeling of Adam combing her hair was luxurious. It made her languid, relaxed to the point of feeling like she was slipping into another place and time.

It had to be something to do with the trauma to make her feel this way now. So amazing.

The gentle tug and pull of the comb felt good. Felt real. It grounded her, kept her from flying completely into a dream world.

When Adam finished, he put away the comb, then took her hand and helped her to stand. The fuzzy dark blue rug felt soft beneath her feet.

"Brought a T-shirt in for you." Adam's voice was husky. "Tomorrow I'll pick up some of your own clothes."

"Can't—" Keri sputtered then laughed as Adam tugged the T-shirt over her head. She let the towel drop as he pulled the shirt down. He helped her put her bandaged arm through its sleeve. Then he handed her panties to her and she stepped into them one-handed.

When the clothing was on, she looked up at him. Her throat felt dry as she swallowed. "I can't stay here."

Adam raised his eyebrows. "Says who?"

"Says me." She raised her good arm. "I'm not going to impose on you more than I already have."

"Who says you're imposing?" Adam said as he smoothed his hands over her shoulders.

"I mean . . ." Keri paused. "Thank you for everything. For being there last night at my house, then the hospital." She raised her good hand. "For bringing me here and even making me dinner and for taking care of Fred."

Adam smiled. "You're welcome." He trailed his fingers along her arm.

The most delicious sensations caused her to shiver.

"Are you cold?" Adam looked so concerned it made her smile. "I'll get you a bathrobe."

"I'm fine," she said, but he was already opening the door of the bathroom.

As soon as he did, cold air rushed over her and some of the steam dissipated.

This time she did shiver from the cool air.

Adam took her hand and led her down the hall. "I have a robe in here."

When he opened the door she saw that it must be the master bedroom. It was a great deal bigger than the guest room, had a huge king-sized bed and attractive cherry wood furniture. The bed was unmade, clothing hung over the back of a chair, and socks were on the floor.

Keri smiled. It looked lived in and comfortable.

"It's a mess," Adam said as he looked over her shoulder. "Maid's day off." He flashed a smile. "Truthfully, I need to hire one."

"Looks fine to me," she said.

After he grabbed an old terry robe he put it around her shoulders, careful not to bump her arm. When he had the robe arranged, he guided her out of his bedroom.

"Let's get you back to bed," he said. "You've had a hell of a time of it."

"I just got up." She came to a stop. "I slept all day."

"You needed that sleep." He gestured to her arm. "Not only do you need sleep to heal, but you just went through some serious trauma. It's not every day that you get shot."

Adam had managed to steer her into the guest bedroom and to the bed.

The thought of this man helping her, being there for her, caring for her in such a gentle way made her feel different than she had felt about anyone for a long time. That and the sight of Adam so close to the bed she would be sleeping in again made her stomach flutter.

"Climb into bed and I'll tuck you in," he said with a smile.

She obeyed and brought the covers up under her arms. He leaned down and brushed his lips over her forehead.

"Good night, Angel," he said and left.

EIGHT

"Tell Mom that I love her and I'll see you both tomorrow." Keri listened to her father for a few moments more as he said he would. "I love you, Dad," she added before she closed her phone, disconnecting the call.

Keri sighed and set her cell phone on the table in the small but roomy house in the Park Slope neighborhood of Brooklyn that her cousin Janice was letting her stay in until it was rented. The furnishings were bare since it was temporary and it felt sterile and not quite welcome.

It had been a week since the break-in at her home in Brooklyn Heights, with no further incidents. But then she hadn't been there since that night. Adam had picked up what she had needed him to.

According to Adam, Edward was reportedly planning to head to his huge home in Miami. Keri had been to it when she and Edward dated and it was an impressive home with Grecian columns, everything made of white marble, from the floors to the pillars to the stairs.

According to Adam's sources, Edward would be making it a permanent move. She prayed every day that was true.

Keri had stayed with Adam for a few days, then had agreed with him to move into a rental house for a while rather than returning to her own home. Edward would be less likely to find her in a different house if he was still after her.

The remaining problem was how she would make it to work each day at her dance studio and how to make sure she wasn't followed home. She'd had substitute teachers take over the classes that she normally taught . . . But she couldn't, and didn't want to, do that for long.

I can't live my life hiding or running. I just can't.

One of the hardest things had been that Adam had also made her promise not to visit her parents for a week. He wanted to make sure she wasn't followed from their home in case Edward had located her parents. The thought of Edward having found her mother and father terrified her.

To Keri's relief, her mother and father hadn't appeared to be in any danger. Adam had made sure their house was under surveillance for the week after the attack in order to spot potential threats.

She'd had her cousin Tessa check in on her parents, telling Tessa she'd had to go out of town unexpectedly. She'd had to reassure her cousin that everything was fine.

Tomorrow she would visit her parents. The thought made her smile. She had missed seeing them.

The back door of the house rattled.

Keri's heart started pounding.

Her gaze went to the knife drawer and she pushed back her chair.

Just as she rushed to her feet, Fred bounded into the kitchen.

She had forgotten. Adam had taken Fred to the vet and she had told him to use the back door. Even after a week she was still so jumpy that she wasn't thinking straight.

"Thank God it's you, Fred." Keri plopped down, then sagged against the back of the chair in relief. She laughed when Fred jumped up, put his paws on her leg, and gave her cheek a sloppy kiss. She hugged him to her, giving him a big squeeze. Her arm twinged a little when she did it, but the pain wasn't too bad.

She raised her head and gave Fred a kiss on his muzzle. "What did the vet say about your leg?" she asked him, as if he could sit down and have a conversation with her.

The golden retriever sat back on his haunches and gave a "woof" along with a toss of his head and a doggy smile. It was as if he was saying he was perfectly fine and to stop worrying about him.

"Vet says Fred is healing amazingly well." Adam came up to the doorway and hitched his shoulder against the doorframe. "How are you doing, Angel?"

Warmth flowed through Keri. She loved the way he called her "angel." When she had been referred to as the "Angel of New York" she had found the society-appointed title a little embarrassing. But coming from Adam it felt entirely different.

"Feeling great," she said with a smile. "My arm's just a little sore, that's all. How was work?"

She wanted to ask about Edward, but let that question hang in the air unspoken.

Adam shifted against the doorframe. "It looks like

Carter is definitely in the process of moving to Florida. Surveillance reported that he's having his belongings packed up in both his Manhattan apartment and the house he has in Jersey."

"Do you think he's really going to go and leave us alone?" Keri asked as she looked up at Adam. "Did he really give up that easy?"

Adam pulled out a chair at the table near her and sat. "There's a lot I can't tell you about what we've been doing, but all intel says he's on his way out. Other than that, all we can do is be careful."

Keri nodded, not quite knowing what to say.

Adam dragged his hand down his stubbled cheeks. "Just in case he is still a threat, I don't like the idea of you putting yourself out in the open."

"What am I supposed to do?" Keri raised her hands as she spoke. "I can't hide forever." It was a conversation they'd had before, but one that apparently bore repeating.

With a sigh he said, "I'm just concerned for your safety."

"I know." She offered him a smile. "And thank you for that. But I'll be okay."

He raised a pink duffel bag that she recognized as hers. "Stopped by your place and grabbed a little more of everything, like you wanted. Hope I got enough of what you need."

"Thanks." Keri took the duffel bag from him, unzipped it, and dug through the clothing to see if he had remembered to bring a set of pajamas for her. A little heat burned in her cheeks when she saw her zebra-striped, leopard-spotted, and red with black lace panties along with matching camisoles in with everything else.

"Well, I can see you don't like pastels," she said when she looked up at him. "A panty man?"

Adam winked and smiled, and she wanted to melt into a pool of sweet chocolate at the sight of his adorable dimple and the whole package that made up the incredibly sexy Detective Adam Boyd.

"Hold on a sec." He scooted his chair back then and disappeared through the doorway. He reappeared again holding one of her little black dresses. "Feel like going out tonight? I promise not to spill any water on you. Maybe a drink, but no water."

She laughed. "You would pick out the shortest LBD that I have," she said. "Yes, I'd love to go out with you."

"I'm guessing LBD is short for little black dress." With a grin, Adam added, "Thought you might like the one with loose sleeves to cover up the bandage on your arm."

"Smart man," she said. "I'll need help with the zipper."

"Planned on that." Adam took her pink duffel off of her lap and started up the stairs. "I'll put these in your bedroom."

Keri trailed him and Fred tagged along. When they reached the master bedroom, Adam placed her things on the bed and Fred curled up at the foot of the bed.

Adam faced her and settled his hands on her shoulders. He lightly squeezed before placing a kiss on her forehead.

"You smell so good." Adam's voice was husky when he drew away.

Keri's pulse quickened and butterflies floated low in her belly.

Adam squeezed her shoulders again. "We'll leave in an hour. Sound good to you?"

Putting aside the crazy feelings wreaking havoc on her, Keri nodded. "Sounds beyond great to me."

Keri spent a good forty-five minutes getting ready to go out on the town with Adam. When she moved it, the ache in her arm made her slower than normal. It was healing well, but the wound would leave a nasty scar.

She left her hair down, loose around her shoulders, rather than make the effort it would have taken to put it up. When the only thing left to do was zip up the dress, she called to Adam.

"You are so gorgeous," he said as he looked at her. "Now turn around so I can take care of that zipper."

Keri moved so that she was in front of Adam. His fingers brushed over her skin as he zipped up her dress. A shiver trailed Keri's spine.

"Cold?" he asked as he leaned close and lightly rubbed her shoulders with his hands, careful to avoid the wound.

She shook her head and turned to face him. "No, but I hope you brought something to put over my dress or I'm likely to freeze once we're out of the house."

"I'll get it." Adam smiled and backed out of the room. "I left it out in the car."

The feeling of pleasure was something that warmed her inside and out whenever she was with Adam. She barely knew him, but she could feel herself falling for him, fast.

She waited for him at the front door and watched as he started the SUV. White puffs rose from the exhaust in the cool night air. Goose bumps prickled her skin from the chill as she waited for him.

The ride to the Manhattan restaurant was fun and Adam had her grinning and laughing from stories he told her about his brother and sister, when they were kids.

Because Adam seemed interested, Keri shared a few of her funnier ballet experiences as well as telling him a little about her career.

Despite the differences in their upbringings, she and Adam had no problem finding things to talk about.

Her parents had never taken her camping or anything else outdoorsy when she was growing up, something she wished they would have. Adam's family went to the Adirondacks and the Catskills a few times a year and they had traveled cross-country in the family van every summer.

Keri had grown up a part of New York's high society, and Adam talked about his blue-collar roots.

Ever since her forced retirement, she had settled into a lifestyle she felt comfortable in, away from the glitz and glamour and wealth she had grown up with. It had been an easy change for her, and she had found that she loved it.

When they reached the city, Adam chose a great seafood restaurant that they both enjoyed. Keri felt so comfortable with him that it was easy to let herself just go.

When she had dated Edward, the relationship had been superficial. What she had thought was genuine had turned out to be a farce. Nothing but a lie.

After dinner, Keri and Adam decided to go to one of the more low-key jazz clubs in Manhattan.

The saxophone was wailing a tune she didn't recognize when they entered the club. Adam took her hand and together they walked through the dim interior, past the bar and round tables with little candles glowing on each one.

It was still early enough that the club was probably

not as crowded as it would be later on in the evening. Probably why they were able to find an unoccupied table off to the side, a little more secluded than other areas of the club.

After Adam seated her, he pulled his chair close to hers, their knees touching. Thrills went through Keri's abdomen. The nearness of him, the scent of him, made Keri heady in a way she had never experienced before. He didn't wear cologne and she loved his natural masculine scent. She met his eyes, falling into the warmth of his gaze.

She didn't hear the server at first when he came to the table and asked what they'd like to drink. Keri chose a chardonnay while Adam ordered beer.

A clarinet solo highlighted the next song and she raised her voice to talk over it when Adam asked her who her favorite jazz singer was.

When their drinks came, Adam left the tab open and Keri sipped her chardonnay. When she set her glass on the table, Adam rested his hand over hers. She smiled and he moved close enough to brush her mouth with his.

Tingles flushed over her body, starting from the touch of his lips and traveling to her toes. A soft sound escaped her, a sigh of pleasure.

He raised his head and looked at her. From just that little contact she felt almost dizzy, intoxicated. As if she had had more than a sip of her wine.

Adam brought his fingers to the side of her face and rubbed his thumb along her jaw.

Keri swallowed and he traced the line of her neck with his fingers all the way down to the hollow at the base of her throat. She let her eyelids close as she listened to the soft tune the jazz band was playing and enjoyed the drift of Adam's fingers over her skin. His hands were callused, but his touch so soft.

She found herself getting lost in the music, lost in his caress. He brought his lips close to her ear. His breath was warm as he murmured, "You're so beautiful, Keri. And I love what I see inside even more."

Her throat was dry as she opened her eyes and looked at him. "I like what I see in you, too."

"You're an angel," he said softly. "My angel."

"Yes." The word came out without her even realizing she would say it. That she would agree so easily with his claim.

She was his.

Hair at her nape started to prickle as if she was being stared at. She turned her head.

And saw Edward across the room. Staring at her and Adam.

Keri didn't know if she could breathe. "Oh, my God."

Adam turned and looked in the same direction. He stiffened, his body going rigid the moment his eyes landed on Carter. The man stood with his back against the wall, his arms folded across his chest, his face drawn into a smirk.

Anger pumped through Adam's body, fierce, hot, and he shoved back his chair and stood. Somehow the bastard had followed them.

It was as if his body was powered by a force other than his own. Adam's legs and arms moved, carrying him across the room, straight for Carter.

Carter gave a broad smile and nodded at Keri, then held out his arms as he stepped away from the wall.

Adam fisted and unfisted his hands as he stopped in front of Carter. His jaw hurt from clenching it so tightly and he felt a muscle tic on his face. He was probably telegraphing loud and clear his desire to kill Carter.

"What's up, Detective?" Carter said. "As I suspected, you're fucking Keri, aren't you."

"Sonofabitch." Adam drew back his arm and punched Carter in the face.

The man stumbled back, his head striking the wall. The fury in Adam only increased. Before Carter could recover, he rammed his fist into the bastard's gut.

"Don't you ever follow Keri again," Adam growled.

He went after Carter again, but his arms were grabbed and he was held back. He fought against whoever was holding him, but it had to have been two or three men who had him.

"He's crazy." Carter wiped blood from his mouth and nose as he looked at the people now gathered around them. "Minding my own business and this lunatic cop punches me."

"I'm a police officer." Adam shook off the men holding him and drew out his shield and showed it to those gathered around. They backed away. "I'd better never see you around Keri or me again, Carter."

"Did everyone hear this cop threaten me?" Carter said as he looked around. "I'm in a public place and I have a right to be here."

"You don't have the right to stalk Keri." Adam said, then ground his teeth.

Carter wiped his nose with more napkins that were handed to him. "Don't know what you're talking about, Detective. All I know is that I was minding my own business when you came out of nowhere and assaulted me."

Adam was about to go after Carter again when some-one said, "I got it all on video on my phone."

"I got pictures," someone else said.

"Police brutality," shouted another.

"Guy wasn't doing anything," came another voice.

Shit.

"Stay away from Keri," Adam said in a growl and turned away.

He bumped into Keri who'd apparently come up be-hind him while he was dealing with Carter.

"Come on." She took his hand and led him through the nightclub. "Let's go home."

Adam realized he was shaking from the amount of adrenaline pumping through him and his knuckles ached. He squeezed Keri's fingers, silently thanking her for com-ing after him and pulling him away from what might have turned out badly for him.

It was going to turn out a lot worse for Carter if he ever touched Keri.

NINE

"That wasn't necessary." Keri waited until they got into the SUV to say anything to Adam about what had just happened. "I don't want you getting into trouble."

Adam dragged his hand down his face. "I don't know how the hell he found us."

"I was wondering the same thing." The thought of Edward tracking them down like he had made her stomach sick. "I'm in a different house now and we've been so careful."

"Not careful enough." Adam banged his palm on the steering wheel. *"Damn."* His face tightened. "Carter must have found out where I live and then followed me to your place."

Keri tugged down her short dress, a nervous gesture because she really didn't know what to do with her hands.

"We need to take you to a hotel." Adam looked at her apologetically. "I'm sorry about this."

"A hotel is fine." Keri gave him a little smile. "For a couple of nights anyway."

With clear frustration, Adam rubbed his face again with his palm. "Carter is supposed to be heading out of town for good. Possibly even this week was what we heard."

"Maybe he just wanted to harass us," Keri said.

"Maybe."

After making arrangements for Fred, Adam picked a nice hotel and she waited in the lobby while he checked them in. Her room was on the twenty-second floor and the room had a great view of Times Square.

Keri stood at the window, staring at the lights, the glitter, the people. Had it really been seven years since she was forced to retire from her life of performance after performance? Seven years since she left behind that craziness that she had loved.

Still looking away from Adam, out the window, Keri said, "Will you stay with me tonight?"

She felt Adam's presence, then his warm hands on her shoulders. He began to massage her and she tipped her head back and closed her eyes.

His touch was strong, familiar, as if he had done this to her a thousand times before.

"Mmmmm . . ." Keri sighed. "Wonderful."

Adam gripped her upper arms and turned her around to face him. His features were shadowed from the dimness of the room, but he looked so intense.

He searched her face with his gaze. "You're beautiful in so many ways," he said quietly. "More ways than I can count."

A feeling like a wave surging inside her belly made

her catch her breath as she stared up at him. His eyes, so dark. His lips, so close.

Adam brought his mouth down on hers. A hard kiss that she met with equal intensity. She wrapped her arms around his neck and bit his lower lip, causing him to groan.

"This should answer your question," he said with another kiss. Then murmured, "Yes, I'll stay with you."

She said nothing back, just kissed him deeper. She had known him just a week, but it felt like she had known him for so much longer than that. Known him and loved him.

Loved him.

He moved his hands from her shoulders, lightly down the sides of her waist, and rested them on her hips. He drew her to him so tightly that she felt his arousal against her belly.

More waves crashed in her abdomen. Need. Desire. A reckless feeling of giving in to everything she wanted from Adam.

He cupped her ass with his palms and moved his mouth from hers. With another groan, he trailed kisses to her ear where he lightly bit her earlobe.

Keri gasped and tilted her head back. Adam kissed her along her jaw and his lips traveled down to the hollow of her throat. She felt herself start to dissolve into his arms. Fall into everything that was Adam Boyd.

"Am I moving too fast for you?" he murmured in her ear. "Tell me if I am."

Keri decided the best response was to show him how fast she thought he should be moving. She reached down and clasped his hands and moved them up so that they were resting on her breasts.

Adam made a sound of approval and palmed her breasts. When he pinched and pulled her nipples, Keri gave a loud gasp and a cry. She arched her back. All he had to do was touch her and she was going to go crazy.

He tugged at the neckline of her dress and drew down the red satin bra with black lace, bringing both hands under her breasts so that they jutted out and her nipples grew even harder. He played with her nipples as she squirmed and then flicked his tongue over them.

As he sucked her nipples he grasped the hem of her dress and brought it up around her waist, exposing the red panties with the black lace that she had worn just for him. He caressed the smooth silky texture of them, a sensual feel that had her moving against him, trying to get even closer than was possible.

Adam reached behind her and unzipped her dress, sliding his fingers along her soft skin as he drew the zipper down.

He pushed her dress from her shoulders, down and over her hips and let it fall to the floor.

Keri gave into every single sensation that rocked her body. She wanted Adam and now was the time to take him. Take him here and now and never let him go.

When she stepped out of her dress, she stood before him in her red satin panties and bra with the black lace, black stockings, and her black high heels. She felt delicious and decadent and loved the way Adam looked at her. Hunger in his gaze, need, and fire.

He showed the fire inside him as he kissed her again and played with her nipples, which responded by tightening, growing hard and even more sensitive.

Adam pinched her nipples hard enough to make her cry out in surprise before he began sucking first one and then the other. He slipped his fingers into her panties and stroked her in a way that made her moan with pleasure.

Keri wanted to see Adam with everything off. She tugged his shirt out of his slacks and began unbuttoning it. Her hands didn't tremble, her fingers sure and quick.

After she finished unbuttoning his shirt she pushed it aside while running her palms across the hardness of his chest, the strength of his shoulders, the power in his biceps. He shrugged completely out of his shirt, then tossed it across the room.

Keri leaned forward and inhaled, filling her lungs with his thoroughly masculine scent. She ran her tongue over his salty skin and licked one of his nipples while she played with the other one.

With a groan, Adam slid his fingers into her hair. It drifted over her shoulders in a caress as he rubbed her scalp and skimmed his fingers down her nape to her shoulders.

She lightly bit his skin and tasted him, small nibbles and flicks of her tongue from his chest, down to his waist, and over his taut abs. As she moved her mouth she eased down so that she was kneeling in front of him.

Crazy sensations zinged through her body as she focused on rubbing her palm over his erection. Adam clenched his hands harder in her hair as she unfastened the top button of his slacks and drew down the zipper, exposing his briefs.

She looked up at him and her insides made more twists and turns when she saw how focused he was on her. How dark his eyes were. How intense his expression was.

Keri rubbed her hand over his boxer-briefs, tracing the outline of his erection with her fingertips. Then she grasped the sides of his slacks and pulled them down to the floor where he kicked them off in the direction his shirt had gone.

Before she could start on his boxers, he pulled off each of his socks, then squared his stance.

It had been so long since she had been with a man and she didn't remember ever wanting someone so badly as she did Adam. Something about him stirred her on some deeper level.

She breathed deep of him again then tugged down his boxer-briefs. His smell filled her, making her want more of him. His erection was so long, so hard. She wrapped her fingers around his cock, then slid her mouth over him.

Adam gave a low rumble in his chest before grasping her hair in his fists while pumping his hips against her face. Keri took all of him to the back of her throat. She loved the way he tasted, the feel of him inside her mouth as he moved in and out. She loved knowing that she was giving him pleasure.

"That's enough," he said after several minutes. "Come here."

Keri obeyed, letting his cock slide out of her mouth before she stood with his hands grasping her shoulders. She noticed he was still careful not to touch her arm. Funny, because right now she had forgotten about it entirely.

When she was standing again, Adam kissed her. Long, slow, hard. He caressed her back, her shoulders, letting her fall into the total and complete pleasure of the moment.

He moved her so that her thighs were against the bed before he lifted her up and laid her on the mattress, which was covered with a downy soft comforter.

Their eyes met and held as he positioned her at the edge of the mattress. He spread her thighs as he bent over her, then braced his arms to either side of her head.

"Bring me inside, Keri," he murmured as he pulled aside her panties.

She bit the inside of her lip as she reached down, grabbed his cock in her hand and guided him inside her.

Keri gave a loud cry, surprised at how much he stretched her, to the point it almost hurt. It had been so long and he was so big.

The initial shock faded into pure pleasure. He moved in and out in slow, easy thrusts that reached her deep inside. It was like nothing she ever remembered feeling before.

Adam ducked his head and sucked and licked each of her nipples, causing her to squirm beneath him. The more she squirmed, the more intense the feeling of having him inside her.

Her breathing grew rapid and her heart beat faster. Adam clasped her hands in his and held her hands up high, over her head. His strokes grew longer and harder.

He began taking her in earnest. Sweat dripped from his brow onto her chest and her own skin perspired more and more until they were both slick from it.

Adam's jaw grew tight at the same time her orgasm started building up inside. Keri let out little cries with every thrust of him inside her.

Her mind started spinning as heat and light swirled inside her. Adam's breathing grew more and more ragged as he thrust harder and harder.

Keri cried out as her orgasm burst inside her. Light prismed and all she could do was feel, not think.

Somewhere her consciousness was aware that Adam

had cried out, too, the sound of pleasure in his voice. He sank against her before drawing her onto her side, pulling her into his arms, and resting her head on his chest.

"I love you, Keri," he whispered.

Keri raised her head and looked down at him. "Funny, 'cause I love you, too."

"Good thing." Adam gave an exaggerated sound of relief. "Because I wasn't about to let you out of here until you said you did."

TEN

"Watch what you're doing," Edward shouted at the idiot who had nearly scraped his mahogany desk as it was loaded into the moving truck. "One more close call like that and you'll be panhandling, dickhead."

"Yes, sir." The mover and his partner stopped and the mover licked his lips, a nervous expression on his face. "Won't happen again."

"Damned right it won't." Edward looked at Johnny. "Have Hector keep an eye on this guy as well as the others. Better not be one fucking mark."

Johnny gave a nod and called to Hector. He gave the punk the instructions and sent him on his way.

"Think they'll fall for it?" Johnny asked when Hector was out of the way.

"They watch my every move. One thing about them, though—like most cops, they've got their heads stuck up their asses." Edward laughed, the sound more bitter than he wanted it to be. "Won't know what the fuck happened."

Johnny was silent for a moment. "Is it worth it?" he said. "Killing the dancer and the cop?"

Edward's body tensed even more and he glared at Johnny. "Don't need you questioning me. I need you doing what you're told."

"Of course, Eddie." Johnny's gaze followed a pair of movers carrying an armoire. "The jet is ready for tonight. Bruce has been here since early this morning and he'll go with all of us to the airport. It'll all work out, just like you planned, boss. He has the right clothes, the right hat, all of it."

"It better work out." Edward felt the press of his PX4 Beretta against his spine. "I don't want anything to screw up my plans."

"So both of them die tonight?" Johnny's face was composed, but he had a nervous edge in his voice.

Edward felt the coldness of his smile as he thought about what he had planned. "I just want the cop to hurt for now. Bad."

"How are you going to hurt him?" Johnny asked.

Edward clenched his hands into fists. "He's fucking that bitch, Keri. The way to hurt him is to kill her. I'll give him a little time to feel the pain of her gone on his watch before I eventually get rid of him, too." He rocked back on his heels. "I have all the time in the world for that."

ELEVEN

"Marcy left her cell phone," Keri said over the phone to her student's mother. "I'll put it in my backpack now so I don't forget and I'll drop it off on my way home from the studio. It's right on my way."

The woman thanked her and Keri pressed the disconnect button on her cell phone while she moved away. Her footsteps were silent as she walked in her ballet slippers across the floor of her empty dance studio. The last student had gone home for the afternoon and Keri was ready to head out herself.

She smiled as she thought of her past two nights with Adam. Being with him had been amazing. Absolutely amazing.

Notes being played on the baby grand caused her to startle and whirl around.

Her hand to her chest, Keri let her breath out in a rush. "Adam," she said and wanted to melt when he gave her his adorable grin. "You startled me."

"Sorry, Angel." Adam sat down on the piano bench. "If you forgive me, I have a favor to ask."

"Oh?" Keri smiled as she walked toward him. "What's that?"

His expression was adorable. For a tough detective he sure was cute. "If I play something, will you dance for me?"

Surprised, Keri paused and stopped at the edge of the floor. "You play?"

Adam shrugged. "My mom is the pianist of the family, but she taught my brother and sister and me while we were growing up. Insisted on it."

"What can you play?" she asked, smiling.

"One of my mom's favorite pieces was 'Dance of the Sugar Plum Fairy,'" Adam said. "She made me learn that when I was twelve."

"I was the Sugar Plum Fairy one season when I was sixteen." Keri began walking toward her office. "It's one of my favorite memories," she said and glanced over her shoulder. "I'll get my pointe shoes."

Keri hurried to put on her black satin toe shoes, which matched the black leotard and simple ballet skirt she wore when teaching. When she finished she went to the center of the dance studio and smiled at Adam.

He played it well as she danced for him. She put her heart into her private performance, her love for Adam becoming a part of the dance.

When she finished, Adam stood up from the piano and applauded. She ran toward him and was met by his embrace. He kissed her, sweet and wonderful.

"So beautiful," he murmured. "You are amazing."

Her answer was to kiss him back and put everything she had and felt into that kiss.

"You look like you could still dance professionally, Angel."

"My knee is fine for a little three-minute dance here and there," she said. "But that's about it."

When they drew apart she said, "What are you doing here?"

"Came to walk you to your car," Adam said. "I want to make sure you get home all right."

"Last night you said Edward was gone." Keri tilted her head. "That he was seen flying off in a private jet to Florida with his entourage of thugs."

Adam nodded. "It's probably not necessary, but I just feel safer knowing someone's watching out for you. Feel better yet when that someone is me. It's a good excuse to see you more."

"Adam, you don't need an excuse to see me more," she said with a laugh. "Whenever you want I'll make time for you."

"That's a lot of time," Adam said and smiled against her lips. "Be prepared."

"I'm more than ready." Keri put her palms on Adam's chest, through the opening in his jacket. He felt warm through the T-shirt. "Okay, I'll grab my backpack and change my shoes," Keri said, then made her way across the dance floor, back to her office.

She took off her pointe shoes and ballet skirt and tugged on a T-shirt and sweats over her leotard before slipping on socks and running shoes.

When they were in the parking lot, Adam gave her a kiss. "See you at the hotel."

They had moved from the Manhattan hotel to one in Brooklyn yesterday, but she hadn't expected to spend another night there.

"Are you sure it's necessary?" she asked him.

"One more night, just to be certain. It's past the cancellation period anyway, so we might as well enjoy the room one last night," he said.

"I love the thought of that, Adam." Keri got into her VW Bug and rolled down her window. "See you there."

In the rearview mirror, she saw Adam watching her drive away.

"Marcy's phone," she said to herself when she neared the hotel. She leaned down and dug her cell phone out of an outside pocket of her backpack.

"Adam," she said into the phone when she got his voicemail. "I promised to drop off a student's cell phone she left at the dance studio. I'm going to swing by her apartment, then meet you at the hotel."

She headed over to Brooklyn Heights, close to her home, and her stomach twisted. To think that she was almost killed a few streets over, and it hadn't been that long since she had gotten the bullet wound to remind her. Thank God for Adam.

When she reached the building that housed Marcy's condo, she got lucky enough to snag a parking spot in the small, dimly lit lot adjacent to the building. She drew her cell phone out of her pack to call Marcy's mother and let her know she was here, then swung her pack over her shoulder. As she started to get out of her car, a van pulled in tight next to her, in the handicapped spot.

She looked at the driver, who glanced over briefly before turning away from her. He seemed totally oblivious as to how he had crowded her. He had pulled in at such an angle she could barely get out of her car and it prevented her from walking to the sidewalk in front of her car because the bumpers almost touched.

What's this guy thinking? She thought about honking her horn and pointing at how close he had parked, but something like that often only roused someone's anger. She would be in and out in a flash, so she would just deal with it.

She squeezed out of the car, shut the door behind her, then started to walk around the back of the van.

The side door of the van slid open.

A large man grabbed her upper arm and began to pull her in.

Fear made her heart pound and adrenaline surge through her body. With every ounce of strength she had she jerked her arm away.

"No!" Keri pulled free. She started to run in the only direction she could go—behind the car and van. "Help!" she screamed.

The thug moved too fast and he was just too strong. Her brief scream was silenced by his hand over her mouth. At the same time he grabbed her with his forearm around her throat and dragged her back into the van.

She heard the sound of her cell phone clattering across the asphalt parking lot as it flew out of her hand.

He tried to throw her into the van, but she fought him. Her cheek burned when it scraped the edge of the door while she was forced up against it. Her body cried out in pain when someone heavy pinned her against the van, smashing her pack against her back.

Air left her lungs in a rush, chasing away the scream as she tried to catch her breath.

Panic seared her senses as she struggled, kicked, and fought the holds of the two men—a big bruiser and the thug driver. Bruiser grabbed her where the healing bullet wound was. The pain was so great that stars sparked in her mind.

For an instant Thug took his hand off of her mouth and she found her voice. He clapped a big hand over her mouth again.

Keri bit the dirty hand. Thug shouted and jerked it back.

She screamed as loud as she could. Thug slapped her so hard her vision blurred, cutting her off in mid-scream.

Keri started to scream again, but Thug grabbed her around the throat and started choking her.

"Don't kill the bitch," Bruiser said. "Carter will take you out."

"The bitch bit me," Thug growled.

"Big fucking deal." Bruiser climbed into the front seat. "Let's go, shithead."

Terror ripped through her. Adam wasn't here and she couldn't fight off two big men. She struggled and struggled, but couldn't get free.

"Put her in," she heard Bruiser say. "Hurry."

She felt herself being lifted. Through the light streaming into the rear of the van from a streetlight, she saw a large open storage trunk.

In the next moment she was dropped in on her back, the pack smashed between her and the floor of the trunk. The heavy lid slammed shut. She heard it being latched and then faint, muffled voices.

When the lid was closed, terror ran even more rampant through her as complete darkness enveloped her. She had to fight to slow her breathing. To not panic in the cramped space.

"Did you get her cell phone?" Bruiser said. "It's lying on the ground."

They had her. Edward had her and he was going to follow through with his threats.

Keri coughed as she tried to calm herself down. She couldn't just give up.

She was locked in a trunk. How was she going to get out of this?

Tires squealed and the car shot forward. Keri's head hit the side of the trunk and her injured arm was squeezed between her and the trunk wall. Her mind spun from the pain.

If only she had her cell phone. Some way to contact Adam.

Her mind went through all the possibilities, which were no possibilities. She didn't have anything sharp to protect herself with.

She was tossed around with the movement of the van.

Her pack hurt her back as she lay on it.

Marcy's cell phone. The girl was always texting or calling someone and Keri had had to make the girl put the phone away more than once. The thing was normally glued to Marcy's fingertips but today she'd actually forgotten it.

The space in the trunk was so cramped Keri could barely move. She struggled to get to the backpack and was barely able to take it off in the close quarters. She tried to rush, knowing that they could get to their destination at any moment, wherever that might be.

The more she rushed, the more she fumbled. She forced herself to take a deep breath and slow down. Her hands shook as she unhooked the top of the pack and pulled at the drawstring to stretch it out. She reached in and groped inside for the girl's cell phone.

She could barely keep her hands steady. Sounds of

traffic were loud. A ship blew its horn. From it and the loudness of the traffic she guessed they were about to go over the Brooklyn Bridge to Manhattan.

Keri dug through her pack and finally clasped her hand over what felt like a cell phone. She drew it out and flipped it open. Immediately the glow of the phone lit up the almost pure darkness of the trunk.

For a second she clasped it to her chest, silently thanking Marcy.

The backlight on the phone went dim. Keri pressed a button and it lit up again. She started to dial Adam's phone number when she saw the battery was almost dead.

She rushed to complete the call, praying he would answer this time.

"Boyd," came his voice.

Keri almost sobbed with relief. "Adam," she said into the phone, "they've got me, Edward's men, and they locked me in a storage trunk and I found my student's cell phone and I don't know where they're taking—"

"Keri, I can barely hear you." Panic was in his voice, then she heard the cop side of him take over. "It'll be okay. I'll get you. Tell me where you are."

"I don't know." She could hear the near hysteria in her voice. "No, wait." *Calm down, Keri, Calm down.* "I think we're going over the Brooklyn Bridge," she said, trying to catch her breath.

"I'm not far," Adam said and she heard the slam of a vehicle door. "Stay on the phone with me. I will find you."

"Okay." Keri nodded, bumping her head against the side of the trunk again.

"Tell me what happened." Adam was trying to stay calm for her and it was helping her panic to ease.

Keri told him how the men had grabbed her in front

of Marcy's apartment and that she had heard one of them refer to "Carter."

She heard the curse in Adam's voice even as he held it back for her.

"Whatever you do, don't shut off the phone. When you notice your surroundings try and describe as best you can where you are. You got that, honey?" he said.

"Yes." She looked up at the trunk lid. It was so close and the space so small that she felt claustrophobia start to set in. She closed her eyes and took a deep breath. "But there's not much battery power left. I don't know how long it's going to last."

"Shit." This time Adam did let it out. "All right, it's going to be okay. Just hang with me."

"I will." Her body rocked as the car jostled her.

Adam asked her about sounds she heard, talking with her while trying to figure out where she was.

They drove for about fifteen minutes and finally they came to a stop.

Finally? Was that what she really wanted—for the ride to end? Would she be killed before Adam could find her?

She heard the car doors slam and then the squeaking of the trunk lid opening.

Right before the trunk lid was all the way up, Keri put the open phone into her backpack and prayed that Adam would be able to hear anything that was said.

Thug jerked her out of the storage trunk and hooked his arm around her throat before dragging her out of the van.

She blinked. "We're at Edward's old house. Why?" she asked, hoping Adam could hear her through the pack. "Didn't he sell it?"

"Doesn't matter, lady," Bruiser said. "What do you care?"

"Furnishings and all," Thug said. "But the boss made sure the two of you could use it one last night, though."

Keri swallowed. "What do you mean?"

"I mean why don't you just shut that trap of yours or I'll shut it for you," Thug said. "For good."

It was then that she felt the gun pressed against her spine.

TWELVE

Carter's house.

Thank God. That meant he was close and didn't have far to go.

Adam's strobe lights flashed and his siren wailed as he tore through the night.

Let me be in time. The place had been under surveillance up until yesterday, when the keys were reportedly turned over to a new owner.

Adam used the police radio in his car to call for backup. From where he was, he'd make it there around the same time his backup would.

He heard muffled sounds over the phone connection, then Keri saying, "Edward."

Adam clenched his teeth as Carter said, "It's the little ballerina slut."

Keep him talking, honey, Adam thought as he drove up the toward Carter's house. *Keep him talking.*

"Why are you doing this?" she said, her voice fainter.

Damn, he hoped her phone wasn't going to die.

"That's a stupid question," Carter said. "Even for you, Keri." The bastard had a sneer in his voice. "Let's see. You give me up to the cops and I get put away for almost seven years. Would have been longer if my lawyers hadn't figured out a way to get the verdict overturned."

Keri's voice was muffled and the connection went dead.

"On your knees." Edward shoved Keri and she cried out as her knees hit the floor.

Her heart pounded and fear tasted sour in her mouth.

"Get out of here, all of you," Edward said in a snarl to Thug and Bruiser. "I'll deal with her myself. I'll have my fun before I take care of her. It won't be messy."

"Right, boss," came a voice from behind her, someone she remembered from years ago. Edward's flunky, Johnny Hill. "Do you want us to wait outside?"

"Yeah," Edward said as he glared at Johnny. "Now get the fuck out of here."

The moment Keri heard the door close behind them, Edward backhanded her. She cried out when pain sparked in her head as he knocked her onto her side on the floor.

He towered over where she was lying. "Hands and knees, bitch."

Shaking, she obeyed. She cried out as Edward grabbed her by her hair and jerked her along behind him, toward the hallway that led to the bedrooms.

"You're slowing me down," Edward was saying. "Crawl."

"Edward, please." Pain was in Keri's voice as he started leading her down the hall while she crawled. "Whatever you want me to do, I'll do it. I promise."

"Sure." Edward came to a stop and jerked her closer by her hair. Her scalp ached with pain. He raised her up so that she was just on her knees and he bent his head to get his face close to hers. "Give me back the years I lost being stuck in that fucking prison. Think you can do that?"

"I'm sorry," Keri said as more panic seized her. "When I turned you in I was scared," she said.

"Are you scared now, Keri?" Edward yanked her head back. "I bet you're scared," he said, then shouted, *"Aren't you?"*

"Yes." Keri's voice was low as she stared up at him. "I'm scared."

Edward laughed. "You know what's funny? As much fun as it's going to be to kill you, it's going to be even more fun to see your detective suffer. When you disappear forever, on his watch, he's going to be real sad, isn't he?"

Keri just looked at Edward as a cold, icy feeling rolled over her. He shook her by her hair and repeated, *"Isn't he?"*

"Yes," Keri whispered. Then louder when he shook her again. *"Yes,"* she shouted.

Edward jerked her harder by her hair. Her eyes watered and she had a hard time catching her breath. She could fight him, but he was bigger than she was. She needed to wait for the right time to try to escape.

She wasn't going to give up hope on Adam. She wasn't going to give up hope at all.

Keri glanced up as he dragged her and saw a handgun tucked in the back of his pants, up against his spine.

Chills made her shiver almost uncontrollably. Was he going to shoot her? But he had said something about it not being messy. What did he mean by that?

They reached Edward's bedroom and Keri gave a strangled gasp as he jerked her to her feet by the collar of the T-shirt she'd pulled over her leotard.

With his grip still on her T-shirt with one hand, he slapped her with his other hard enough that she stumbled. Her T-shirt ripped in his hand and she almost fell.

He released his hold on her torn shirt, then shoved her. This time she dropped onto her back on the mattress. "You hurt me in more ways than one, Keri. We were meant to be together, but you threw that away."

"I—" she started.

Edward raised his hand and slapped her. Keri's mind spun as lights and colors erupted behind her eyelids.

"Here is what I am going to do, Keri," Edward said with a cold look in his blue eyes. "You violated me. Now I'm going to violate you. You took some of my life away. I will take all of yours away."

Keri's skin prickled from every word Edward said. She knew she didn't have a chance if she didn't keep him talking. Adam had to get here and she had to stall until he did.

Keri swallowed. "I thought you were in Florida."

"I knew these loser cops were following me," Edwards said. "They're so stupid. It's not like it's hard to outsmart them. I have a double. Name's Bruce. Idiot cops watched him go to the airport and get on the private jet I chartered. So as far as they are concerned, I'm in Florida and I won't be blamed for you disappearing."

"Edward," Keri said, "I was frightened back then. I was afraid of what you would do to me after you crushed my knee. I cared about you, I still do, I just didn't know what to do. I was young. Please Edward, don't do this. I am sorry."

"I love to hear you beg," Edward said in a growl. "But your lies don't help you here."

Keri clenched her hands in the bedspread beneath her.

Edward reached for the buckle on his belt. "Time for payback, bitch."

Adam was a few blocks down the street from Carter's house when Captain Wilson's voice came over the radio. "Boyd," she said, "House is empty."

Adam's skin crawled. "Empty? What do you mean it's empty?"

"I mean nothing's here," Wilson said with impatience in her voice. "Place is clean. Not even a stick of furniture in it, much less Carter or the woman you say he kidnapped."

Confusion made Adam's head spin. "She said Edward's house—" Then he realized his screwup. "She meant his old house."

Adam couldn't believe how stupid he'd been. Carter's *old* house. Carter had used it sort of like a guesthouse for friends or meetings. He'd kept it and rented it out. Not long ago he'd sold it to a fellow lowlife friend. When this started up again, Adam had gone by the house, not knowing it had been sold.

"His what?" Wilson said over the radio.

"Carter had another place two streets over." Adam whipped his SUV down a side street in the direction of the other house. He gave the captain the address he had in his Blackberry as he drove. "I'm almost there."

"Damn," the captain said, but Adam barely heard her as he neared the house.

Twenty seconds and Adam was parked down the street from Carter's old house.

He killed the engine and quietly climbed out of the SUV. Lights were on inside the house, downstairs and up.

In front, a van was against the curb and three men were standing nearby, having an animated discussion. One of them looked up and down the street every so often, but it looked more like it was ingrained in him as opposed to real concern.

Adam drew his Glock and crept through the darkness. He avoided the streetlight as he ducked through the shadows and walked toward the house.

Gravel shifted beneath one of his shoes. He paused and held his breath, waiting for one of the men to say he'd heard something.

"What's the boss doing with her?" one of the men said as he rubbed one hand with the other, as if it bothered him. "The bitch bit me."

"I told you to quit whining like a girl," the big guy next to him said. "My bet is he's having some fun before he takes care of her for good."

Adam gritted his teeth. Keri had to be okay and he'd get there before anything happened to her.

Gripping his handgun, carefully, slowly, Adam made his way to the side of the house. When he reached the wall he leaned against it and took a deep breath, then let it out.

He had to find Keri. He was running out of time. Keri was running out of time.

One-handed, Adam grabbed the short fence that ran along the side yard. He vaulted over the fence, and rushed into the shadows, and pressed himself up against a wall, melting into the darkness.

He held his Glock in both hands as he peered in the windows through gaps in the curtains. The house was furnished and it looked lived in. But he didn't see any-one and he definitely didn't hear anything.

Adam tried to keep his professional cool as he prayed he wasn't too late. He ran around the house to the back. Lights came from windows on one corner.

Holding his handgun tight, Adam tried to peek into the windows on the east side of the house, but the curtains were shut too tightly.

He made his way around the corner. Just as he tried to get a look in through that window, he heard a woman's scream coming from upstairs.

Keri.

Adam's heart pounded faster. He ran for the back door of the house and tried it. Locked.

Keri screamed again.

Adam used the butt of his Glock to knock out a small pane of glass from the window on the door. He reached his hand through and unlocked the door.

"Hold still, bitch," Carter said loud enough for Adam to hear.

Adam ran toward the staircase and bolted up the stairs as quietly as he could.

Keri cried out and Adam opened the door. Carter's back was to him, but Adam could see that the bastard had a hold on Keri.

"No." Keri was fighting Carter, trying to get away. *"No!"*

Gripping his Glock in both hands, Adam bolted into the bedroom. "Police!" he shouted. "Hands in the air."

Carter whirled, his arm around Keri's neck, a gun pressed up against her temple.

Adam's gut tightened as he raised his hands and pointed his gun to the ceiling. "Let her go, Carter."

The bastard smirked. "Looks like I'm the one holding all the cards—and the bitch. Slide your gun over here, dickhead."

Very slowly, Adam eased down, careful to not make any sudden movements that would set off Carter. He slid his gun and it clattered over the tile floor to Carter's feet.

Keri thought her heart just might burst out of her chest. Edward's gun pressed into her temple and her throat hurt from how tightly he was holding it.

Her eyes met Adam's. He was here, but Edward would probably kill them both.

Keri could barely swallow. Still with his grip on her, Carter moved his gun away from her head and started to reach out his foot kick away Adam's gun.

She had to do something.

She dug her nails into the arm he had around her throat. At the same time she slid down.

With her countless years of training, Keri was so limber she was able to swing her leg over her head and drive her foot into Edward's face.

She felt the crack of his nose against her toes, which were strengthened from years as a ballerina. He screamed in pain. In the shock of what she'd done, he released her.

Keri twisted out of his grip and kicked the gun out of his hand.

Edward shoved her and she fell back and hit her head against the tile.

Blood pouring from his nose, Edward grabbed Adam's gun and started to point it at Keri.

A shot rang out from behind her at the same time she saw a spot of red appear in Edward's forehead.

He slumped face-forward onto the tile.

Stunned, Keri couldn't move. She felt frozen for a moment, not comprehending what had just happened.

"Keri. Honey." Adam was there, his arm around her shoulders as he helped her sit. "Are you okay?"

She looked up and saw Adam, a deadly look in his eyes as he held Edward's gun.

Keri looked at Edward's body, then she met Adam's gaze again.

"It's over," Adam said. "It's over."

THIRTEEN

"Thank God he's gone." Keri leaned up against Adam, her back to him as she looked into the crackling flames in his fireplace.

It was the night following the horror of the ordeal with Edward. She still couldn't believe the terror had ended.

Adam stroked the side of her neck with his fingers. His touch was feather light, soothing against the areas that had been abused by the thug who had tried to choke her and by Edward.

"You were amazing, Keri." Adam pressed his lips to the top of her head. "But you scared me to death."

She tilted her head back and looked up at Adam, meeting his warm brown eyes. "I thought we were going to die." She swallowed. "I was so frightened."

"Everything is all right now," he said. "Everything is fine."

She nodded. "He's out of my life, forever." With Edward dead, there was nothing for her to worry about anymore. She could move on with her life without looking over her shoulder ever again.

"Where did you learn a move like that?" he said. "It was pretty amazing."

"Dancing." She smiled impishly. "You should see the positions I can get into."

Adam touched the side of her face with his hand. "That's one position I never want to see you in again."

Keri shifted so that her head was against his chest. She felt the heat of his body against her cheek. "Don't worry about me. I plan to stay out of trouble from now on."

Adam wrapped his arms around her and rocked them both from side to side. "I'm holding you to that."

For a moment they sat together, looking into the fire, neither of them saying a word. The only sound was the pop and hiss of flames as they danced in the hearth.

Being careful not to hurt her arm, Adam moved her so that she was lying on the rug in front of the fireplace and looking up at him.

She reached up and touched his jaw, the feel of her fingers light against his skin. "You're almost too good to be true," she said. "I'm so afraid of losing you."

"To tell you the truth," he said, "it's the same for me. I've never felt this way before. You make me want to take care of you. Always."

Suddenly, Keri's eyes grew wide. "I almost forgot," she said, "I have two things, just for you."

Keri shot up and ran into the next room. A moment later she returned and said, "Okay, close your eyes and don't open them until I tell you."

Keri walked out with a wrapped package and set it on the table next to Adam. She grabbed his hands. "Keep your eyes closed until I tell you," she ordered. "Okay. Stand up."

She pulled Adam up and he stood in front of her. "Open your eyes," she said.

There Keri stood, in her Catwoman mask, with the biggest grin on her face he had ever seen.

Adam laughed. "The most beautiful Catwoman ever. I can't believe you remembered."

"So I guess you like the look," she said, still grinning.

"Like the look? I love the look." Adam said.

"But it didn't come with the whip," Keri said.

"Awwwww, it's not the same." Adam pretended to look disappointed. "Catwoman without a whip."

"Maybe I will just have to find one," she said. "It's important for Batman to get what he likes."

"Oh, I got what I like," he murmured. "Right here."

"What are you waiting for?" she said. "My permission, that you may kiss the Cat?" Keri tilted her face up. "Wait, you have to open your gift."

Keri handed Adam the package and Adam opened it.

"Just what I always wanted," Adam said with a laugh. "A Batman mask."

"Just what *I* always wanted," she said. "My own Batman. Now put it on."

Adam put on the mask.

"It fits you perfectly," she said. "Something about a man in a mask . . . You just might be in for quite an adventure tonight, Batman."

"You do look like quite the adventurer right now, Catwoman." He rubbed her upper arms as he met her eyes. "Time to kiss the Cat."

"I love you, Adam. I—" she said before her words were smothered by his kiss.

"I love you too, Keri."

Then he kissed her again.

CAUGHT

RED GARNIER

PROLOGUE

Phoenix, Arizona—August 2005

He did the same thing every year.

On August 22, at 6:00 p.m. sharp, Cody Nordstrom would drop whatever he was doing in order to head straight home.

He'd have trouble getting to his front door sometimes; phone calls, unsolved cases that suddenly needed his attention, always popped up on this day. But he'd ignore them as best he could.

He'd ignore the tempting call of a cold beer after work, and the buddies clamoring for him to come over to the Starbucks by the station, and the paperwork on his desk and the meetings with his superiors, and he'd drive straight home.

He would start a cold shower, put out his clothes—a black Armani suit and a crisp white shirt he had dropped off in the morning at the cleaners and picked up on his way home—and for this day, the only day in the entire year, he would wear them with a solid black tie.

By 6:15, toweled dry and somberly dressed, he would stop by the corner neighborhood florist and purchase two dozen white roses. Then he would climb back into his car and drive with care, glancing now and then at the petals riding shotgun beside him, starkly innocent against the dark upholstery and caught in mid bloom.

By 6:30, he would reach the cemetery.

This was his destination, and he'd stay here for hours. Until the traffic waned, and the hot desert day began to morph into a cool night.

He'd keep his face downcast, his thoughts to himself, and those white roses would lie on the ground, right on the spot where the bodies of his two parents had been buried.

There was comfort in this routine, and maybe there was some punishment in it, too; punishment in the gloomy sight of the graves during the evening. Yet today—

The hair at the nape of his neck pricked, and Nordstrom raised his head in puzzlement.

He scanned the cemetery for signs of disturbance, noticing how this one time, this strange time, the sun was shining bright, casting an orange glow across the scattered grass, hitting the only tree nearby at an odd angle. He didn't know that what followed would rock his world— for he hadn't seen her yet.

"Oh, is that nice girl with you?" a female passerby asked him, noticing that he was looking in the direction of the tree.

Uncertain of the curiosity prodding him to find out to whom she was referring, Cody stared at her hard, then he glanced back at the tree. There, leaning against the trunk, was a . . . female.

"That girl, is she your sister?" the woman insisted.

Cody honed in on the girl. No. Not a girl. *Too curvy to be a girl*.

"She comes to visit this same grave every Saturday, too," the stranger offered before hauling her bag closer to her chest and walking away, dragging a small toddler behind her.

Fixated on the slim figure by the tree, Cody narrowed his eyes as he tried to place her. Blond hair to her shoulders, brilliant eyes even from afar. His pulse stopped.

Something about her, the way she held so still and quiet as she looked back at him. Her skin, the shade of her hair. Time stopped as they stared at each other across the graves and trees and grass.

Megan.

Holy fuck—it was her. It had to be.

But she was there, and she was . . . walking over? Holy hell, she was walking over.

He stood slowly, wondering if she knew it was him— Cody. Of course she knew. Megan had never looked at his twin quite the way she used to look at Cody, quite the way she was looking at him now.

Ahh, fuck, his groin was heating.

She was a woman now—a very sexy woman—and he wished he hadn't seen her, for she'd plague his mind from now on.

He hadn't planned to look for her. Not after social services took him away—he sure as hell hadn't returned for that. He was just plain bad luck, should let the girl continue on with whatever kind of life she was leading, which was for certain better off without him in it.

She should stay away from a problem like him.

True, he had become a cop. Homicide detective and all that.

He was supposed to be a good man, but the same blood as that of a killer ran in his veins, and he knew what he really was. Soiled. Unfit. And *responsible* for what that sick bastard had done.

Thoughts of his twin brother made his lips curl in disdain. Theirs had been a complicated relationship, spawned by parents who did not pretend that doing things halfway was okay. They liked to challenge their other son to become more like his responsible brother, but he never seemed to make it to the bar they raised.

This did little to encourage sibling harmony between the two, and somehow Cody, as the eldest, had felt compelled to allow for Ivan's rebelliousness. Until that day. What Ivan had done was so sick, so twisted, there would be no going back from it.

"I killed them," he said that fateful day when Cody had been taking Megan to the lake, intent on stealing a first kiss from her. Cody would not have believed him had his parents not been lying there, in a crimson pool. Dead.

Dead at his brother's feet.

"I told you I would." Ivan had looked at him with hard blue eyes, a monster with Cody's own face.

And deep down, Cody feared that a monster lived inside him, too.

One that made him steal that kiss from Megan. One that imagined taking her virginity, the virginity of the only girl he really cared for. The monster that even then, after seeing with his own two eyes what Ivan had done, urged him to hide his brother, to protect him.

Maybe that monster would have surfaced if Megan

hadn't been there, her face pale and frightened, her eyes round as moons. The horror and pain he felt that day, that she be witness to what had become of the Nordstroms, made him want to tear off his face, the face of a murderer, and forget he'd ever had the last name Nordstrom.

But his parents' sightless eyes, staring from the ground, seemed to yell their disappointment. And he knew that he'd spend the rest of his life trying to make amends.

"It was my fault," he told her, when Ivan dropped the weapon and ran. "It's all my fault, Meg." And he'd hugged her for as long as he could, until the first officers on scene pried her away.

Those were the last words he ever said to her before his new family claimed him. He saw her little face in the windowpane watching him being taken away. He didn't know if she was crying, he could hardly raise his face to see his neighbors, knowing they all thought: *One of those boys did it.*

His brother had, yeah, but Cody could have prevented it.

Your fault, Cody.

He fisted his hands at his sides and reminded himself he was a cop now, a detective. He put bad guys in jail. He shouldn't be ashamed anymore.

"Hey?" Only an arm's length away from him now, she blinked at him, her gaze wide, and he didn't know what to do except stare.

Up close, her eyes were maybe a little greener than he remembered. A little smarter. Her lips a bit fuller. Her breasts a hell of a lot more—*you're staring at them, asshole!*

He brought himself up short and shook his head. "Hey."

She stared at him, her eyes teary as though she had expected more contact from him through the years, a better hello right now, and still he stood there and willed himself to grow cold against this woman. She wasn't the girl he'd lusted after as a teenage boy.

He imagined ice growing in his veins and that ice moving up to his heart. Nothing got to him, ever. He didn't feel, not after his parents had been brutally murdered. No feeling. Ice man. Ice cold on the inside. But that cracked when she beamed at him, and before he knew what the hell happened, she was hugging him like crazy and just like that it felt like she was squeezing his heart. "Welcome home, Cody."

Right then and there, she had him.

She.

Had.

Him.

But he'd be dead before he ever let her know.

ONE

Six years later

He was home early.

Megan Banks stole a peek out the window as the motor of his SUV shut off, and her breath seized in her throat when she caught a glimpse of him. There he was: the man of her dreams. Her every dream. Her every want.

Her eyes greedily took in his form as he stepped out of his car, the tailored cut of his suit molding to his broad shoulders, his muscles bulging under the fabric of his pants as he strolled over to the house. Cody.

Sensation spread down her thighs as she realized Cody would be here, in his room, any minute. And he'd see that she was here, too. Almost naked. *Oh, God.*

"Hellooo? Meg? *Meg*—you still there?"

The voice from her cell phone snapped her back to attention, and her heart began to thunder in her ears. "Yes! Yes, I'm still here. He's just pulled into his driveway. He'll walk in any minute."

"Okay, don't freak out and stick to the plan," her friend, Paige Rivers, voice of reason, said. "Just relax, look gorgeous, and whatever happens: Stick to the plan."

Oh my God, I'm really going through with this . . .

Megan's stomach twisted painfully. Her plan had been so simple, initially.

When she'd surveyed it in bed, alone, in the cloak of obscurity: simple.

When she'd driven on her way to his place: simple.

But it seemed so complicated and impossible now.

Her knuckles knotted painfully as she gripped her cell phone. "Remind me why I'm wearing only my bra and panties under my coat please," she hissed urgently. "Remind me why I'm doing this now, before he walks in through that door." *And I make a complete and total fool of myself.*

"You're seducing him," Paige said sternly, "because he won't."

"But if only I gave him a little more time—" Meg began.

"Time for what, Meg? You've been friends since you were kids and although you can't seem to date each other, neither of you dates anyone else."

"Still, that doesn't mean the plan is sound enough to—"

"Oh, it's sound all right. And it's happening—as soon as he comes in," Paige decreed.

A thick ball of nerves and emotion piled up in Megan's throat, and suddenly she wanted to wail at the injustices of the world.

There were a thousand reasons behind her seduction, but only one that made her hesitate. She wanted *him* to do it. Him, the man of her dreams, to break down, and seduce *her.* "But if he truly wanted me, he'd have done something about it already. I wouldn't need to break into his home dressed like a—I look like a slut, Paige!"

"Meg—I've *seen* the way he stares at you, and I'm surprised your hair hasn't caught fire yet. Can't you see why Cody's always protective toward you—he *wants* you. In some part of his labyrinth of a mind, he thinks you're *his.* But if the guy has some hang-ups about not being good enough for you, then you're going to have to show him you *don't care!*"

A pang of longing struck her as all the years of pent-up wanting washed over her. All those looks he gave her, all those smiles.

Did any of them mean anything other than friendship?

Every single night, Megan replayed the ways that cornflower blue gaze of his took her in. She wondered: Was that a little heat in his eyes today? Was his smile a little higher on one end? When he grazed my elbow with his, did he mean to? But if he did, why did he pull back?

And even when she was 99.9 percent certain she'd seen a spark of something wonderfully heated in his eyes, she would end up shaking her head in denial.

If he'd wanted her, a man like Cody would not hesitate. Not for an instant.

He was a leader, a charger by nature, a doer. One of the city's top homicide detectives and one that lived for the chase.

No. Cody Nordstrom was not one to stand by idly and let what he wanted get away. If he'd wanted her . . . *he'd have caught you long ago, Megan Banks.*

A weight of sadness settled over her shoulders at the

realization. "He doesn't want me, Paige. He thinks I'm still just a young girl. He'll always see me like that fourteen-year-old girl that walked in on . . ." No. Why, oh why, had she thought about that awful day right now?

"He won't see you as a little girl when he sees you naked, so stop with the pity party. Just take off your coat, seduce him, and let him come to terms with it later. Zach loves it when he comes home to find me partially dressed."

"But Zach's your husband," Meg countered.

"He didn't used to be," her friend shot back, and she hung up.

Right. Okay. She could do this. She was here already. Had successfully mastered some of the most difficult parts like "breaking in"—although, technically, the door had only needed a little nudge. Still, she was in his bedroom this evening and she was going to do it.

Megan Banks was going to seduce Cody Nordstrom. *Oh, God.*

Searching the trembling depths of herself for courage, she tossed both her coat and phone on the chair by the window and nervously ran her hands down her curly blond hair to make sure it wasn't sticking out or doing anything weird. *Six years—six years of being ignored—* and oh, yes, Megan had been counting ever since that day she'd seen him at the cemetery. She'd been counting every second since he'd returned.

Well—the counting ends tonight.

Listening for the front door and trying to stop her tummy from quaking, Megan waited, all the while trying not to imagine the enormity of what she was about to do, of what it would mean if she failed to seduce the tall, blond hunk who made her heart race, her mouth water, and her insides twist with unfulfilled desire.

She tried not to think that she'd rather the earth swallow her up if Cody didn't respond like she was hoping, praying, that he would.

Megan loved him.

She loved him so much that it ached most of the time.

She loved his hard-boned face. His cool personality. And the way his wide white smiles hid the somberness of his thoughts.

She loved his arresting features and his tanned hands, how big and thick those hands were, and how effortlessly he handled a gun with them.

She loved the way he dressed, and how his suits were always so dark and sharp and contrasted beautifully with the blond of his hair. And she loved those snowy white shirts that were at all times matched with a tie that would kick any other cops' ties' asses.

Most of all, she loved his stubbornness and his determination, and the way he protected her like she was the only thing the world had of value.

She thought of him day and night, and every evening prayed that one day, one day soon, those cool blue eyes that twinkled with humor when he teased her would become hot and dark with desire for her.

He'd looked at her like that before, like he wanted her, when they first met as teens.

His family had just moved in, and Megan had bumped into him as he helped unload their truck.

He had seemed stunned at his first sight of her, and he'd stared for what felt like minutes, all while keeping a big box balanced on his shoulders. Then he'd smiled crookedly and said, "I'm Cody," while an identical-looking fifteen-year-old with eyes not quite as intense stood looking on. He'd jerked his head toward that boy, too. "He's Ivan."

They were identical.

Except, maybe, the way they looked at her. One, with hot, friendly blue eyes. The other . . . with dull, shuttered ones.

"How can people tell you apart?" She'd surveyed them back then, trying to determine their differences.

But Cody had flashed her such an amazing smile, she felt like he—the one with the box and the gaze that made her toes curl—had just become the center of her universe. "That's the fun part: They can't."

He'd made her laugh that day. But when she introduced herself as their next door neighbor and offered him help unloading boxes, he'd shaken his tousled blond head and said, "Nah, we've got it. Thanks though."

But Megan had wanted to talk to him, could not make herself go home to her boring little room and her boring homework, so she'd grabbed a duffel anyway and helped lug it inside.

That had been the mark of their friendship.

Cody would always deny anything Megan offered, like he was too much of a gentleman to take something from her, but she always seemed to know what he really meant and gave it anyway. Then on that day long ago, they had walked into his house only to find Ivan . . .

The memory of the grisly scene made her heart stop. It had been surreal, like something out of a Freddy Krueger movie. Megan had been so shocked and appalled she'd just stood there as Cody brought himself to ask, to demand of his sixteen-year-old brother, *"What have you done!"*

She didn't cry that day. Not when she saw the motionless bodies, saw Ivan toss the weapon aside and break into a run. She didn't cry at the funeral of Cody's parents either.

But Megan Banks cried the day they took Cody away from her.

She kept each and every letter she received from him during the years, and sent back letters of her own that told him how scared she was at night—she was certain that his brother Ivan would do something horrible to her family, too.

For years the police had searched and failed to find him, but Cody vowed to her that *he* would.

But the years passed, the letters stopped coming, and one accidental day while at the cemetery, Megan found herself staring at the shiny blond head of that somber boy to whom she'd confessed her every fear and weakness. Except now he was a man, and he hardly seemed to remember her.

He didn't say much when she came over to say hi, but then it's not like she had much to say, either. Her heart had been fluttering so hard she could barely remember what she'd said, or what he'd said back, she only remembered how fast she'd been back in her car, alone, and brokenhearted.

He also seemed to be haunted by that event, for he appeared on her doorstep and said he had three things to tell her: He'd joined the Phoenix Police Department, he'd captured his parents' killer, and she didn't need to be scared anymore—he'd be around if she needed him.

If it's possible to lose your heart twice to the same person, then that was the second, and last, time, she fell in love with Cody Nordstrom.

But while her nightmares of murders were replaced by unsettling fantasies of her and Cody, the unsuspecting man of her dreams had been treating her like sister, friend, and nun for the past couple of years.

She'd been patiently waiting, wasting away the best years of her life while Cody saved the world from scumbags like his brother. She'd hoped that he would notice she wasn't a little girl anymore, but he never did, so tonight, she'd put it all out on the table and seduce him.

She nervously glanced down at herself—sexy red heels, sheer leopard thong, matching sheer leopard bra, hair perfectly mussed for that just-got-tumbled look—or in this case, tumble-me-now look—plus lip gloss that matched her stilettos . . . a total transformation from the usual cardigans and jeans with ballet flats.

Cody might not even realize it was her. *Oh, no, please please let him get turned on when he sees me.*

Meg backed from the bedroom door when she heard a sound downstairs, her heart pounding in anticipation, her palms sweating. The front door creaked and, just as quickly, slammed shut. She tensed when she heard him below—

"Megan?"

His voice. Deep and lush, even from afar it stroked her insides, the sensual baritone a warm caress to her very soul. Her heart skittered as she realized that parking a couple of houses away in order not to spoil the surprise had been a big mistake—the guy was a detective and he rarely missed a thing. Obviously while he'd been out there, surveying the streets before coming into the house, he'd spotted her Altima by the Ellisons' home.

Spurring herself into action, Megan quickly rushed

across the room and jumped on the bed, assuming a sexy pose.

"*Nice tie*," she would say when he appeared at the door, recalling a movie that happened to be a favorite of hers, but no no no, she always admired his ties and she should look for variety.

How about something forthright and sexy and innocent sounding. Something like, "Do you like my new panties, Cody?"

Her pulse skipped as she imagined seeing his eyes, blue as cornflowers, go dark with arousal when he realized she had transformed from the girl next door—literally—into a real woman. Laid out right on his bed for him to feast upon. Would he finally take a bite?

Her ears strained to hear his footsteps on the stairs, but seconds passed, and they didn't come.

Frowning, Megan stumbled out of bed as she heard puttering in the kitchen. She peered through the door, and saw lights from below. She also thought she heard the microwave. Great. Just perfect. She'd have to either go down there in her underwear, or put on her coat and get cooked in it while he stuffed himself, or just wait by the bed. As planned.

She went back to the bed, wondering if he'd sounded tired and not necessarily happy when he'd said her name. This was the first hour of his first day of a long-deserved vacation.

Should she have waited until tomorrow?

Or maybe never?

Maybe he's not happy, genius. Invasion of personal space and all that.

She frowned. Well, had he not left the door practically

open? A hardass detective like him, always leaving home on the rush, never locking up—was that even logical? Protect-the-others-while-I-happily-get-myself-killed was probably Cody Nordstrom's motto.

She sighed drearily and then readjusted herself along the length of the mattress, plumped up his pillow behind her head and tried to relax.

Cody was far from perfect—under every joke lay a troubled man.

But her troubled little body just adored her troubled man, and she'd like to think that she understood him better than most.

He felt responsible for what his brother did all those years ago, and because of that, Cody didn't know that he was a higher caliber man than most.

He was one of the best homicide detectives the force had ever seen, but when it came to his personal life, he could stare at something and just not see what stood before him. Now, Megan would do anything to finally be seen. Even strip.

Be sexy, she thought as she stretched out over the bed in a way she hoped would flatter what she considered her plain, none-too-curvy figure.

She was dying for him to get up here and let her put his rough-hewn, pretty-boy, Armani-ad face between her hands and kiss those lips she dreamed about for the first time, when she heard *squeeeeeach* from the closet door.

Frowning, Megan raised her head and sat up straighter, when a flash of movement in the shadowed interior caught her eye.

Her heart stopped. The fear was so overwhelming that it paralyzed her. Ice started to build, chilling her skin, her

hands, her feet, her brain. Once again, she became statu-
esque as a shockingly familiar face materialized.

Lungs burning for air that could not make it past
her throat, Megan stared into the darkness, a part of
her numbed mind screaming at her to move, do something, because *someone was staring back at her*.

She had been so wound up in her plan, she had not
realized she was not alone. Something was inside Cody's
room. Something, some monster, seemed to have been
waiting, had been watching her, intent on doing—what?

An image of fifteen years ago, of Cody's brother
standing over his parents' dead bodies, assailed her, and
like she had back then, she remained frozen with fear as
the figure stepped out of the shadows.

Panic gripped her by the throat, blocking out the
commands of her mind for her to run run run, overpow-
ering her so that she could do nothing, think nothing,
only see him coming . . .

"No," she croaked helplessly, starting to scramble
back against the headboard.

"Shhhhh," he said, and the fact that he was speaking
to her only alarmed her further.

She'd never been so scared in her life. Not even that
time long ago, because that time she'd been a girl, and
at first she'd thought that what she'd witnessed was a
dream. Now she knew for a fact that some little boys did
kill their parents.

She knew that the man she had grown to love spent his
days hunting down the scum of the earth, all of whom
had taken someone's life, just like his brother.

Life was not pink anymore in her eyes, and it had not
been pink for a long, long time . . . this shadow . . . this

criminal . . . coming toward her was REAL. He was real and he was closer and he was talking to her!

Her every nightmare, her nightmare of being murdered, of dying a stupid virgin, was real.

Suddenly fear kicked instinct into action. She opened her mouth wide, panic and fear tangling together for a voice, tumbling to form a big, loud "HEELP MEEE!!!" that the entire world would be able to hear, or at the very least, Cody, her hero, but a black rag came over her nose, and she had no time to scream.

TWO

"Meg?"

Cody rubbed the tension in the back of his neck as he waited for the microwave to ping, then he scanned the staircase, expecting Megan to appear, her clover-green eyes bright and excited as she came up with an explanation—and it had to be a *good one*—for breaking and entering into his home.

He knew himself well enough to know that he'd glower at her only for a minute—or perhaps a couple of minutes more because, dammit, she could've gotten hurt! Plus where the hell did she learn how to pick locks? Especially his state-of-the-art locks?

Then again, Megan Banks was the kind of woman who always surprised a man, and he knew that even if he glowered for a whole damned hour, as soon as she flashed one of those pearly white smiles, he'd be done for.

Heck, he might as well just give her a key so she could come in and make herself at home whenever she'd like to. *You wish, don't you, asshole? Come home to her for a nice warm meal, a long, wet kiss, and then it's upstairs together to make a couple of babies.*

His treacherous blood began to boil at the thought. Yeah, Megan was the kind of girl any man would kill for. Would travel worlds just to be able to come home to. The kind of girl for whom any man would spend a lifetime doing hero work, putting scumbags in jail, just so a girl like her could sleep at night.

The kind of girl Cody would never, *ever*, touch with his callused, bloodied hands.

Since the night of his parents' murder, Cody knew that he would never get married. He would never get the girl, the kids, the dog, or the happily ever after.

He would get the killers.

There were always casualties in a story, and his personal life would be one of them.

It seemed a small sacrifice at the time, in exchange for justice and capturing his parents' murderer. Now, the criminal—his brother—was behind bars, and although he hadn't gotten the death penalty due to his being a minor at the time of the crime, the bastard had gotten life. Which was mighty fine with Cody.

And yet Cody's thirst for justice was still not appeased. He needed new cases, tougher cases, meaner criminals, all to keep his head buried so deep in work, he wouldn't think of what he'd lost in the blink of an eye. With one bad call. One bad day.

He heard footsteps up in his bedroom, and he cocked his head as he pictured Megan coming down the stairs, doing that hip-swing thing she did that drove him crazy. His eyebrows furrowed when she took her goddamned time. What in the hell was she doing up there? Wrestling?

"Megan?" he growled, annoyed.

Ding.

He ignored the microwave when a thump was followed by an eerie silence, and a chilling premonition slid up the back of his neck. His hackles rose. Legs tensing as his blood began to pump faster through his veins, he yanked his Glock out of its hip holster and climbed the stairs, two at a time, silent as death.

All was quiet upstairs—unnaturally quiet. Not natural, when Megan was around, for things to be still for more than a second. *If she gets hurt . . .* He pushed the thought aside, narrowed his eyes and scanned the hallway, dark at this time of night.

A window screeched from the guest bedroom, but it had been the master bedroom where he'd heard the noise, and it was from that direction that he heard a soft moan.

He parted the door and peered into the darkness, gun carefully doing a one-eighty-degree turn. "Megan?"

Again, that damned tickle in the back of his neck. It had happened far too many times to ignore. Something was wrong. Megan wasn't answering.

The moan became louder, as if pained. He hit the light switch and he saw, sprawled over his duvet and pillows, a little bundle of flawless white skin and loose honey-wheat hair.

"Megan?"

He froze one step into his bedroom, and his cock shot up like steel. *Holy Mother of God, I'm not seeing what I'm seeing.*

But he was.

Megan. With skin that looked air-brushed and sweet. Hair you could wrap yourself in. Sweet little Megan was in his bed—wearing the cutest, sexiest, out-of-this-world outfit.

His heart pounded as his mouth watered, and for this moment, this one moment, he didn't wonder what she was doing there. It felt like she belonged there, like every time he had dreamed her there had summoned her to do it for real. Make his every wet dream come true.

He pulled his eyes away, off her chest—a chest he wanted to taste with his tongue—no, he didn't just think that, fuck, this was Megan! Meg, dammit, not some bimbo, and he glanced up, swallowing thickly.

His voice came out raspy, and what he said made not one lick of sense. "That's my bed you're in."

She stared at him with those big, wide, green eyes, and he stared back. No, he wasn't staring, he was *gawking* like a stupid idiot, like a complete moronic idiot with his gun still in his hand, but he couldn't stop. He had worked on his discipline, for twenty years he had worked like a dog to one day be able to forget what the monster inside him was capable of doing, but damned if this girl didn't tempt him.

She moved, a sinewy undulation like a ribbon being made into a twist, and when she kicked her legs, more of her perfect, nearly-nude body became exposed.

His gun trembled in his hand as he slowly put it back in its holster, but he could not tear his eyes away from that shadowed valley between her legs, a V of curls glistening dark under the sheer leopard print of her panties.

Greedily, he took in the length of her toned thighs, down to her slim, creamy white ankles, and his blood rushed through his veins as he imagined . . . imagined what it would be like with *her*. With the one woman he'd sworn to himself to never touch.

And the only one you've ever wanted.

She moaned, softly, the sound sexy and making a growl get trapped in his throat as he fisted his hands at his sides and reined himself back, locked his legs in place. And then it finally registered that she did not seem happy, that the moisture shining in her eyes wasn't desire, but tears.

Another muffled sound came, and he noticed her mouth was not moving as she spoke, and she was . . . struggling in her binds? *Binds?*

"What the hell?" He took a step closer and his heart sputtered when he saw the words scrawled on dark red marker on her navel. A name. *His* name all over her perfect skin. One for every year he'd served in jail . . .

IVAN IVAN IVAN IVAN IVAN IVAN IVAN.

But Ivan was locked up.

Cody had *locked up* his own brother.

The kid he'd protected when he was young.

Against his every raging instinct to protect his own kin, he had trained like a mad man. He'd chased him for years, in his dreams and fantasies, and later, for real, so that he could have the pleasure of finding him, catching him, and locking him in.

And he had.

He had come back to Phoenix, hell on Earth, if you asked him, and he had the bastard convicted for their parents' murder—even though evidence had been scarce, he'd still managed to prove him guilty. And yet now . . . his name was written on Megan's body. How the fuck was that even possible?

Never, in his life, had he ever felt this all-consuming frustration, except the time he'd seen his parents lying sightless in a pool of their own blood.

His eyes flew up to Megan's tear-filled ones, while an icy rage hardened his veins until the cold of Antarctica would've seemed like a warm summer. "Who did this?" he demanded, pulling—there was no easy way of doing this—at the clear packing tape that covered her mouth.

She gasped for air and Cody yanked out his knife and cut her binds with two swift moves, listening for any strange sounds other than the wild pounding of his own heartbeat and Megan struggling for words.

Instantly his senses became alert, ears, mind, eyes, all over the house, for he could still be there. The bastard could still be in the house. He had an urge to chase him, but first he pulled her up and checked her pulse, and stared into her wide, scared, tear-streaked eyes.

With a quick check he realized she was breathing, gazing up at him with a strange expression of disappointment and fear in her face. When she opened her mouth to speak, he was about to tell her to "save it" when he heard them, footsteps racing down the stairs, and his insides kicked into overdrive.

Fury, red hot and scalding, poured over his veins, and before he knew it he was on his feet, kicking open doors of the other rooms, running down the stairs, outside, gun drawn as he chased—he didn't know who he was chasing, he was chasing something, some bastard he had to catch and beat down to a pulp.

Who? Ivan was in jail—what bastard dared come into his home and leave a message with Megan? *Megan*. His one weakness. The one person in this world who could make Cody forget about justice, the law, and common sense.

In some cases, when a man loves a woman, he takes her in his arms.

But in his case, if he loves a woman, he stays the hell away from her—and that was exactly what Cody had done his whole life.

Megan had seen death at an age when all girls her age only saw balloons and flowers and sun. The killer she saw wore Cody's same goddamned face, which was enough to disgust anyone.

He had spent his life with one mission: to protect her, to keep an eye out for her, to make amends. To make sure that she never again in her life had to see an ounce of injustice go unpunished, never see more darkness than what she'd seen that day with him. He had been her friend because that was all he could be, when many nights he had wondered who was her lover.

He had even prayed that if Megan ever decided to marry some nice respectable guy who added numbers for a living, Cody would be transferred to Timbuktu or some other faraway place where he never had to watch her with him. He had done all this—everything—for her. And some crazed man had touched her, hurt her, in his own home, under his very own nose.

Someone who wants to fuck with your head . . . who knows how much she means to you . . .

He pushed the unsettling thought away and after one final scan of the guiet neighborhood, he went back, climbed up the stairs, and yanked out his cell phone in annoyance while it rang its little buzzer off. He picked up with a growl.

"Nordstrom, bad news." His partner, Zach. Like he ever called with good news.

"What is it?" he said in exasperation, storming back into his room. "I'm kind of busy here, man."

He glanced at Megan across the room, on the floor now, shivering, beautiful, vulnerable, and he wanted to howl at the moon, a call to all the desert wolves to come out and have this perpetrator for dinner.

"You're not going to like it when I tell you he's escaped," Zach warned in his ear.

Nordstrom's entire frame tensed. "Excuse me?"

"Ivan." The word came out like a death sentence, and then came the hammer: "He's out."

THREE

Megan tried to get dressed for the third time, but her fingers were cramped, and she couldn't seem to make them work.

She felt like she was wafting in a dream, but not her sexy, delicious, making-love-to-Cody dream, but one where a bad man came in and . . . what had he done to her?

She glanced down at her body, swallowed back the bile when she read the message he'd written on her skin. She wadded the sleeve of her coat and spat on it, then gritted her teeth from the effort it took to try to erase the words.

Still unable to resume her normal pattern of breathing, she didn't hear Cody's footsteps until he was back in the room, standing at the door with a wild look in his eyes.

Her heart could not handle much more of this, but even now, it responded to his utter virility by giving a vigorous kick. He stood there, all ripped, marked, and pissed, and she realized in the working part of her brain that she had never seen him so enraged. He might not be pacing, or ranting, but that was *not* how Cody raged. No. Control was his weapon, and he never lost it.

Jaw so tight she feared it would crack under the pressure, he surveyed the room as though for clues. His eyes glimmered murder.

"I'm okay," she said softly as soon as he pushed his cell phone back into his suit pocket.

His striking blue eyes settled on her. Time stopped as he searched her face, the muscles of his temples slowly working. Her heart stuttered when he then began his inspection of her body.

With soul-searing slowness, narrowed blue eyes trailed, totally unreadable, down the length of her almost naked form then dragged back to meet her startled stare. Their gazes held for a long, electric moment, and Cody's eyes flashed so bright, the light was almost unholy.

What did she see there? Was it . . . God, was it hunger?

Feeling avalanches in her tummy, Megan licked her lips and refused to be the first to look away. Impossible, but Cody was looking at her as if—as if he were imagining—

No.

Whatever emotion glowed in his eyes, it was swiftly concealed, tightening the muscles of his face. Cody seemed to recall who she was, and what had happened here this evening.

"I want to know," he said in the lowest, most threatening voice ever, "why a puke slime of a bastard had you tied up to my bed, why *you* didn't seem to be wearing any clothing save for—" in three seconds he'd covered the space to her, and in one more, he was raising her lonely little coat up to his line of vision—"this one coat, and I really, really want to know who that bastard was and what he has to do with my *sick ass of a brother*!"

She blinked. Her head must have gotten banged, because Cody Nordstrom never lost his cool. Never, ever. But now he didn't sound all that much in control. He didn't sound like a detective, asking cool questions. He sounded almost, almost, like a jealous husband.

Not the smartest thing, she knew, but it turned her on. It really turned her on, the way he was on the verge of losing control. Nordstrom was a master of appearances, of control, always outwardly cool, outwardly composed, but now—her nipples pricked in excitement and even though it wasn't the moment, her body didn't care.

After being so scared, her hormones were raging, she was on overdrive, over-sensitized. The place between her legs clenched with wanting. The adrenaline coursing through her veins seemed to have summoned other hormones into play, and she was aching everywhere. She wanted to be touched. Held.

Suddenly sexual frustration and fear needed some outlet, and she trembled with the need for release.

Seething with another kind of tumultuous energy, Cody set her coat on the bed, opened his chest of drawers, and yanked out a folded white shirt. Immediately he brought it to her, lowering his voice as he offered it for her to wear. "Did you see his face?"

"He was wearing some kind of hood," she murmured, cradling his shirt to her chest, trying not to think of how good it smelled.

Cody glanced over at the window and restlessly plunged a hand through his blond hair. He wiped the back of his mouth and then yanked open the closet door, inspecting for differences inside.

"Perp was hiding here when you came in?"

She nodded.

He traced the steps to the bed, the exact same steps the man had taken. She didn't know how he knew, but she was glad she didn't have to explain the events that had transpired here, word for word.

"Was there a struggle?" he inquired, his brows furrowed. God, he was so handsome when he was all business.

Megan tried to remember what happened but only recalled the hands, the stench, the blackness that had enveloped her. She was still breathing loudly, and for the first time, she realized, so was Cody. The discovery brought a fresh pang of longing to her heart.

She'd imagined how they would sound, their breaths, as they made love.

Now she wanted to die when she realized she'd never find out.

This had been such a bad idea. She was such a needy, foolish little slut, she wanted to whack herself with a stick.

When she'd been tied on the bed, afraid, and had seen Cody, a little part of her had still gotten aroused. For a nanosecond, she hadn't wanted him to set her free. She'd wanted him to take her. Like that. Caught and trapped, take her, all of her.

But he didn't. He hadn't.

He was so obsessed with protecting her, he never would, which was the saddest thing of all.

Cody sighed and came over. "Tell me what happened, Meg."

His delicious scent teased her nostrils as he dropped down beside her and it made her want to erase that horrible name from her skin, made her want to forget the past hour entirely.

She furiously scraped the first I, but Cody caught her hands, stilling their movements. Her lashes rose, and their gazes held. He squeezed her fingers in reassurance, and the exquisite contact made her shiver with need. Solid. Warm. That was what his touch felt like. *What I've always wanted.*

She surveyed his expression, but there was no lust in his eyes, only anger. "Don't scrape it off yet—" He urged her into his shirt and his face hardened, his jaw tightened as he explained, "Evidence."

He gazed at her stomach with indecipherable eyes, but when he lifted his hand to trace her chin with the pad of his thumb, the touch was sensual. Lush. Sexual.

As the adrenaline left her body, something else arrived in its stead, something hot and wanting.

She caught her breath as he lowered his hand and, with that same callused thumb, grazed his brother's name on her navel.

"Is it tender, does it hurt?" he asked in a low voice.

She didn't know how to interpret the gruff emotion there, but his timbre wasn't cold, and she knew that he was not unaffected. Was it her nearness that made him seem on edge? Unlike himself?

No. It was the fact that she had his brother's name over her underwear.

"It's sensitive," she admitted, just a whisper at the blond top of his head. *Sensitive because you're touching it.*

His finger trailed the last word, and then stopped, somehow, at the edge of her leopard panties. She felt so stupid all of a sudden, like this, with his shirt hanging at her sides, her red heels, her failed plan. She'd dressed for the perfect evening to seduce the man of her dreams, and instead, another man had seen her. Another man had tied her to Cody's bed, and it had not been the man she wanted, nor quite in the way she'd dreamed.

She shuddered involuntarily, feeling vulnerable.

He sat back and stared at her beneath his eyebrows, his golden-tipped lashes so heavy his eyes appeared slits now.

His voice became so rough it scraped through her like sandpaper. "What the hell were you doing here dressed like this?" he murmured, pinning her on the spot with a penetrating stare.

She wanted to tell him the truth, and at the same time, she was still chicken enough to want to lie and say that she *had* been dressed and all her misery tonight was that criminal's fault! But Cody was a detective, and he'd know it was a lie. There were no womanly clothes scattered about, and at the moment, she feared that he was already realizing that her being in a panty and bra had been deliberate.

She could see, by the way he slowed down his breathing, the way he did not look up while he was composing himself, that it was just dawning on him why she had come here. Tonight. For him.

"I'm going to assume," he said, and cleared his throat when his voice got too thick to speak, "that your state of undress was a one-time thing, not to happen again?"

He raised his eyes, and, was there disappointment there? Or, God, *please don't let it be pity.*

Megan flicked her eyes down at his tie, unable to look at him, her dearest friend, the man she wanted.

"I wanted to show you my acquisition, all right? No big deal." She had to say that. Just had to save face somehow.

His brows flew upward, and he almost coughed. "You wanted me to see the underwear you bought?"

"You're my friend, aren't you?" she countered.

He looked flabbergasted, his mouth hanging open for a moment. "I happen to know shit about women's underwear!"

She said nothing, and Cody glanced at the door, then back at her. Slowly, as though he feared he would detonate with a touch, he set a big, cautious hand on her shoulder, and his voice went raspier by the second. "Aren't women supposed to wear that kind of thing to their dates?"

Because she still wouldn't look at him, and he continued touching her shoulder, a touch she was sure was not meant to be sensual but *was*, her blood sang—and this feeling of being alive after thinking she would die was exhilarating.

Megan wanted to wrap her arms around his thick neck, draw his plush lips against hers and bite and lick them. She was about to just kiss him, throw caution to the wind, when he asked, with a gentle squeeze, "Did he hurt you?"

This time he did not allow her silence, but tipped her head back until she answered,

"No. He—he put a rag over my nose, and I blacked out. That asshole!" she exploded.

Suddenly furious at herself, at the criminal, hell, at *Cody,* she stood and tossed Cody's shirt aside, angrily pushing her arms into her coat. It had been an awful idea, to come here. Awful.

This sick intruder had ruined her perfect evening. He'd ruined the rest of her life! Now when was she going to gather the courage to try this again? Damn him. And damn Cody for acting like a detective when what she needed was . . . *what you need is to leave, Megan Banks!*

"Whoa there, where do you think you're going?"

When Cody pulled out a camera—no doubt intending to take pictures of the "evidence" on her stomach—Megan closed her trench coat tight, knotted the belt around her waist, and shot him a scowl that could melt an ice pyramid. "Put that thing away. Last thing I heard, you needed to be dead to become one of your cases!"

"Meg," Cody stopped her, his forehead creased in annoyance, "I understand you're in shock and want to submerge yourself in hot water so there's not a mark left on you, and I promise you when it's time for you to leave, I'll be the first to drive you home and scrub it off. But I'm afraid the procedure—"

And for the first time since they'd known each other, Megan let Cody know what she thought of him and his rules and procedures. She went around him, and from the door, said, "*Fuck* the procedure!"

It took Cody five seconds to register, digest, and act upon Megan's parting words.

And no, he never, ever, fucked with his procedures. Or, okay, almost never.

He caught up with her on the stairs, his grip firm on her elbow. "Next time you invite me over for Christmas, I'm going to tell your mama all about that mouth of yours and all the words it can say. But for now, you're going to put it to good use and tell me exactly what happened."

Megan pulled away and jumped the remaining two steps to the first floor, then whirled around and shot him an acid smile. "I'm not saying another word to you, so arrest me if you must."

She slammed the front door in his face, an inch away from his nose, and Cody was really, really reaching the end of his patience here.

Suddenly it dawned on him that Megan was the worst victim, the worst damned witness, Cody had encountered in all his years at the force. He yanked the door open.

"Megan Banks! I represent the law, and as a representative of the law, it's in *your* best interest that *I* remain informed—if we screw up the evidence you screw with your chances in court. Now get back here and talk, dammit."

She stormed back, but she was fuming. "I can't believe all you care about is taking pictures of his . . . argh, forget it." She poked a finger into his chest, her cheeks flaming bright red in fury. "But next time a woman gets accosted in your bedroom, do yourself a favor and drop the questions, ditch the stupid camera, and just *hug her*, you idiot!"

She dashed across the street.

"Goddamit, Meg!"

He chased two steps after her, then he stopped, torn between staying put for the team he'd summoned to arrive or following her. His male instinct said follow her. Chase her down and then—no, he wouldn't pursue that train of thought.

Procedure told him to remain on the scene. He could gather the evidence himself, but that meant paperwork and a whole lot of trouble for a case that may or may not be treated with the importance it was due.

No. Damn procedure—this was one time when Cody had to trust his instincts. He could arrest the little chit for jaywalking but she knew damned well he wouldn't do that. Maybe he should show her that he had the balls to—oh yeah, he had the balls all right. But she had them in her tight little grip, damn it.

Charging up the stairs for what he needed, he determined that this invasion of his home, his girl, was personal. If that murdering sonofabitch Ivan was out, then yeah, it was personal.

Nordstrom had a vacation week, but he had not even planned to rest. He had, by circumstances and tragedy, become filthy rich—so Cody didn't need to work to make a living.

He'd inherited his mother's money, substantial from the sales of some produce farms down in Texas, and his father's savings, which had amounted to a couple of million. He didn't need to work to live; but he needed to work to feel alive.

Nobody could give him back his father or mother. Nothing could give him back all the time he'd lost, all the mistakes he'd made, not even all the millions the family had in the bank. And no matter how many cases he nailed, or how many women he took to bed instead of one, he felt empty, discontent, like fucking shit. But at least now he had a purpose.

Get that motherfucker once and for all.

He might even relish the chase, if he hadn't messed with Megan tonight.

A sinking feeling settled in the pit of his stomach as

he remembered her words. "Next time just hug her, you idiot!"

Megan.

If I hug you I'll lose control.

No. He wouldn't hug her. But he'd die before another guy ever set a finger on her.

Heart pumping as adrenaline rushed through his veins, he grabbed his duffel with his spare guns, his knives, a set of extra clothes, passport, cell phones, laptop, and then drove like a shot over to her home, only a few minutes away. He called her cell phone the whole ten minutes it took him to get ready, leaving three messages ranging from, "Meg, call me, you're in danger," to, "Meg, pack your bags. I'm on my way."

He checked the perimeter of her home as he arrived, then rang the doorbell three times. Relief assailed him when she called out through the intercom, "Who is it?"

"The damned hug patrol, come on! Open up."

Meg opened, and for a moment he lost his breath, for the moonlight cast her face in an almost angelic glow. The flaring streetlights seemed to work entirely in her favor, casting a captivating shine to the lighter streaks of her hair, damp from a recent shower. The scent of peach shampoo drifted to his nostrils.

She still smelled like his childhood. And she looked like his dreams. Her hair was perfectly combed back, all wet and slick. The perfect symmetry of her face, the innocence in her eyes. She looked . . . like a goddess.

Like a virgin goddess that you could never have, never touch.

But he could protect her.

He could try to make up for what she'd seen, try to

make sure no crazed fuck ever got near her. She would never know he loved her. He loved her so badly his gut ached.

A raging thirst to drink from her mouth consumed him. A rampant hunger to bite her skin and taste how soft and sweet it was. *Calm the monster, calm the fucking monster—now.*

Her blond curls were springing as she shook her head. "I'm not home."

He cocked a brow. Oh, so she was pissed at him? Why? For doing his goddamned job? "All right then, can I leave a message for you?" he asked dryly.

She shrugged and stared down at her nails, suddenly engrossed.

"Pack your bags, Meg. You're coming with me. If you have anything to say about it, you can say it in the car."

She stared at him blankly for a moment, and then she pulled the door open wider, where—aha!

There sat her bags on the foyer medallion behind her.

So she *had* been listening to his messages after all.

"You didn't think I was staying alone here with Mom and Dad out of town and a killer on the loose, did you?" she asked, her lips curving into a mischievous smile.

Cody flung his arms up in the air. "At last, the woman starts to make sense!"

"I'm sorry I lost it back there, Cody," she murmured, grabbing the smaller bag as he went for the bigger suitcase. "I'm sorry I didn't pick up my phone, I was in the bathroom. I just needed to get that . . . name . . . off me. This was just not how I pictured my Friday night," she added sadly.

Cody's jaw clenched. "Yeah, well, I'm sorry I let you go off like that. You could be in danger, Meg. From now on, you're either with me or with a cop of my designation, but not alone, you *got* that?" He tossed both suitcases into the trunk of his SUV and slammed it shut for emphasis.

Padding out behind him after locking up, Meg leaned against the passenger door, watching him as he came back around, her arms crossed under her breasts. "You know, Cody, you don't have to look so satisfied; I wasn't going to knock on your door tonight. I did that earlier, and it didn't go so well, remember?"

He opened the door for her. "I'm sorry." It came out just a gruff whisper.

"Sorry I erased the evidence?" She plopped down on the seat and pulled her sweater an inch above her belly button, enough to let him see her cleaned navel, enough to make his eyes bulge and leave him salivating with the door in his hand and aching to look at more.

"I'm sorry, shit happens."

And he was. Guilt assailed him as he climbed in behind the wheel. *It's always your fault, moron. You get everyone around you killed. You're jinxed. Cursed.* And if he were smart about it, he should go deposit Megan somewhere where she would be safe.

Megan noticed the gun bag in the backseat. "I thought you were on vacation."

"I'm never on vacation, I only pretend to be on vacation." He geared up the car and pulled into the traffic, heading to his partner's home. The only place he knew she'd be safe tonight.

"Where are you taking me?" she asked.

She sounded serene, but somehow, hopeful. In fact, she sounded like a young bride asking the groom whether he'd booked the Ritz Carlton or the Four Seasons. And of course he was the shithead who got to tell her he'd

booked *neither.* "I'm taking you to Zach's, you can stay
the night with them."

The shine in her eyes died an abrupt death. "Oh." She
stared out the window and he wished he could see her
expression. When she spoke, her voice was devoid of all
emotion. "So you called your partner, because . . . ?"

"Because Zach can protect you while Paige enter-
tains you with baby talk."

She shot him a withering glance. "Why doesn't Zach
handle this, then? You stay with me and *you* can entertain me with caveman talk. You're supposed to be on
vacation anyway."

"Zach's home wasn't broken into. His girl—" He broke
off, shook his head. "He's homicide—and this bastard's
not dead yet. Not until I'm through with him. I'm the one
who needs to find him."

"You did not just call me your girl," she said, incred-
ulous.

"No, I did not," he snapped. "But you're my responsibility, especially now, since the bastard escaped from
prison."

"He did? When?" Her eyes widened to saucers.

"Couple of hours ago—tops. I know I don't need to tell
you he's *my responsibility,* and I want you out of this, as
far away as possible. Understand?"

He'd already touched her today, frightened her, and
the memory made Cody feel like a loaded grenade, about
to explode.

He clenched his hands on the wheel, fury and jealousy blurring his vision so hard he had to slow down in
order to avoid a collision.

Probably sensing that, Meg softened her voice. "Ivan

wouldn't hurt me, Cody, not really. He always liked me," she said.

"I'll bet that's what my mother said." The memory of her sweet face always defending him to their dad made him angrier. "Ivan doesn't like anyone."

He couldn't have, not anymore, not really. Hell could not get scarier than his brother. Sick. Perverted. Hurt. Lonely.

"He can't know the meaning of the words like or love," Cody snarled. "People like him have people like you for lunch, Meg."

"Well, Paige won't have me staying over, I know she won't. She'll . . . she'll feel I'm much safer with you." Megan smiled, but Cody didn't.

He surveyed her with a bit of puzzlement, and she looked away with an attractive blush, staring straight ahead with an odd expression, one of determination and conspiracy. He didn't know what she was plotting in her head, or what she and Paige had ever said about him, all he knew was that she was wrong.

You're not safe with me anymore. You never have been.

When he'd left Phoenix, he'd thought the violence, the blood, evidence of a sick and twisted gene pool, would have wiped the stars out of Megan's eyes, but the truth was, he still lived for a glimpse of the looks she gave him.

Maybe Ivan had been born a monster, but it was Cody who'd kept him from being caged. It was all his fault. Long before the murder, Cody should have told his parents that Ivan beheaded squirrels in the backyard. He should have put in more of an effort to stop him.

But no, he had been too consumed with his crush to see straight. Too consumed fantasizing about the blond, curly-haired fourteen-year-old neighbor. His judgment would not be clouded again.

But dammit, what was he supposed to do with her?

His concentration was out of whack and her nearness wasn't helping. Every damned second he remembered her: tied in his bed, with those beautiful breasts, that perfect skin.

Was she the kind of woman who enjoyed being tied up, under other circumstances? Did those moans she let out sound the same, when she emitted them with pleasure? His cock pushed up so hard into his pants he could barely sit straight.

Okay, so she didn't want to go over to Zach's, but he didn't want to bring her along on his hunt either. Bringing her along was wrong on so many levels he wasn't even going to get into them. And yet: Another man might do a better job keeping his hands off her, but no one would give his life for hers the way Cody would.

"Cody? It really was him, wasn't it?"

Cody shot her a sidelong glance, wanting to deny that the man who'd tied her to the bed had any links to him. Wanting to deny that he had shared a womb, a childhood, shared a family name, with that man.

He couldn't. And found himself nodding grimly. "In all probability, yes, it was him."

He saw her fear, her uncertainty, drain the color from her normally rosy skin. She could've been sedated if the cloth had a hallucinogen, which meant she could've seen all kinds of things that weren't real, and all kinds that were. She had had nightmares about him for years.

Every night when she closed her eyes, she told him, she saw Ivan. It killed him that he wasn't there to comfort her; he almost sickly wished she'd have those nightmares again so he could be there, coo her back to sleep, hold her for security, make love to make her forget.

That she would see that criminal's face, that he would be the first thing a woman like her thought about when she woke up, and the last thing in her mind when she went to sleep, enraged and obsessed him. It was unfair, and it made him angry to the point it pissed him off to even think it might be jealousy, even though he didn't want it to be.

"You know what he's after, right?" He swerved to the right and pushed the pedal, ramming the car deeper into traffic.

Her curls bounced as she shook her head. "After all this time? I don't know." Turning in her seat, she reached out and ran her hand over his arm—a touch, then gone. He felt it everywhere. In his chest, his stomach, his balls. He wanted to hold on to her, pull that hand back, put it everywhere at once. "Tell me," she urged softly.

Cody laughed a dark, humorless laugh. Tell her? What? That he was a monster? That at night he imagined he rutted with her until they both passed out? That her most insignificant touch or smile aroused the socks off him . . . or that it was his fault?

There was so much she didn't know.

How both Nordstroms had had crushes on her. How both would stare at her, fantasize about her. How Cody and Ivan had made a brother's bet, that whoever took her virginity would keep her.

The next day, Cody had made a move, certain this was one bet he couldn't bear to lose. He'd bragged to

Ivan, "She's agreed to go for a walk with me after school, so I'm going to win."

And Ivan hadn't liked it. "Yeah?" he'd said. "If you take something I love away from me, I'm going to take something you love away, too."

Cody hadn't listened, hadn't cared about his brother's threats. All he'd cared about was winning, winning *her*, making sure she would be his and not his brother's. He'd been determined to claim her. Being a teenaged idiot, he'd had raging hormones twenty-four hours of the day and he'd planned to expend them all inside of her that afternoon during their picnic in the woods.

Never mind he hadn't gone through with it, had changed his mind and led her back home to walk in on that nightmare of a scene. Never mind that after the murder he could never bring himself to touch her, take her, like he once dreamed of.

But they hadn't, and now they never would. They weren't minors anymore, but Megan Banks was more unreachable to him than ever.

If Cody touched Megan, it meant Ivan won. It meant that motherfucker knew Cody's weakness and had made him go caveman on the one woman he cared about.

No. He'd never touch her. Ever.

Which was why his life sucked like blue balls.

If given a choice to be born again, in all likelihood Cody would say no just to keep his brother from coming into the world along with him. But then who would watch over Megan?

"Meg," he said, softly. "He's after *you*."

FOUR

"Why are we here?"

Meg glanced around the abandoned front yard of what used to be the Nordstroms' old home, her skin crawling as Cody kicked the front door open.

"Detour," he said, and crooked his finger so that she followed.

At her refusal to be dumped at Zach and Paige's home, Cody had driven all night, stopped by his office for paperwork, coffee at midnight, and in between errands, Meg had dozed on and off.

When she woke up it was 6:29 in the morning, the sun was beginning to light the empty streets, and they were back in a neighborhood her family had sworn never to return to.

Swallowing a lump of fear, Megan cautiously stepped inside, surveying the place in horror while Cody inspected the rotting wood beams above.

My God, it seemed like nothing could have ever

thrived here. No evidence of life remained. The furniture was mostly gone, and what remained contained layers and layers of dust and maybe termites. The marble floor was cracked and uneven, making walking a hazard.

Assailed by a wave of pity as she remembered the once-cozy ambience of this household, Meg dragged her fingers over the dusty dining room table surface, then she recalled Ivan's face across the table, young and predatory at sixteen and gazing at her as if she were lunch, and she yanked her hand back. "Are you looking for something in particular?" she asked Cody's broad back.

"I always come here when I need to think."

She didn't imagine it; there was wistfulness in his tone, and it made her feel incredibly sad.

Standing here, while a truckful of memories threatened to burst through her walls of forgetfulness, Megan wondered how Cody could possibly bear it. Come here to "think" and at the same time, confront the horrors that had happened here. And it *had* been horrifying. *Don't think about it*, she thought frantically as she felt herself grow faint.

But an image of Ivan standing over the bodies, bloodied and screaming as he continued hacking away at their flesh, flashed through her mind, and her blood froze in her veins. "You don't think he would be here, too, would he?" she squeaked in sudden fear, rushing up to stand close to him. Suddenly she had the distinct sensation of being watched. The hair all along her arms rose to attention, and her heart began to thunder.

Oh, God, he was watching.

"Not sure he'd risk coming here."

Calm and cool as ever, Cody crossed the cluttered length of the old kitchen, then went to check the glass

doors that led to the back yard. As he checked for the
kind of stuff detectives always check for, he said, without looking up, "You'd be amazed how many cases crack
open with the most stupid mistakes—criminals returning to the scene of the crime, that sort of thing." He
straightened and pulled a fistful of hair in apparent frustration, and when he let go, part of his hair remained
standing up so adorably, making him look so handsome
and irresistible, that she felt her fear begin to ebb away.
"What I want to figure out is where this bastard's hiding," he admitted.

*And what I'd like to figure out is what a girl needs to
do to make you notice her.*

His face was so virile, Cody would make the perfect
Armani model. And with that killer tie, a solid, satiny,
crimson one that brought out his tan, he could be on TV
right now.

Oblivious to her thoughts, he walked to the book-
shelf that used to contain the world's largest collection
of family photographs, and she wondered if Cody remembered the sounds of his mother's cooking.

Megan did. The clang of the baking pans, the *click
click click* of the oven timer. It could've been yesterday
that she was here, playing Life with Cody and Ivan and
even Mr. Nordstrom, while the Mrs. pulled out home-
made Margarita pizza from the oven. Ivan hadn't seemed
happy here, nor had Mr. and Mrs. Nordstrom ever been
proud of Ivan the way they had, clearly, been of Cody.

"Where would you hide, if you were him?" she asked
as she watched him, loving the way his muscles bulged as
he reached out and wiped the dust off the empty shelves.

His head came up, and the corners of his lips formed
a barely-there smile. "Here."

"Here?" she asked, shocked. "Really?" In this decrepit, smelly old house? *Well, maybe he remembers the Life days, too.*

"Yep. I'd hide right here." He banged the wall with his fist. "Under everyone's very own noses."

She made a face and crossed her arms. "We could say Ivan's got that pegged, too, you know. He *was* hiding in your home just hours ago, and something about the way he hesitated before approaching me made me think he hadn't planned on me being there."

Cody's expression darkened; his entire face tightening with anger. "And then he saw you in your . . ."

"My purchases, why, yes!"

The nonchalance she tried injecting into her admission seemed to pass by him unnoticed, for Cody stared at her for a long, tense moment, his blue gaze dark and shuttered and so personal she felt the muscles of her legs turn buttery. He walked over to her, moving slow and sure, like a panther. His voice dropped a decibel.

"What where you doing there?"

The gruffly spoken question stroked her insides more than any seductive whisper.

His manly stance, his hot, possessive gaze, ignited her need and hunger until her throat hurt with the need to tell him how he made her feel.

Those beautiful blue eyes he stared at her with now had seen the same thing that haunted her nightmares. Those beautiful blue eyes were exactly like the killer's, except she liked to think that she knew their small differences.

Cody's lashes were longer, the tips blonder, and the way he used those eyes—to control, to intimidate, even to seduce—was a power his twin had never mastered.

Those eyes made her want to *melt*.

Now those eyes demanded she answer, but her pride would not allow her to admit the truth out loud.

"I already told you."

Unsettled by his stare, she pivoted around and headed to the small study, crossing all the way to the back of the room, determined to pretend to be engrossed in the sight of her old home from the arched window. She was sure that a man like Cody—a cynic by nature and a detective by trade—did not buy her tale in the least.

But then again, maybe he did. Because he wanted to.

For years, Cody Nordstrom had been chasing killers. His focus generally was aimed toward evil motivations, revenge and jealousy, the kind that inspired people to kill. He was not focused on the good emotions so much, like how and why someone sought out happiness and comfort. She was sure that if he had any inkling of how she felt for him, he would stop tormenting her and either buy a one-way ticket to Mars, or buy a roundtrip for two for their honeymoon. And yet, evidence pointed to the fact that he couldn't see, didn't realize that Megan wanted him . . . beyond bearing.

"You know," she began tentatively, "I think Ivan was trying on your suits while hiding in your closet. That's why the closet door burst open; there was some movement going on inside."

Cody didn't seem surprised, but he also seemed preoccupied.

Wondering what he wasn't telling her, Megan went fishing for information. "You'd make lieutenant if you weren't so blind to what's right before you sometimes. I bet you hadn't noticed he messed with your closet, huh?"

He laughed and shook his head. "Trust me, I noticed."

She could tell by his amused tone that he knew he was being baited, and that he didn't plan to fall any further than that.

Plus being that he was surveying the place like a hell-hound, she suddenly felt a little stupid for telling him he was missing a point, because he was definitely being very thorough. But then hadn't Paige said she needed to do something because he never would?

Yes, she had. So Megan let her top slip from one of her shoulders, low enough so that when she baited him a little more and he finally glanced at her, he would notice that her bra was falling off one shoulder as well as her shirt, and he would see the top of the creamy globe. "So you never miss a thing, Nordstrom? Ever?"

He straightened and stiffened when he saw, then seemed to have trouble finding the right words to say: "Meg, can't help but notice. . . . your shirt's falling off."

She met his glimmering blue gaze head on, and just smiled at him, not bothering to fix it, issuing him a silent dare . . .

Okay, maybe he'd failed to say it loud enough. Heck, maybe, he was so wired-up he'd only *thought* it.

"Your shirt's falling off," Cody repeated.

His voice faltered, so he cleared his throat and then, when Megan remained motionless, leaning against the wall and looking like a lovely pinup girl, he pointed a shaky hand down at her . . . beautiful, almost exposed, perfectly shaped wet-dream of a boob.

"Your shirt—Meg."

Eyes widening in surprise, Megan looked down at that perfect half-exposed breast, then innocently up at him, her eyes so green he could get lost in them, like in a rainforest. His hands itched at his sides. His whole body itched under his suit. He wanted to tear off his tie and curl it around her rump and use it to pull her up against him.

He could imagine her . . . *Wanna take her upstairs, in my old room, my old bed, where I thought of her so many times* . . . No, dammit! He'd come here to think, but instead she was driving him crazy, and this was not the time to indulge in teen fantasies. He'd stopped being a teen at sixteen, when his parents had been murdered.

In this very house!

He gritted his teeth and pointed once again at her cotton top draped over that creamy shoulder almost all the way down to what he was sure would be the pinkest, perkiest little nipple he'd ever seen.

His eyes fastened to it, and suddenly he knew he would not be able to pull his gaze free if she didn't pull that damned top in place.

But Megan did nothing to fix the problem, to remove the temptation.

Instead, she made a slight sound, like a sigh, leaned back, further back against the wall, and aroused the fucking daylights out of him when she closed her eyes and pushed her breasts out like she was taking the sun outside.

"I could really use some coffee later," she murmured sleepily, her eyes still closed. "Mind if I wait here while you do your thinking?"

Like hell. Like he could think about anything with her here, almost naked.

He wanted to pounce on her. He wanted to warn her to run, but then that would only make him want to chase her. And what would he do when he caught her? *Fuck I'm going to lick her calves like an ice cream cone . . . suckle her breasts till there's no tomorrow . . . taste her honey and suck every last drop . . .*

He wanted the killer, yes, his no-good sadistic brother, but right now all he really wanted was to take little Megan Banks in his arms and . . . God, his cock was about to explode.

She pushed from the wall with a soft smile and moved toward him, enough for his nostrils to flare in his need to inhale all of her. The air became oxygenless; heavy with need, charged with longing. The breeze outside moaned, as though the rasping against trees were erotic. Her incoming scent continued to draw him in, make him think of his childhood, and strangely, of his kids, how they would be if he ever had a couple. A daughter with her eyes, her hair.

Megan wrapping her legs around me . . . pulling me closer . . .

His breathing accelerated as he tried to maintain control, stay in place, but her eyes were shining with welcome, and holy God, were those hard little points her nipples against her top? She licked her lips. "So," she said, a hint of nervousness in her voice.

He took a step. Bad idea, Cody, stop stop stop. He couldn't help himself and reached up, stroked her lips with his thumb. His hand trembled; she shuddered at first touch.

Ecstasy swarmed him when she closed her eyes, a bubbling sensation in his veins as he allowed himself the luxury of stroking that mouth, driving himself way too hot just watching the way her breath changed. "So," he rasped back.

She held her breath, but when she opened her eyes, there wasn't desire there, but fear. "Someone's watching us."

Silence reigned. A knife of possessiveness sliced through him, and he pulled her close, hugging her while he assessed his surroundings, whispering in her ear, "Don't move."

Her body felt perfect against his, perfectly female, and just to give the monster a little of what he had for his entire existence begged for, he cupped her ass to distract whoever was watching them, keep them from noticing his other hand, reaching into his jacket. As he felt the grip at the tip of his fingers, he continued to savor the shape and pulled her tight against his aching groin.

"It's him, isn't it," she whispered, pulling her top over her shoulder and smashing herself against him, her voice scared. "He's here."

The prickle at the back of his neck didn't lie.

"Yeah." Almost there; he curled his fist around his gun. "Give me one more second."

Had they not felt a presence, he could've kissed her and urged her to tell him that she wanted it, his cock, against her, *inside her*, but when she squirmed restlessly closer against him, he knew she did, and he knew he couldn't do shit about it, never would, and it drove him to the edge.

He groaned, keeping her pinned against his body as he turned, and called out, with his gun firmly in his grip. "Ivan, I need to talk to you."

It was his twin, it had to be. The only damned bastard that had ever crept so easily past Cody's radar. *Megan shouldn't be here, dammit.*

A noise came from up above, and when a book landed *splat!* three inches to her right, Megan jumped in alarm.

Cody curled an arm around her waist, bending over so that only she could make out his whisper. "You're all right, you're with me."

She nodded fast enough to get dizzy. "What does he want?" she squeaked.

"I don't know, but I sure as hell would like to find out. Let's talk to him for a bit, hmm?" He raised his head to scan the room, sure that Ivan was somewhere up in the rafters. "Ivan, if it's you, come out here and talk to us."

A voice broke through the space as if spoken through a microphone. "Last time you talked to me you tossed my ass in jail, *brother.*"

Cody almost stumbled back when his brother's baritone struck him. Holy fuck, genetics were amazing. Cody could've been doing the talking, their voices were identical. And then it barreled into him: and he knew exactly how this bastard would have managed to escape prison.

Get his hands on a badge and a suit and—whoa, a crimson tie—and he'd look just like Cody.

Heart pounding at the possibility of Ivan being smarter than he remembered, Cody searched for him up in the wood beams and the second level library, but failed to find him. He'd be climbing up there by now, he'd already have the bastard by the throat, if not for the scared little kitten currently holding on to his arm.

"I'm on vacation this week," he told his brother, as easily as though he were speaking to Zach in an attempt to inspire his confidence. "So what do you say we lunch together and talk? Noon? Meet me at Marcel's Bistro in the Western Plaza." He needed answers, and more than that, he needed that bastard back where he belonged. *Serving a life term.*

The silence gave him hope, so he yanked out his business card, set it over the tome on the floor—*Moby-Dick*—and guided Megan out of there, calling behind his shoulder, "I'll see you there."

Ivan wouldn't follow.

Not yet.

The bastard wanted something, and Cody was pretty sure that she was currently walking in his arms.

Megan turned out to be quite the stubborn little package.

She didn't want to sleep at her house, and she refused to stay at the Rivers place if Cody wasn't, and after Ivan had picked his locks, Cody couldn't very well take her to his home, either. Plus, considering the fact that he only had one bed and the thought of Megan Banks's juicy derriere sleeping in it drove Cody's libido out of whack, his place was definitely out of the picture.

So he ended up setting them up for the night at the Candelabra, a small, boutique hotel that was close enough to the Western Plaza shopping center to make his meeting with Ivan on time tomorrow.

Since keeping things businesslike was the way to go, he got two connecting rooms with king-size beds, shared an early dinner downstairs with her, and once they went upstairs, threw himself into his research.

At least, that was his plan.

Megan seemed to have another idea.

While Cody surveyed all the paperwork he'd brought, she padded out from her room and curled up next to him on the couch, cuddling against his chest.

Within minutes she fell asleep, the soft sounds of her breathing audible in the silence, while Cody did his damnedest to concentrate and review everything he'd written about his brother on his first capture. Where he'd caught him last. Where he'd been seen before.

"No!" Megan suddenly murmured in her sleep.

She tossed her head to the side, her hair falling in a waterfall of golden tresses across her cheek. Damn, it had been a mistake to go back to his parents' place. Abandoned, falling apart, and the stench of death still lingering. But it was a place that would always be a part of him, a reminder of his origins, his failure. Every time he visited, he felt angry, determined, and many times, enlightened.

But what in the hell had Ivan been doing there?

Could he be hiding there now? No, he must have left.

Another moan filtered through his thoughts, soft and deep. It struck him that she sounded like a woman being made love to. His dick jumped at the thought.

Stiff as a flagpole almost instantly, Cody tried pushing her off his lap, but Meg whimpered again, and he felt a pang of sympathy.

Okay, he could do this. Comfort her. She'd wanted a hug before, maybe she just wanted that now.

He ran an awkward hand down her hair, attempting to soothe her. Not to touch her hair or any of that stuff; he'd always tried to touch her as little as possible. But tonight she was whimpering and he wasn't deaf—he heard her moans. He ran his hand down her hair again—silky delicious hair, not that he was really noticing. "Shh. Relax. Go to sleep."

She whimpered again, and Cody shut his eyes tight, trying to block out the sound. Damn it was hard. He pitched himself to the darkest day of his life, the only thing that could bring him out of any sensual haze.

It had been awful, that day. He'd been sharing looks with her for weeks. Heated looks. And he'd been standing closer only to find out that she didn't move away. Cody was certain, certain, that she liked him.

"She wants me," Ivan had taunted that evening. "It's me she wants, not you."

"Shut up," Cody had said. "You're just jealous she's walking with me tomorrow and not you."

"I'm not jealous. You can't even get her to kiss you."

"Of course I can, you dimwit," Cody assured him, but really, he wasn't so sure. She was different than the other girls; special. He didn't want to screw it up.

"I could make her have sex with me," Ivan offered.

"I can make her have sex with me, too," Cody countered, angry, "and when she has sex with me she'll be mine, all mine, no one else can ever touch her, especially you."

"Ten dollars you can't get her to do it tonight."

Cody had been pissed, but he'd been challenged and he'd shaken that asshole's hand.

For ten fucking dollars.

Now he could never bring himself to imagine being with her; he felt like that moment would be tainted, forever, because he'd shaken his brother's dirty hand and had boasted that he'd lose his virginity and take Megan's for ten dollars.

He remembered leading her into the woods and how they began arguing about something. He didn't remember what, it was so inconsequential. Something about him being too quiet and acting weird, according to her. Apparently he wasn't good at appeasing perceptive females either, because she said, "You know what, Cody? I don't feel like walking with you today after all."

They walked back through the woods back to the house, and that's when they saw them.

In the living room that adjoined the kitchen.

His parents, in a pool of their own blood. The family cat.

Every living breathing thing in that house had been killed.

And at the ages of sixteen and fourteen, they witnessed their first murder.

One week later, he was taken in by his mother's Texan relatives, and Cody left town. He thought that he'd died the day he'd seen his parents' murdered bodies.

But he'd been wrong.

Some part, some small part of him, had been clinging to life. That last part had died the day Megan watched him drive away through that window.

He stopped dreaming. He stopped wanting to live. He stopped thinking. He became an animal. Was labeled aggressive in school. Antisocial. Rebellious, even though he was still naively innocent—every act of vandalism he committed, he later came to clean, every property he damaged in his raging fits would be mended the next day. It was a need to make things right that kept him coming back, and a need to hurt something that made him do something wrong. And it was that need that made him come back to Phoenix, Arizona, to the dry weather, the cacti, the Southwestern flair homes, every year on the anniversary of his parents' death, and then later, to make a home here. And make things right.

He hadn't intended to look for Megan, at least, not at first.

He supposed she'd put the past behind her and didn't need to see his big ugly coyote face every day as reminder. But then he saw her, that day at the cemetery, and when she spotted him across the graves of his parents, he knew she had not forgotten him.

She had not forgotten him, or that night long ago, the one they would never forget.

"No," she gasped now, and when she squirmed, her ear grazed his groin—more exactly, the muscle awakening there—and Cody bit back a growl as pleasure shot up his spine.

She snuggled with her nose, caressing that aching part of him without knowledge, and it was so unexpected that his grip loosened on the papers he'd been holding. They cascaded to the floor, all at once, in a whisper.

He murmured in a breathless prayer, "God don't do this to me," and gave up, dropping his head back and taking a deep breath. He wanted to push her away. No. He wanted to pull her closer. Wrap her legs around him. And make her forget every man but him. Make her forget every pain with the pleasure he could give her.

Before he could control himself, his palm cupped the soft, perfectly round swell of her right breast, just to discover that it fit so right in his . . . no!! What the hell was the matter with him? He yanked his hand away and, shocked, glanced down: saw that she still had her eyes closed.

The breath shuddered out of him as he eased away from her and set her back on the sofa.

"Banks, Megan . . . Meg," he said, his voice laced with warning. "Stop . . . making noises."

She did not stir, but parted her lips to let go a sigh. And those lips, holy God, they were so wet and pink.

He growled.

"You better wake up and tell me to get the hell away from you," he said, his starving eyes fastened on her parted lips. He had wondered many times what they would feel like. Taste like. And then he'd cursed at himself for wanting to know. He'd caused her enough grief. He was *cursed*.

But now it didn't matter, it was difficult to feel anything other than hot inside, and itchy in his skin, and hungry. Now he saw her lips and if he did not take them soon, if he did not taste her with his own, he would die all over again like the day he'd been taken away.

He bent over, feeling their breaths mingle, thinking this was so so goddamned wrong, even if Cody wanted her like nobody else in their lives would want her.

With an unsteady hand, he reached out and ran the pad of his thumb across her lower lip, and his heart started to pound as he tested the soft, silken puffiness of that lip.

If only she weren't so pretty, her lips so soft, so pink . . .

He lowered his mouth to graze hers, softly, so that she would not wake, murmuring, "This never happened, Meg."

But it had, it *was* happening.

Just a graze.

Though he wanted so much more he felt like yelling down the damned hotel until she gave all of herself up to him. Feeling a growl trapped in his throat, he brushed her lips one last time, softly, igniting the hunger inside him so badly it took an inhuman effort to pull back, get up without waking her, and step away. "Ahh, shit!"

Storming across the room, he escaped through the connecting door, breathing hard as he bolted the lock behind him.

He needed much more than a cold shower.

But he couldn't have what he wanted.

So the cold shower would have to do.

She woke up afraid.

A sense of being watched crept over her again. Her bones felt cold.

Afraid she was becoming paranoid, Megan hugged the couch pillow tight to her chest and groggily glanced around the hotel room. Her mind flashed to Cody, honing in on his smile. His blue eyes that made her think of Hawaii when they sparkled warmly like that. Where was he?

She set the pillow down and stood, spotting him by the door.

She smiled at him, feeling herself blush. "Hey," she said sleepily. He had not moved an inch, was still and silent. "What time is it?" She glanced at the clock on the nightstand and saw it was 4:10 A.M. "So early. Don't you sleep?"

She saw a smile form on his lips, and it filled her with pleasure, but she wanted more than smiles. Wanted the clean, cool forest scent of his hair filling her lungs.

Watching her strangely, he ran his fingers down his tie as though its weight was a burden on his chest. As she watched his hands, she could only think of how rough his fingertips were and how they would feel if they ever reached the tender parts of her skin.

He took a step forward, moving differently, not as stealthily as he normally did. But slowly. Very, eerily slowly. Megan held her breath, her head swimming with anticipation. The shadows pulsed, the breath of each somehow synchronized to begin when the other ended.

"I want you," he said gruffly.

Her heart skipped, and for a moment she could only stare while holding her breath, unsure she'd heard right.

"I . . . want *you*," she hastily returned, her heart hammering. *This is it*, a part of her screamed in excitement, while another could not believe it, couldn't give credit to this happening.

Cody wants me, Cody wants me, he really wants me!

He reached out and pulled her close, and his scent was different. Her nose twitched as she attempted to place the strange scent, struggling to find the essence of Cody in it, but it was difficult to retain an idea when he started stroking her rump. Shock raced through her system, and then, slow as ice melting, she relaxed against him and moaned. "Please," she murmured. "Please kiss me . . . please . . ." she heard herself say.

He held her face and kissed her while pushing his fingers deep into her hair, his tongue rough and hungry. His taste . . . so unexpected. She opened her eyes, confused, but he groaned and the sound undid her, so she closed them once more and let him sweep her away. Something inside of her whispered, *this can't be. He's stronger than this. You'll wake up soon, and he'll be in the other room, and you'll be alone.*

But she silenced that voice with a moan of pleasure, another whispered "please" as she sank her nails into his shoulders and rocked against him.

Way in the back of her mind, she heard footfalls in

the adjoining room, then a bang on the door, followed by a crash as the door thrust open. And still Cody deepened the kiss, as though proving to her that nothing would tear him apart from her.

Megan shuddered wantonly. His attention had been so desired, so cherished, she wanted to beat whoever was coming in—get lost in Cody's kiss. But she couldn't. The intruder made Cody stop kissing her, and suddenly he instead wrapped his arms around her windpipe. "I wouldn't if I were you," he told the one who'd broken through the door, in a voice so cold, Megan felt a chill down to her ankles. Was Cody threatening to throttle her?

Then she saw that the man by the door was Ivan. And he was . . . bare-chested. Wearing only something like checkered sleep pants. His hair was wet, his chest gleaming with moisture. "You're *not* me," he growled, in a voice so deadly, Megan feared for Cody's life. But for a full second, she became riveted by Ivan's phisique.

He looked . . . muscular.

Too muscular.

When she'd pressed against him right now, Cody didn't feel as hard as Ivan looked as he walked over. And he moved, wow, like a killer. Like a trained killer.

Goodness but jail had done him wrong. They had made him into a killing machine, and he had eyes only for Cody. Murdering blue eyes.

Noticing that his hold on her throat had loosened, Megan pushed him aside. "Cody, run! Go get your gun!"

But before Cody could move, Ivan knocked him to his knees and pushed him to the ground. "Son of a bitch," he hissed, grabbing his hair and slamming his forehead on the carpet. "Having fun in my closet? *Huh?* Having fun *watching her* while you play with my *fucking ties*?" He tightened the tie on his neck with a yank and Cody began choking.

Panicked, Megan didn't register what Ivan was saying, only registered what she saw: Cody being killed by his tie, just like his colleagues joked he would.

She had to do something. She lunged at wet, bare-chested Ivan and pummeled his ribs so hard he turned around to face her with a look of utter annoyance, and when he did, she launched a kung fu kick in the air, slamming it right in his nuts. He bowled over with a yell.

Megan twisted around and reached for Cody on the floor, who seized the moment and punched Ivan one, two, three times, then broke into a run. She was about to follow when a bloodied Ivan caught her hand and pulled her back with a growl of displeasure. She was about to hit him again when he snarled, "Don't . . . Even . . . Think it!"

She blinked, registering the glimmering blue eyes that flashed pure anger at her. Long-lashed blue eyes. *Cody's* blue eyes. Cody's . . . wet chest?

"THAT SICK FUCK WITH THE TIE"—he gritted through his teeth as he tried to stand, still bent over from the pain—"WAS NOT"—he put both his hands on his knees, dragging in hard breaths—"ME."

FIVE

Megan wasn't talking.

Her throat was clogged with emotion and she doubted she could take any more of this crap for much longer. When Cody had grabbed her stuff back at the hotel, haphazardly put on a suit, but not a tie, and informed her that they were going to Zach's house, she didn't protest.

When they arrived and a fussy Paige brought towels and clean sheets for the guest bedroom, Megan didn't offer anything.

And when Zach came in and discussed what had happened with Cody, Megan only sat there and listened, still dazed about it all.

Nordstrom and Zach just had to be the best-looking pair of homicide detectives the force had ever seen. Paired with a group of men that were neither tall, nor short, nor fat, nor slender, the tall, athletic hunks were definitely a standout.

But Cody . . . how could she have mistaken him for

his twin? The man she *loved*—of whom she should know every mark, every flaw. And she didn't. Her mind was already screwed up.

She wanted him so much she had wanted to believe that it was him, kissing her.

"Here," Paige whispered, handing her a cup of tea.

Megan took a slow sip and nodded her thanks. They sat in the living room of her friend's spacious apartment, a warehouse loft that Zach had made into his home and Paige had comfortably moved right into when he proposed.

Megan had met her only a couple of years ago, but had felt like Paige was one of the best friends she'd ever had. She seemed to read right into her.

"Want to talk about it?" her friend asked softly.

She shook her head. Cody wouldn't look at her. He hadn't said a word to her. Meg couldn't bring herself to look at him, either. She felt so dirty, so ashamed.

"So I guess the plan wasn't a big hit, huh?" Paige tried, sad-eyed.

Meg shrugged, because she figured she had to respond to that and didn't feel like talking much.

"Who knows," Paige reached out and patted her knee, "maybe you'll get lucky tonight sharing a room?"

"His brother kissed me" Meg blurted.

Paige blinked, and Meg set the teacup on the coffee table and rose, ready to head for the bedroom even though she doubted she'd catch much sleep.

"I can get the murderer to kiss me but not the cop."

The disgusting image of Ivan and Meg kissing was permanently embedded in Cody's brain.

Megan in his brother's arms, Megan moaning as she kissed him.

If Ivan had wanted payback for his years doing time at the Maricopa County Jail, then he'd succeeded. Cody was insanely, inhumanly jealous. He'd wanted not only to kill, but to die.

After updating Zach on the recent events, Cody made his way to the guest bedroom, the last door down the hall, where Megan had disappeared only moments ago.

He didn't know what he'd say to her, or do. Fact was, he planned to sit there and do nothing.

Nothing but keep his brother away from her until Cody managed to get his hands on the bastard tomorrow.

The door stood slightly ajar. Uncertain if she was asleep, he parted it wider and saw that the lamps were on, and a pool of light illuminated the snowy white bedsheets.

Megan sat there, gazing at the door, as if . . . waiting.

He felt a trickle of blood sliding down his swollen lips. His eye had already started to swell, and his rib-cage stung like a sonofabitch. But none of that hurt as much as watching her being kissed . . . by a man that was not him.

Rage spread through his system like a blazing torch.

He could use his twin as a punching bag. Good God, he'd kill him this time, do what the state hadn't been able to do. Ivan wasn't a minor now, and he would pay for this. For everything.

As she gazed up at him from the bed, her eyes were teary, but less than an hour ago, they had been watered with desire. *Desire for my murdering brother.*

His fingers curled into his palms and tightened. He should back away, to any other room but this one.

No. He couldn't leave her. Suddenly, he noticed the outline of her nipples under her thin sleep shirt and became hard as a rock. She wore no bra now . . . her beautiful breasts were there to hold, to touch, to kiss . . .

His heart pumped steadily as she stood uncertainly, staring at him, while Cody didn't know what to do with himself; he had never imagined he could ever love someone so much, or feel so powerless when he was with them.

He took an involuntary step closer to her, and as he reached out to cup her face in his hands, he stopped himself. "You okay?"

A sob caught in her throat and her face came down in disappointment and embarrassment.

During the evening she had been frequently wiping her mouth, and sometimes, she whimpered softly as though he'd bitten her. Desire and jealousy ricocheted within the walls of his body, painful in their force.

That should have been me . . . kissing her . . . biting her sweet lips . . .

Breathing hard, he suppressed the urge to smash her against him and hug her as hard as he could. To kiss her like his brother had, do more to her, do everything to her.

"I thought it was you!" she burst out, weakly hitting his chest with her fists. Tears welled in her eyes, her words striking him where it hurt. "I thought it was you, you bastard." Tears spilled one after the other, and she looked so fragile and alone he wanted to take his gun and just shoot himself with it. "Where did you go? Why did you leave?"

His harsh breaths made it difficult for him to speak, to explain to her. No words could explain. "I needed to get away." His voice was low and raspy, his hands hanging at his sides as he allowed her to vent.

"Why? Why, Cody! Am I that repulsive?"

His heart squeezed painfully. "No."

She began shaking her head, furiously wiping the streaming tears from her lovely pink cheeks. "Didn't you hear what I told him, Cody?"

He shook his head, barely holding his shit together, trembling with the sheer and utter agony of seeing the woman he loved cry like this.

He had heard voices, had been locked in his room, had been too panicked to make sense of what those voices were saying. Now, he stood there, noticing the flush creeping up her neck and cheeks, fearing that he was about to find out.

"I told him 'please'," she whispered, covering her mouth on a sob. "I told him to please, please kiss me! I begged, Cody, I would have kept on begging!"

She was killing him with every tear, with every word. He shook his head, his voice uneven, his throat tight. "I'm no good for you, Meg."

She started storming away, but impulsively he caught her before she could take a step. Making a small sound of grief, she fought at first, then she swallowed a sob and let him reel her back into his arms. "Shh. Just listen to me," he murmured. "I'm no. Good. For you. Do you understand me?"

She squirmed in his hold. "Let go of me."

"No." He started hugging her, his arms enveloping her whole.

"Let go of me! I hate you!"

He should listen to her. He knew he should listen, but instead he hugged her tighter, feeling her squirm against him, closing his eyes to savor this one moment with Megan Banks in his arms.

What she'd said had left him flabbergasted. She'd begged for his kiss. It left him shocked, feeling like he should throw caution to the wind and—*kiss her. Make her yours. Yours. She's yours. Don't make her beg. Never make her beg*.

"I hate myself, too, Meg," he whispered hotly as he seized her waist. "It's all my fault. Everything. But I still think I should kiss you, so that there will never be a doubt in your mind when it's me."

A shudder coursed through her, but she shook her head. "But you won't. You never do."

He pressed the front of his body against hers, so she could feel everything—everything. His hardness. His desire.

He needed her to know there was one man, one man, who'd die for her. That he truly believed no other would ever want her the way he did. Groaning as he lost control, he nuzzled her hair, his blood pumping hot and primal in his veins.

"Can't stop thinking that if I'd kissed you before, you'd have realized"—he pulled her face with both his hands up to his lips as her breasts crushed against his chest—"I wasn't the one kissing you."

She flung her arms around him as he pulled her close, slanted his head, and hungrily covered her lips with his.

The contact was amazing. Electrifying. Terrifying.

Fire raced from the tip of his lips to the soles of his feet. She moaned against him; tasted sweet and minty and warm, making him dizzy with arousal.

"Meg," he rasped against her, turning his head to take her lips from another angle. "Mmm. So good." He nipped, and licked, and gently bit. "Say it, say it's me you want."

"Please, Cody, please . . ."

The gasped words were so powerful he could barely take them, caught her wrists before she kissed him again, pinned them up over her head before she ripped his control to shreds.

Her chest heaved, her nipples jutting out and pushing against the fabric of her T-shirt, drawing his eyes. He bent his head, heard her catch her breath when he caught a nipple through the material with his lips.

She pulled her arms free and clutched the back of his head closer, gasping, "Oh, God, yes."

He growled. "I feel so starved. Every time I hear you humming to yourself, every time you take a sip of whatever it is you have in your drink, I want to be tasting that sweet, sexy mouth."

He came up and seized her lower lip between his teeth, swiping the plump flesh with his tongue, devouring her as softly as he could while he raised his hand and cupped her breast, kneading it.

She gasped when he pinched her nipple, and the sound drove him wild. He bent his head and suckled the taut bead through the thin fabric, his cock an aching pain inside his pants, his balls gathered high and straining in pain, they were so full.

Her breathing escalated, and when she mewled for him, his blood stormed through his body like an avalanche of need. He flattened her against the wall, grinding his hips against her, kissing her lips as his hands squeezed her hips, her waist, then dragged up to cup both her breasts. I love you, he thought. I love you I love you *I love you.*

But he pushed the words aside, the thoughts. This was sex. Animal attraction. He could never love her like she deserved, could never be the solid, dependable guy she needed. His brother was a murderer. He wasn't the man for her. He wasn't even man enough to stop.

Hungrily, he kissed her creamy neck and tasted her skin, soft and sweet. *Mine. Mine. Mine,* an angry primal part of him said, insisting he claim her, once and for all. No one else would touch her. Ivan could no longer stake a claim, not even try to.

Mine.

He pressed his lips over hers, and as her tongue came out to play, her taste flooded him, sparked him up like a fire. He made a moaning, groaning noise of need as he luxuriated in the soft feel of her in his arms, under his moving hands, the intoxicating taste of her. He tore his mouth away and set his nose against hers, rolling his forehead against hers as he tried to capture his breath.

"I'm losing it." He crushed her lips with his again when all she managed was a moan, her fingers tunneling through his hair, pulling him down to her.

This was the stuff of his wet dreams, of his every forbidden fantasy. Kissing Megan, hearing the way she moaned, the fast way she breathed, feeling her, smelling her.

He dragged his lips up her jaw, to her temple, to her ear, cupping her face, hating that his hands trembled, hating that he couldn't stop himself, not now, not anymore. He wanted to memorize the exact taste, the shape of every part of her, he wanted his tongue, his teeth, every cell in his body to know her tonight. "Mine . . ."

* * *

". . . all mine."

Her world was spinning in heat, in colors, in beauty. Cody's lips, his hands, his words. She was floating in a sea of sensation and didn't want to stop, ever.

Megan tightened her arms around his neck, moving restlessly as she kissed his neck, his jaw, his lips.

His fingertips trailed under her T-shirt, caressing her softly, and against her throat he said, "This is me." Meaningfully his erection scraped against the side of her hips. "And this, Megan, this is why you needed to stay away from me."

He backed her into the bed and, before she could lie down, his tongue surged into her mouth, and as it plunged, his hands moved to her jeans.

He panted as he unhooked the top button with one hand, then stroked her cheekbones with the fingers of his other hand. "Tell me I'm out of line."

"I hate you," she breathed, shivering, seeing his jaw tighten, his handsome face darken.

She brushed his lips against his, whispered, "I hate you for not doing this sooner."

"Jesus, take your shirt off." Cody yanked his shirt off faster than she could discard her T-shirt, and when they were bare-chested, he couldn't seem to stand the distance between them.

When he pushed her breast up to his mouth, she gasped in surprise. As he thrust his tongue around the pebbled tip of one nipple, her eyes flew open in shock. Oh, wow.

Wow wow wow.

Her eyelids drifted shut as she licked her own wanting lips and moaned. Her dreams were made of this stuff. Of the stuff of Cody. Nordstrom. THE One. The one that made her heart race, her stomach twist, oh goodness, he was *good*.

He came up with a ragged breath and nipped at her bottom lip, then tugged and dragged his lips up her jaw, where he breathed into her ear in a craggy, pained voice, "I want you."

Her stomach clenched. "Please."

He nuzzled her ear, his voice dropping another decibel. "I've always wanted you—always."

Megan couldn't breathe.

Oh, God, please let this be happening.

Cody captured her mouth again and she tasted hunger, the rawness he hid behind the suit, the polished veneer.

Oh, Cody. Cody, Cody, Cody.

She wanted to say his name, to say *touch me,* to say *please never stop doing this*. But instead she heard her own whimpering moan as he unzipped her jeans and she felt them slip down her body in a whisper. He grasped the edge of her panties and tugged until they dropped to her ankles in a puddle of lace.

Naked, trembling with lust and a need pent-up for too long, she reached out with trembling hands and pulled his belt off his waist.

A protesting rumble vibrated up his chest as he nuzzled her face and whispered against her lips, in between licks, "I'll handle this, you get down on that bed and I'm going to take you like you've never been taken before."

She hadn't been taken before. Ever. Any way would be amazing to her. But his words triggered a new, fresh bolt of arousal, and her head spun.

Rushing to kick off her shoes, she edged barefooted to the king-size bed, her heart thundering.

She could make out his body in the moonlight, beautiful and surreal as he pulled off his shirt. His eyes glowed in the darkness, full of promise, of male need, as he tossed it all aside.

She lay back against his pillow. The fire between her legs spread to her entire body, her head, her toes.

"Please don't let me be dreaming," she whispered, but then could not say any more.

He was walking toward her practically nude—gloriously, lethally nude—except for a pair of crisp white trunks that hugged his lean hips. In that state of undress he advanced, his eyes smoldering. She couldn't imagine a bolder, rawer image of masculinity than the one Cody presented. His body was all sinew, all steel, all hard. *Every*where.

Her breath hitched when the bed dipped. In less than a second, her body was covered by the hot, heavy weight of man. Her man.

Never had she felt something so erotic as the touch of his bare, naked flesh against hers. Her nerves were alive, singing to him. He studied her with dark, liquid eyes.

"You okay?"

She slipped her fingers into his hair and pulled him down so she could kiss him instead, and he responded with a low sound of need in his throat, his kiss so deep and fierce she felt devoured like the tastiest candy.

He tasted of danger, darkness, heat.

"Let me touch you," he growled.

Her heart leapt when his hands moved down to her navel. His fingers were gentle, but firm and strong, as he caressed, and then he shifted his strong hard body above hers to get a different angle and slowly inserted one finger where she'd grown achy and moist.

Gasping as his finger entered, long and strong, Megan clamped her hands on his shoulders and bucked. "Cody."

"Ask me for more."

"More."

He pushed in deeper, so deep that she couldn't seem to keep a whimper of pleasure in check. Paige and Zach could hear . . . but suddenly it didn't matter.

Today she had mistakenly kissed his brother. But oh, it seemed her life had all been leading to this one moment, this one night, in bed with Cody.

He moved inside her while expertly twirling her clit with his thumb, and she arched back and tossed her head in abandon. "Oh, God, Cody."

He ground his palm against the tight little pearl, while pulling out, and pushing in, sending her heated body into oblivion.

She whimpered softly each time he penetrated, aware that he was gazing down at her with piercing dark eyes that seemed to know her very soul.

He cupped her breast with his free hand, causing her to moan because it felt so right, and her breast swelled ripe under his kneading.

She turned her head into the pillow and closed her eyes, fighting the intimacy of it all, the swelling tenderness that washed over her as he touched her—as she moaned for him. Why had he broken down? Was it the adrenaline of the danger? Did he just need to feel alive? "Am I just any woman to you, Cody?" she whispered.

She wanted to know—needed to know if this would only happen once.

He stopped for a moment, and then his hard chest vibrated as he released a slow, rolling chuckle. "Wouldn't that be easy," he said wistfully.

Reaching out, he tortured both her nipples with his thumbs—and she was ashamed at how fast and tightly they puckered. How sharply they throbbed. "In my mind I've only taken one woman, Meg, the woman I've wanted for years."

"You don't have to say this. Don't lie."

A palpable tension whipped through him at her words, and his entire face hardened. "This, here, now, is no lie. Out there, I have to. Here . . ." He signaled down at her, the bed, them, and shook his head, "no lie. Not in this bed with you." He ducked his head to where her breasts awaited in sensory peak. "Waited too long for this to be a lie." He took her nipple into his mouth, drowning it with a hot, ravenous kiss that left her gasping when he went onto the next. "Too damned long."

His long, wet kiss on that sensitive crest made her burn from both embarrassment and pleasure. Trembling down to the arches of her feet, she moved against him, stroking his cock between their bodies.

He delved one hand between her legs and cupped her sex once more.

His eyes glittered like a rascal's as he explored, expertly fondling. Through the quivers and warmth taking her over, she sensed his dark gaze on her face, watching as he gently eased two fingers inside.

"*Ahhhh, Christ, so tight.*" It was a reverent whisper, full of wonder as he stretched her.

Her hands flew to the back of his head, clutching him tight as a marvelous pressure gathered inside her. "Cody."

He kissed her lips, his tongue probing her mouth in the same sinuous way his finger did. "Am I your first?" His eyes smoldered as he gazed down at her—expressing his desire in ways that couldn't be put into words. "You are so tight. Am I your first lover, Meg?"

"Yes."

His face went tight with emotion. "Who were you waiting for, Meg, tell me."

The fire was building, stronger and stronger, hotter and hotter, but his eyes were deep and dark and they were hungrier than she'd ever imagined. She wrapped her arms around him and pulled him close. "You have no idea for how long I've wanted you."

"Fuck, I'm trying to be gentle, but I can't—your words—the way you feel—the sounds you make—"

Unable to tame the flutters his words caused, she sat up and rubbed against him, burning all over. "Don't be gentle, Cody."

It was all the permission he needed. He growled and snaked an arm around her and flattened her against his side, pressing his mouth to her throat. "Then fit my body to yours." His rough, ragged whisper fanned across her skin. "I feel you against me and know how good it will be. I can't wait to be inside you." She felt the moment his control was gone, his full passion unleashed, and it drove her feverish when he rolled off her to get fully naked.

He quickly returned, then ran his hands up the outside of her legs, nudging them apart with his body, making room for him.

His hips burrowed between her splayed thighs. Hard to soft. Heat to heat. "Ready?"

Yes. *Yes.* She had been ready for years, forever.

She widened herself for his entry and dropped her forehead on his arm, where, under some ungodly impulse, she placed a kiss on a hard, rounded bicep that left the salty taste of his skin on her lips. "Hard," she whispered, "Take me." *Make me yours. Just yours.*

He remained as rigid as a granite slab above her. "It'll hurt, I believe."

"Not as much as you keeping your distance."

"Jesus—hold on to me." He rocked in a slow, powerful move that brought them close to joining, teasing her, taunting her with his nearness. He was panting hard now, as hard as she was. "I planned to make you beg . . . but you're so ready, baby. I'm so ready . . . I've been ready even before I saw you naked and tied to my bed."

She tensed as she felt him grab his shaft and guide the engorged tip into her opening. He was enormous. Stretching . . . Opening . . .

One heartbeat passed. Two. Then his hands clutched her waist. "Oh," she gasped, her nails digging into his back as she absorbed the thick length of him.

He impaled her fully. *Yes.* With a moan of frenetic desire she thrust her hips up and curled her legs around his hips, dragging him closer. Deeper. Thick, hard, thrusting, filling her with a wrenching relief of having his pulsing flesh deeply embedded inside her.

He growled in relish, then seized her waist in his big hands and pinned her in place as he thrust again. Deeper.

They moaned together. Megan tossed her head, swimming in pleasure, in wicked thrill, peering through her eyelashes and seeing his face ravaged with pleasure.

He thrust again, and this time she wildly reached behind him, grabbed his buttocks, and dug her fingers into his muscles—urging him for more. More!

"Ahhhh, God," he growled, and he thrust so hard her knees skewed sideways, bringing his balls to slap against her, for every hard inch of him to be sliding in her tight channel.

"Ahhhh, God!" he cried again, undone as she twisted her head to the side in a frenzy.

The complete look of passion in his face drove her wild. Cody was no more the cool detective, but Neanderthal caveman who'd just dragged his woman into the cave.

Cords had popped out of his arms while a distinct buzz of sexual energy vibrated around him. His cock stretched her beyond capability with his need, sending a rush of renewed warmth through her system on each thrust.

He set a pace, a primitive pace. A pace where Megan was licking his neck, rubbing his shoulders with her greedy hands, his lean, muscled back, as he took her. She rocked her hips to his, and he was growling, plunging, penetrating, losing his head in a way she'd never imagined Cody Nordstrom could.

Then it happened. Her first orgasm with him, the first time she ever truly let go of her fears, her everything.

It happened when she felt him stiffen over her, heatedly hiss in a groan, "come with me, baby," and she did. Boy, she did! A sweeping climax crashed through her and she shuddered, and shuddered, and clung to him and shuddered. She heard him growl and his great big body trembled against hers, too. She felt heat explode inside her. Warmth, heat, heaven . . .

At last.

SIX

Meg woke up disoriented, but within seconds, memories of last night rained over her like petals. She smiled to herself, stretched, and looked around. "Cody?"

There was no sign of him, so she slipped into the bathroom to check her appearance and gaped at the first sight of her reflection, appalled that Cody could've seen her like this. Her normally reckless-looking blond curls looked even more tousled this particular morning, while her lipstick was smeared across her lips. But as she stared longer, she encountered something she had never seen before. An odd serenity in her eyes, like that of someone who knew a deep, satisfying secret.

A woman's secret.

Heart clenching as she remembered their lovemaking, she smoothed her hair with her hands and carefully wiped away what remained of her lipstick. Out in the living room, she found Paige by the window, peering outside.

"Good morning," Meg said.

"He's gone," Paige decreed, lips pursed. She pivoted around and planted her hands on her hips. "What happened? He didn't look very well slept or too happy, either."

Meg blinked. What?

Had this become an alternate universe? Last night had been surreal. Amazing. Cody should be grinning, ear to ear. And yet he might be unhappy because—*his brother's still out there, dummy.*

"So?" Paige asked. "What's the story?"

Meg's cheeks felt toasty, so she whirled around and marched to the kitchen. It felt weird to admit to her friend that they had got it on in their home, and it embarrassed her. Especially when Cody didn't look too happy about it. Damn him!!! Anger surfaced, and she pulled out a chair from the kitchen table and plopped down. "I guess you could say we may have fucked up."

Paige's eyes widened, then she grinned. "Oh, so that's what's got him in a knot. Want some breakfast?"

Meg rose. "I'm not very hungry, but if it'll take my mind off what I did, yes."

Together they searched the cupboards and 'fridge; eggs, ham, bread, napkins, and place settings.

"You know my mother always used to say to me, only when we are no longer afraid do we begin to live," Paige offered.

"How eloquent," she said as she raised her hand and discovered that Cody had left a love mark on the inside of her wrist. Something warm and mushy spread across her tummy.

"Live with no excuses and love with no regrets," Paige said as she whipped up two omelets.

"Ahh."

"Life is a quest, and love a quarrel."

Meg's eyebrows flew upward. "Wow. Your mother was full of sayings."

"She was." Paige nodded, then frowned. "I think she just refused to talk about herself, so she quoted Hallmark." She smirked, Slicing thinly through the ham.

Meg was only partly present in the conversation. Her mind kept drifting to last night, the sensations. The total hotness of the man. *The way he kissed me. The way he lost control . . .*

Her skin pricked in remembrance of his touch, and her sensitized nipples beaded under her sleep shirt.

"So," Paige said, clearly noticing, "I don't think you got around to telling me what happened."

Urging herself to get busy, Megan slipped two slices of bread into the toaster, and when she opened her mouth to reply, swiftly closed it. She didn't *know* what had happened. There was more to the man than his organized clothing attested to, and something about Ivan touching her, kissing her, had sent Cody's instincts flaring to life.

So would he have never kissed her if his dirty brother hadn't first?

The thought left her miserable, especially when he was gone this morning. Would it have killed him to leave a note?

"Plates?" She offered them to Paige.

"Please." Paige finished the eggs, added a slice of ham and toast to each plate, and carried them with her to the kitchen table. "You know, he looked like shit this morning—but he was wearing a kick-ass tie."

Meg laughed softly and set two cups of coffee on the table. "Yeah, Cody and his ties."

"He left a message for you."

Her heart tumbled to her toes, then she jumped to her feet. "Where? Give it to me!" She snatched the envelope from Paige's outstretched hands.

She didn't expect him to say something mushy and sweet. Cody wasn't like that. But she didn't expect what she read either.

I'm sorry.
C.

At first, she did not react, only stood there, staring at his note. Then, she sat down, thinking.

During the first week after his parents' murder, there was a fury in Cody's gaze. Rage. Megan had hoped that later, there would be understanding. His brother had murdered them: not Cody. But the day he left with his adopting relatives from Texas and he'd looked at her window from the car, she had seen a horrible emptiness in his eyes. No rage. No understanding. Only a terrifying emptiness.

She had been haunted by that boy, had made thousands of wishes on his behalf. He had left a broken boy, but had returned a mended man. Though only Megan knew the depths of the little cracks he hid inside.

Cody could be Mr. Hollywood to his colleagues. He smiled, and joked around, and ribbed, but the truth was, he didn't allow anyone to get close and the tactic had worked for him.

He was on his own.

But last night, he had not been alone.

Last night, he had let down his carefully constructed walls, and he had let her see how much he needed her.

Wanted her. Never, in her wildest dreams, had she imagined a man could make love to her like Cody had.

He had explored every inch, had gobbled up every inch, and his face, his breathing, the tension in his body, the fire in his eyes: she could not believe it didn't mean something to him.

After the sex they had spent hours awake in bed, talking lazily, looking at each other. His eyes had sparkled, there had been a tiny crinkle at the corner of each, a brilliant shine to them as they talked. They'd had a midnight snack and in between morsels he would find an excuse to nibble on her, and Megan had felt like a blushing bride must feel on her wedding night.

No. He could not do this to her. He would not kick her back out to easily resume playing his Iceman role. She refused to let him, to waste another day waiting for him to realize he was "The One." The *only* one. For her.

She clenched the note in her hand and slammed it down on the table.

"That bastard!"

"Come again?"

"That jerk! That insufferable buffoon!" She stood and marched to their bedroom, grabbing her purse, her shoes, Paige close at her heels.

"What? Where are you going?"

"To find that asshole and tell him exactly what I think!"

Paige grabbed her elbow and squeezed. "Hey, calm down, he's out catching a killer, you know, not having an affair. Zach's with him. He'll be fine!" When Meg remained unconvinced, Paige gave her a sympathetic pat on the back. "But I guess he's no longer officially on vacation."

An idea flashed in her head. What if Cody ditched Zach because he wanted to face Ivan alone? What if the man she loved finally managed to get himself killed? *Oh, God.*

Struck into motion by her mounting dread, Meg pounced into the master bedroom and rummaged through the drawers. "Does Zach have any extra police radios we could tune into? It might give me an idea of what they're planning before he gets his stupid buffoon ass killed." Before Paige could protest, Meg yanked one out and turned it on. "Bingo."

She was going to help them.

Ivan wouldn't kill her. She knew it with every bone in her body, that if Cody got in trouble, not even Zach Rivers stood a chance of manipulating Ivan like Megan did.

Plus she was certain that now, after last night's fireworks, Megan would be the only person on this planet who could truly distinguish between the twins if that devilish Ivan chose to wear a tie.

Cody had once said he'd die for her.

Well, Nordstrom, I'd die for you.

She'd be the bait, if need be, but she was not standing by idly another day in her life. And if Cody had lied to Zach about the meeting at Marcel's, then Megan was going to make sure Nordstrom was covered.

Face your fears.

Take charge.

Protect him like he's always protected you . . .

"You're not going, Megan Banks!" Paige stopped her at the door, hands on her nonexistent waist, her pretty face scrunched up into a scowl. "There's a *killer* on the loose."

Megan nodded complacently. "Which is why you are staying here. I've got a man to catch."

Ivan was a no-show at Marcel's Bistro.

At 12:39 P.M., as Cody sat at a small, round window table, he received a message from the waiter, informing him there was someone on the phone for him. Surveying his surroundings for about the hundredth time, Cody walked to the bar, lifted the phone, "Yeah?"

"Think he smelled a trap?" It was Zach.

Cody glowered, not for the first time, wondering if he should've informed his team of the meeting or have faced Ivan today—solo. "I don't know, man, but he obviously thought you stank."

Cody's heart stopped when he spotted her through the window. Across the street, she was hard to miss. A bright spot of color in a sea of cement and buildings. God, she looked lovely in a pair of jeans and a yellow shirt, with her blond curls flapping behind her as she gazed up at the glaring red sign above the window that read MARCEL'S BISTRO.

His hands started itching with the need to go out there and just . . . *hug her*. Then, he noticed the man creeping up beside her. He'd been leaning against the lamppost, covered head to toe in a black gabardine coat. Yeah, a damned gabardine, in this stinking hot weather. Alarm bells clanged inside his head, and his instincts kicked into overdrive.

"Two o'clock," Cody barked. "Megan's here. Dammit. Fuck! Goddammit!"

He slammed the phone back on its cradle and pushed past the waiter and shouldered through a party of eight that was just coming in through the revolving doors.

"Excuse me! *Move*." When no one seemed to think he was serious, he pulled out his badge and roared, "GET OUT OF MY FUCKING WAY!"

He charged outside, his heart thundering, his gun drawn, his thighs burning as he kicked them into the hardest run he'd ever taken in his life.

She was gone.

Zach Rivers stood there in their stead, his eyes shielded by a pair of aviators, but Cody didn't need to see his gaze. The grimness of his stance, his mouth, said it all.

He took her. He took her. That murdering motherfucker took her.

"I'm sorry, man, he was armed," Zach grumbled. "I couldn't stop him without risking her getting hurt."

For a wild second, Cody refused to believe what he was witnessing. Hearing. Zach fucking Rivers, a reckless motherfucker, just standing there while his murdering sonofadevil killer of a brother took Megan into the underworld.

"What the fuck are you doing standing here!" Cody exploded. He spun around and scanned his surroundings, wildly searching for a direction, a clue to where they'd gone.

"He wants you," Zach's words made him stop. "Just you. No monkey business. No wires. No cops. He asked you to meet him at the Tonto National Forest, and if you do, he'll let her go and no harm will come to either of you."

"Like hell I buy that!"

"Your call, man, just tell me what you want."

And Cody had one second, one second, to decide. He would have liked to have an army follow him. He would have liked to drop a missile right over that sick gorrilla's head. But he had Megan, and Cody wouldn't risk a hair on her body.

His entire body, his entire system, was having a short circuit. He couldn't think right, couldn't focus. Every cell in his body burned with the need to kill Ivan Nordstrom. And get Megan back to safety, somewhere far away from Ivan. Far away from Cody.

"Just stay the hell put," he snarled. "If I'm not back with her in half an hour—you know what to do."

"Don't piss him off, Cody," Zach warned.

Cody charged to his car and yanked open the door with a glare. "You should've said that to *him*."

As he drove full speed in the direction of the national forest, he told himself he was focused. Focused on one and only thing: Ivan. And getting both Ivan and himself out of Megan's life forever. He was not thinking of what Ivan could be doing to her now—no, he couldn't function if he considered the possibilities.

He was not thinking of how well her body fit to his last night. Or how hard they'd moaned.

Or the fact that he was completely, indisputably in love with her.

Yeah, this morning his mood had been perfectly morose. Even the guys at the station had wondered why he wasn't joking today, or ribbing someone, or acting like all was well.

Because it wasn't well.

It hadn't been well for fifteen years.

And it would not be well until his brother was out of their lives. Until Cody no longer posed a threat to Megan—a danger.

He had, what? Like two hundred and twelve homicide cases under his belt? So why did he continue to feel like the foolish teenager who'd been too engrossed in his cock to see what was happening in his own home?

Because that woman makes you a nitwit! Now focus!

He pulled over into an empty parking spot, expecting Ivan to be waiting in the shed by the clearing. In the vast rocky terrain, there was plenty of space to hide a body or two.

Was that what Ivan planned?

Disturbed by the thought, he yanked open the car trunk, armed himself with as many weapons as he could without them being too obvious, then let the trunk slam shut behind him as he made his way through the dirt path.

To the right the clearing led to a lake, which usually allowed for campers to park their RVs, toast marshmallows by a fire, and dip their toes into water. But this afternoon the space was flat and empty, and the lack of noise lent a gloom to the area that Cody found quite the match to his mood. In fact, a morgue was quite the match to his mood.

He spotted Ivan sitting down on a red boulder, dressed like their mother used to dress them to go to Mass: in suits and ties.

Except Ivan was wearing Cody's suit and tie.

So not only was his brother a murderer and a kidnapper, but he was a thief, too. A fact that Cody had noticed the day Ivan had broken into his home, but had not dwelled upon until now.

Yeah, in that silky blue tie that happened to be Megan's favorite, Cody could tell Ivan thought he was the man. Cody planned to knock him down a peg or two.

"Nice tie, asshole."

Ivan smiled. When he did, he looked regal. Decent. Exactly like the man that stared back at Cody from the mirror. "I hope you don't mind it when I strangle you with it," the bastard replied.

"Game on." Cody took a step, flashing him a dangerous smile. "Now where's Megan?"

Ivan signaled to his right, and Cody saw her, arms and legs tied, bundled inside a net and hanging from the branch of a mountain mahogany tree. "You all right, baby?"

She nodded, squeaked, and squirmed inside that net like a little fish.

"You know, I've heard my wooing tactics need a little softening," Cody grimly told his brother. "I'll bet yours need a one-eighty turn."

A crimson color spread up Ivan's jaw and neck, turning his face red.

"It's over, Ivan," Cody said, counting his steps to her—*eighteen . . . nineteen . . . twenty . . .* "She's not for you, man. And she's not for me. She's too good for both of us, so if she's the reason you escaped, I suggest you do your time and reflect on what you did."

"You made me do it!"

"Bullshit." Hearing it, Cody realized that it *was* bullshit. He shook his head. "We were stupid boys, with hormones for brains."

Ivan spat. "You lie. You took her already, didn't you? She's yours? She fucking loves you, doesn't she? Doesn't she?"

"No," he began, intending to placate him while he found a way to set Megan loose, but Megan spoke out at the same time.

"Yes, I do. I love him. I've always loved you, Cody.

Always." Her voice broke near the end, and it could've been the last little string that held Cody's sanity together.

A thousand emotions bombarded him at once. He felt hundreds of different sensations. Like when lightning strikes, and you land on a fire pit, and you're trampled by a pack of elephants, and you fall from a parachute, all at once.

"You don't love me, and what in Christ's last day were you doing at Marcel's, Meg?" he demanded because she shouldn't have been there.

She should not love him.

The monster, the monster had marked her little wrist, had bruised her lips . . .

"You were a bet, did you know that?" Ivan sneered. "Did loverboy here tell you?"

"She leaves, Ivan. Right now. This is between you and me."

But Ivan was talking to Megan. "He knew I'd kill them if he took you out that day, and he still did it! He's the monster, not I!" Ivan rammed his fist to his chest, shaking his head as he fought back tears. "I'll bet fucking her has been the most exciting thing you've ever done in your life." He shot the accusation like a missile at Cody and took a few steps forward. "How about I show you how a real man fucks?"

Shaking with fury, Cody spoke through his teeth. "How about you eat my shit."

"Why don't you eat this, brother?" Covering the space between them in a flash, he pulled out a Glock just like Cody's and rammed the gun into his mouth and pulled the trigger.

Cody shut his eyes as he expected to explode.

Click.

He didn't.

He opened his eyes to meet his brother's bloodshot blue ones.

The chamber was empty. Ivan's sick laugh echoed in the forests silence as he shoved Cody back. "I'm not killing you yet."

"I'm getting that sense," Cody grumbled, reaching into the back of his waistband for his own weapon . . .

Heart pounding, watching both men below, Megan realized that she was a fool. She was an idiot. Cody was a professional. And she had thought to follow him and do what? *Face your fears . . . Save Cody . . .*

What an idiot! Now she was stuck in this net, and the man she loved was down there, at the mercy of this killer, all because he'd taken the advantage by kidnapping her—oh, God.

Cody seemed to be plotting. His eyes were narrowed by the sun, but she could see him reaching behind him, weighing Ivan, and measuring his distance to the tree.

"Let me down, let me down!" she screamed, hating the trapped sensation hanging here gave her.

Ivan cut the rope so swiftly, Megan crashed to the forest floor like a falling rock. The air was knocked out of her with a *whoomp,* and quickly Ivan put the knife away then pulled her to her feet, his face contorted as he forcibly untangled her. "You always got the pretty girls, didn't you, Cody? Made the football team. Made Mom and Dad so proud. Even now, you're a goddamned cop." He smiled thinly, cupping Megan's breast in his free hand as he put the gun to her temple. "Does it bother you when I do this? When I have something that you want?" He massaged, and Megan bit back a strangled protest, revolted by his touch, when Cody took a menacing step forward.

"Fuck you." Cody's breathing became ragged, his eyes so dark, they could've been black. Megan feared for him, for herself, kept remembering the bodies, the way this man, this man, had killed two adults at the tender age of sixteen.

"Fuck me? No, brother. I'd much rather fuck her."

When Megan kicked his shin and broke free, it took Cody only seconds to reach for her, but by then Ivan had grabbed her by the throat. "You're not going anywhere, Maggie."

Cody whipped out his gun and aimed. "Let her go, Ivan."

Ivan's cold, hard laugh made the hair rise in her nape. "Ahh, Cody, always wanting to boss me around 'cause you're a minute older. You're not boss here, *I* am. I have the girl now."

"She walks, Ivan. She walks now and we'll settle this."

"Oh yes? But you see . . . maybe she doesn't want to walk—" he licked his tongue into her ear and her stomach roiled in disgust. "Do you know why I killed them, Maggie? Because of you. Did you know what your boyfriend did, Meg? Huh? Did you know what he did? He said he was taking you from me. My parents thought I was not good enough for you. Because I was not my brother." He shot a look of venom at Cody. "But for a moment I was able to make you believe I was him, didn't I? Last night?" he cooed into her ear. "When I touched you, you believed I was that guy, the perfect guy."

Bile rose up to her throat at the memory, and she wanted to scrape her mouth clean of him once more.

What a fool she'd been.

So desperate to be touched, loved, by Cody, that she had not seen the difference of the touch, of his taste, until she'd seen him—the man she loved—with a gun pointed to his head.

They were nothing alike.

Ivan had tried to look like him, but his essence, his goodness, his decency, had a scent, a feel, a vibe. Oh God, she wanted that strength around her, that scent, that man.

Ivan curved his hand around her nape and wound his fingers into the blond curls of her hair. "You think I haven't thought of this, too, Maggie Meg?" He massaged her scalp. "That I didn't fantasize about this even when I was just a boy?"

"LET. HER. GO." Cody's trigger finger was trembling, and Meg wondered if she ducked . . . would he shoot?

Cody was so damned decent inside, she wondered if he'd kill his own brother. Despite the fact that he was a murderer, Cody had not killed him before.

Ivan yanked her head back so hard the pain burned across her scalp, tearing a gasp and a whimper out of her. "Toss me the gun. And the other gun. And the knife."

"You won't kill her, Ivan," Cody hissed in a low, threatening voice, "but I have no qualms about killing you."

"I'll scar her for life! I'll make her suffer, you son of a bitch!"

"We have the same mother, you moron."

"Drop your weapons and she goes!"

The silence was deafening in the nature. And then, one by one, Cody tossed everything to the ground, and Megan's hopes of coming out of this alive plummeted.

"Okay." Ivan pushed her aside with a smile. "Forty steps, Maggie Meg. Make them quick before I change my mind and shoot."

Megan began walking, uncertain as she sought out a pair of blue, blue eyes that seemed to urge her to do as Ivan said. As she passed him, the man she loved, Cody ground out under his breath, "Keep going."

But it was difficult to take another step. "I don't want to leave you," she said anxiously, fearing Ivan would do another stupid thing, another crazy thing.

"Keep going, Banks."

She still couldn't. "I don't want to!"

"Go, goddammit!" Cody exploded, framing her face between his hands. "My life is over if anything happens to you." He kissed her hard and long, pushing his tongue into her mouth in a long, hot wet thrust that sent her senses spinning. "I love you. Now go."

I love you.

Now go.

Megan didn't know why she obeyed, why she headed out off the clearing, dazed with those parting words, taking those words into her heart, even as she heard Ivan curse Cody in the background for what he'd done. Fifty steps later, down the rocky path, eighty heartbeats later, and about a hundred haggard breaths later, it struck her: Maybe . . . Cody would never have said he loved her if he thought he'd have another chance to.

She'd certainly never expected him to say the words except at gunpoint.

Oh God. What had she done?

And where in the hell was Zach Rivers?

When Megan disappeared in the distance, Cody's heartbeat roared in his ears, like a wave crashing against the open mouth of a never-ending cavern.

He was stalling for time, time for her to get the hell away from his crazy brother. He met those blue eyes just like his with a taunting smile, wanting to get Ivan's gaze back on him rather than on Megan's rear, the crazed man's full attention on him.

"She'll call nine-one-one, you know." Cody smiled thinly, enough to goad him, but the victory in his brother's gaze took him aback.

"I'm counting on it." He smiled triumphantly. "By the time they get here, you'll be dead. And I'll be you."

Megan found a bar of signal after running around the forest like a lunatic. "Zach!" she cried into her cell phone when a male voice picked up. "Zach, where are you?"

There were men's voices in the background as he answered. "We're on our way. Are you okay?"

"Yes, but I'm afraid Cody won't be. We're at the—"

"Tonto National Forest, got that. Just whatever you do, get out of harm's way or Nordstrom'll kill me," he commanded.

"Not if he's dead!" Meg screamed, and hung up.

Putting the phone on silent, she started running back to the clearing.

Her heart felt like exploding with each step. And then, she heard it. Gunshots.

"Oh, no." Megan kicked up her speed, her throat closing in. "Oh, no no no."

She reached the clearing, and instantly Megan saw him, dead, on the ground. A pool of blood surrounded him. Him. Cody. It was him; she saw the tie he wore today, his most horrible tie, an orange color she wanted to throw away for the first time ever. Oh my God.

She began to shake her head, refusing to believe what lay right before her eyes, already feeling her heart begin to crack. Then she spotted him. Ivan laid back, clutching his chest, bloodied and panting. Megan's eyes began to spill tears. She reached for one of the guns on the ground and raised it. "You son of a bitch!" she screamed, and shot.

"Mega—" His eyes widened when the bullet hit him, somewhere close to his heart, and he slumped back against the tree trunk. She squeezed her eyes and was about to shoot again when he barked, "Son of a bitch!"

She opened her eyes, lowered the gun. The voice. It was unmistakable, its effect on her, its timbre. "Cody?"

"Fucking hell!" He was scrambling to tear a fabric of his shirt to cover his wound, which was seeping red all along his right arm.

"Cody?" she screeched, dropping the gun to the ground. "Ohmigod, what have I done!" She took a tentative step forward, then halted, doubting herself, what she was seeing. That blue tie . . .

She glanced at Cody, dead, sightless, on the ground.

"Come here and kiss it better, damn it, stop looking at that asshole unless he's better-looking than me."

"Why is he wearing your clothes!" she protested angrily, then went to help him rip his shirt open. She was relieved to note the bullet had hit his arm and not his chest, but was still so shocked at what she'd done she considered using the gun on herself.

Cody grabbed her with one hand and kissed her like a starved man, sloppy tongue and panting breaths and everything, which, lucky for her, meant he probably was not near death. "He wanted a new life—to kill me, and make it seem like he'd died, while he became me. Just the thought of him laying a hand on you enrages me . . ."

She scowled. "Nobody's laying a hand on me, and if we don't get you to a hospital soon, neither will you."

"I'm fine, baby. Just a scratch," he assured.

With wide, unblinking eyes, she stared dazedly at his wound as they knotted his shirt around it. "I almost killed you," she whispered.

The soft reproach in her voice made him raise his eyes. He covered her little hands with his, squeezing reassuringly. "You should have, Meg, I'm no good for you."

"You are good, you're the best, you're my *everything*."

"Then you're a fool, Meg." He grabbed her cheeks and kissed her again. "Thank God you're a big, silly fool." He deepened the kiss, and dragged her with effort to his lap. "You're mine, do you hear me? Forgive me for not explaining that to you sooner. No one touches you. No one kisses you. No one drives you nuts but me. Got that?"

"I didn't get the last part . . ." she said sheepishly.

"You're not getting me to say I love you again."

"And if I threaten to shoot you again?"

"I'll deny it." He hugged her to him, kissing her neck while she kissed his. "But you're mine, never doubt that, and if you run, I'll catch you, on my word."

"Hmm." She smiled and snuggled against him slowly, afraid to hurt him. "Then I better stay put."

"*Police!* Hands over your heads!" a set of voices yelled in the background, but Meg remained right where she was, and before all hell could break loose, Cody grumbled at them over her shoulder.

"I'm a little busy here, partner, as you can see."

Meg turned to see Zach approaching, scowling menacingly at the corpse, then even more menacingly at Cody. "So how am I supposed to know it's you, man?" he asked, annoyed.

"Because, moron, Megan's with me."

Want more HOT reads from the authors in this book?

Also available from #1 *New York Times* bestselling author

Lora Leigh

The Sin series

DEADLY SINS
ISBN: 978-0-312-38909-3

MIDNIGHT SINS
ISBN: 978-0-312-38908-6

Elite Ops series

LIVE WIRE
ISBN: 978-0-312-94584-8

RENEGADE
ISBN: 978-0-312-94583-1

BLACK JACK
ISBN: 978-0-312-94582-4

HEAT SEEKER
ISBN: 978-0-312-94581-7

MAVERICK
ISBN: 978-0-312-94580-0

WILD CARD
ISBN: 978-0-312-94579-4

The sexy SEALs series

KILLER SECRETS
ISBN: 978-0-312-93994-6

HIDDEN AGENDAS
ISBN: 978-0-312-93993-9

DANGEROUS GAMES
ISBN: 978-0-312-93992-2